The j...
"Gentle on My Mind"

And Betsy realized, with a start, that she was falling in love with this man. Nothing could come of it, of course. But it felt wonderful, quite wonderful.

"Yeah," Hutch said, as if he could read her thoughts. "Funny, isn't it?"

He kissed the corner of her mouth. Shyly, like someone doing something for the first time, she kissed him back.

They parked in Ruth and Tyler's unfinished driveway and necked like the youngest and most innocent of teenagers. Transported, Betsy found herself doing unthinkable things. She wrapped her arms around his neck. She did not simply accept his kisses, resolutely and without emotion. She shared them and returned them.

For Hutch, it was sweet, but a nightmare of self-control. He ached to do far more than kiss her, but he knew she wasn't ready. Any real sexual aggression on his part would terrify her. It would break the spell that seemed to have bewitched them both. So he kissed her mouth, her extraordinarily adorable mouth, and he held her. That was all.

It was intoxicating, it was addictive, it was maddening, and he thought it might kill him.

Bethany Campbell is acknowledged as the author of this work.

Special thanks and acknowledgment to Sutton Press Inc. for
its contribution to the concept for the
Crystal Creek series.

ISBN 0-373-82532-3

GENTLE ON MY MIND

Copyright © 1994 by Harlequin Enterprises, B.V.

Bethany Campbell

GENTLE ON MY MIND

Harlequin Books

TORONTO • NEW YORK • LONDON
AMSTERDAM • PARIS • SYDNEY • HAMBURG
STOCKHOLM • ATHENS • TOKYO • MILAN
MADRID • WARSAW • BUDAPEST • AUCKLAND

Dear Reader,

Reviewers have hailed Bethany Campbell as "one of the brightest stars of this series." In *Gentle on My Mind,* the twentieth installment of Crystal Creek, the author of the critically hailed *Rhinestone Cowboy* explores her fascination with the relationship between the McKinney brothers, the serious Tyler and the lighthearted Cal. This book is about them and their marriages, but also focuses on two new characters to Crystal Creek: Ruth's aloof cousin Betsy, a woman with a secret, and her polar opposite, Cal's friend Hutch, who seems to live by the maxim that "freedom's just another word for nothing left to lose."

Next month, prepare for double-barreled drama as Penny Richards returns to lead us poignantly down memory lane. When the new marriage of Rio and Maggie Langley takes a heart-stopping, unexpected turn, the author uses the opportunity to share with the reader the surprisingly touching story of the courtship and marriage of Maggie's parents, Crystal Creek mainstays Eva and Howard Blake.

Watch for *Unanswered Prayers*, available wherever Harlequin books are sold. And stick around in Crystal Creek—home of sultry Texas drawls, smooth Texas charm and tall, sexy Texans!

Marsha Zinberg,
Senior Editor and Editorial Coordinator,
Crystal Creek

A Note from the Author

The hero of *Gentle on My Mind* is modeled in part on my adored uncle. He seemed to me a truly free spirit, a man of enormous originality, and he was a wonderful storyteller and one of my childhood heroes.

He was tall, blond and handsome. Like Hutch, he was nearly a professional baseball player, but an injury sidelined him. Like Hutch, he took it philosophically. Like Hutch, he turned his back on formal education and went out, whistling on his way, to see what the world would teach him. It taught him a lot.

He was funny enough to make a cat laugh, yet he was also a kind and deeply compassionate man. Once, I opened the evening paper and saw a news photo of a child who'd been injured by a car. A man identified as "a passerby" was holding him. The look on that man's face was of such pain, concern and sympathy, it wrenched my heart. It took me a moment to realize the man was my uncle. He didn't know the child. He would have reacted so to any child in pain.

Most of Hutch is fictional, but part of him is inspired by fact. My uncle was an American original. He was in a way indescribable, but perhaps my cousin—his daughter—described him best. Her eyes shining, she once said, "I thought he was like a prince." She meant it, and she was right. He was.

I wanted to give my heroine, Betsy, a prince. I tried to give her one like the one we loved. He was a man of light heart, yet deep spirit, and he always waits in my memories, as the songs says, "gentle on my mind."

Bethany Campbell

Who's Who in Crystal Creek

Have you missed the story of one of your favorite Crystal Creek characters? Here's a quick guide to help you easily locate the titles and story lines:

DEEP IN THE HEART	J. T. McKinney and Cynthia
COWBOYS AND CABERNET	Tyler McKinney and Ruth
AMARILLO BY MORNING	Cal McKinney and Serena
WHITE LIGHTNING	Lynn McKinney and Sam
EVEN THE NIGHTS ARE BETTER	Carolyn Townsend and Vernon
AFTER THE LIGHTS GO OUT	Scott Harris and Val
HEARTS AGAINST THE WIND	Jeff Harris and Beverly
THE THUNDER ROLLS	Ken Slattery and Nora
GUITARS, CADILLACS	Wayne Jackson and Jessica
STAND BY YOUR MAN	Manny Hernandez and Tracey
NEW WAY TO FLY	Brock Monroe and Amanda
EVERYBODY'S TALKIN'	Cody Hendricks and Lori
MUSTANG HEART	Sara Gibson and Warren
PASSIONATE KISSES	J. T. McKinney and Pauline
RHINESTONE COWBOY	Liz Babcock and Guy
SOUTHERN NIGHTS	Lisa Croft and Tony
SHAMELESS	Rio Langley and Maggie
LET'S TURN BACK THE YEARS	Hank Travis and Mary
NEVER GIVIN' UP ON LOVE	Brock Monroe and Amanda
	Neale Cameron and Clint

Available at your local bookseller, or see the Crystal Creek back-page ad for reorder information.

CHAPTER ONE

"NOW THE REASON he stopped eatin' fire and swallowin' swords," Hutch said, "was he started gettin' fits of the hiccups."

The truck driver laughed, as Hutch had intended.

Hutch kept his own face carefully deadpan. "Hiccups interfere somethin' fierce with eatin' fire and swallowin' swords. So he and his wife decided to retire. To Lewistown Lake. Did I say she was a snake charmer?"

"A snake charmer?" the trucker said with a snort. He was a big, fortyish man with a receding hairline and a curly black beard.

He shook his head. "I never knew no fire-eater or snake charmer. You must of been everywhere, done everything."

"Pretty near," Hutch said. He'd hitched this ride in Austin just after his van broke down. Much of what he owned was in the worn army-surplus duffel bag stowed in the storage compartment behind the driver.

The driver had said he was tired and had picked Hutch up for company, to keep from falling asleep. Hutch held up his end of the deal by spinning tales.

He knew a thousand yarns, both true and strange. The one about the escaped python and the ensuing panic over the sea serpent in Lewiston Lake was one of his newer ones. He needed to practice it, perfect it.

So he drawled on in his laid-back way, shrewdly building to the story's climax. He seemed artless, but there was a good deal of art to what he did, and he did it well.

Hutch was long and lean, with high cheekbones and thick, dark brows set at a quizzical angle. His faded jeans were torn at one knee, his denim jacket had seen better days, and his old black cowboy boots were down at the heel.

He wore his broad-brimmed gray hat pulled down over his eyes—which were his most exceptional feature, a piercing blue green, as clear as spring water and startlingly alert. They were all that belied his cultivated air of laziness.

"So she went wadin' into that lake like Rambo," Hutch said, "and that python looked up from the log he'd been restin' on, and he *knew* he was in trouble. I swear that snake got guilt written all over his face."

"Snakes don't got expressions," the truck driver interjected, laughing.

"This one did," Hutch insisted mildly. "And she says to him, 'Bad Cuddles. Bad, bad snake.' She gives him a kind of little pop on the nose. Bap! Like that."

Hutch demonstrated, flicking his fingers with a flourish. "That's how she disciplined him. Then she grabs him and hauls him back to shore, all fourteen feet of him. The three of us carried him back home, like we were a parade or something. And that was the end of the Lewiston Lake sea serpent."

"I heard about that there sea serpent rumor," the driver said, shaking his head. "But I never knew it was true."

"As true as I'm sittin' here," Hutch maintained. He dug into his back pocket, drew out his wallet and flipped it open. "That's a picture of her and him and Cuddles. That's one thing you can say for a snake. He's never got his eyes closed when you take his picture."

The driver glanced at the snapshot and grinned. "I'll be danged," he said. He settled back against his seat and stared at the highway again. "You say it's the Double C you're goin' to?"

Hutch nodded and gazed out at the rolling Texas hills, drab with November. "Yeah. The McKinney place. Know where it is?"

"Yep. Pass it at least twice a week. You got work waitin' there for you?"

"No. A friend. Supposed to meet him and his wife in Austin, but they said to come on here."

Hutch felt in his jacket pocket, touching the crumpled note. Cal McKinney had left an envelope with Hutch's name on it taped to his front door. "Change of plans," the note said. "Got big news. Meet us at Double C. You can bunk there. Come round back. See you, you hopeless yahoo—Cal and Serena."

Hutch cocked his head reflectively. If Cal had important news, it must be about business. Cal had quit rodeoing and taken charge of promoting Serena's bootmaking business. He'd done a hell of a job. Hutch knew there was a big deal in the works, and it must have finally come through.

Good, he thought, the ghost of a smile playing on his lips. Cal had always come across as the world's wildest hell-raiser, but he had a good business head on his shoulders, better than anybody'd suspected. Hutch liked anybody who could throw a good, fast curve and upset expectations.

"You just visitin'?" the driver asked. He wasn't nosy, Hutch sensed. He just wanted conversation.

"No. Gonna check out the town," Hutch said. "Thinkin' of stayin' in one place awhile. See if I like it."

The driver cast him a dubious glance. "Stay? In Crystal Creek? It's a small town for a footloose man like you."

"Been travelin' a mighty long way," Hutch said, watching the landscape roll by. "Startin' to feel like I've seen it all. Hell, if I don't like it here, I'll move on, like usual. It's simple as that."

"Wish my life was simple," the driver said with a note of regret. "Me, I got a wife, three kids in Waco. The youngest needs braces on his teeth. You know what braces cost these days, man?"

Hutch made a sympathetic sound. Wives, kids, houses, mortgages, all the ties that bind, were foreign to his nature. He was thirty-one years old and free as the wind.

He'd read once that a man who takes a wife and children gives hostages to fortune. That man was trapped. Hutch prized freedom above all things, and he planned never to offer fortune any such hostages.

"So what you aim to do?" the driver asked. "Ranch work?"

Hutch shook his head. He'd rodeoed awhile, and ranch work was fine, but he had other plans. "I aim to open a chili parlor," he said. "See how I like it."

The driver whistled appreciatively. "A chili parlor? There's a thought. The town don't have one. Myself, I'm fond of a good bowl of red. Food of the gods, is what I say."

Hutch nodded, feeling in perfect accord with the sentiment. For one of the few times in his life, he had money, and he could think of nothing more noble to invest it in. A chili joint that served beer on the side, an old-fashioned jukebox, and a little floor space for honky-tonk dancing. Paradise enough.

Hutch's rakehell great-uncle, Harlan, had died and surprised everybody by having money socked away in the bank. Nobody'd thought the old man had two dimes to rub together, but he'd had nearly fifty-five thousand dollars, and he'd left most of it to Hutch.

The old man had left instructions for the use of the money in his will. They were short and sweet. "Have fun, and if you lose it, so what? Don't cry and don't look back." Seemed like a pretty good philosophy to Hutch.

He and the truck driver traded chili lore for the next dozen or so miles. They discussed the great factions and schisms in the creed, tomatoes versus no tomatoes, beans versus no beans, ground beef versus chopped.

Hutch was a purist—no tomatoes, no beans, beef chopped, not ground. The trucker was a heretic, who admitted even to trying chili in Cincinnati, where they put cinnamon and spaghetti noodles in the stuff.

But when the truck reached the lane that led to the Double C, the two men parted amiably, with the trucker pumping Hutch's hand, slapping his shoulder and wishing him luck. He called Hutch a "good ol' boy" and said he'd sure stop into that chili parlor once it was going, yes sir, he sure would. He said Hutch was good company, sure as hell, and wished him luck again.

Hutch swung his duffel bag over his shoulder and hiked the last mile to the ranch house with easy, swinging strides. He didn't look any too presentable, he knew. He needed a shave, his brown hair was too long, and its unruly waves fell almost below his ears.

He'd intended to clean up and change clothes at Cal and Serena's place in Austin, but they'd headed for the

Double C early. He hoped nobody'd try to run him off the ranch for a drifter.

He knocked at the back door of the ranch house, marveling at the size of the place. Hutch had known Cal a long time, but never suspected he'd come from a place this fancy.

A slender black woman with salt-and-pepper hair swung open the door. She wore a white apron over her blue pantsuit, and she had a smart, no-nonsense glint in her eye. She put a fist on her hip and looked Hutch up and down.

"We don't give handouts," she said in an authoritative voice. "You want work, that's different. You see the foreman, Slattery. He's down at the stock pens."

"I'm not askin' for a handout, ma'am," Hutch said, unembarrassed. "I'm lookin' for Cal and Serena McKinney. Was supposed to meet them in Austin. He left me a note to come here instead."

"He didn't say anything about it to me," the black woman said suspiciously. "Where you know him from? His rodeo days, I bet."

"Yes, ma'am," Hutch said. "You'd be right."

"His daddy told him years ago not to bring you crazy cowboys 'round. He was always comin' home with some *compadre* with a hard-luck story. One nearly stole us blind."

Hutch smiled. He'd heard the story. Cal could do a fine, rumbling imitation of his father's decree. "You will *curb* your goddamn charitable impulses, boy. And keep that rodeo trash out of my house."

"Ma'am," he said, "my rodeo days are behind. And I'm not of felonious disposition. If Cal's not here yet, I'll go back up the lane and wait. I won't trouble you."

"Felonious disposition," the woman echoed dubiously, narrowing her eyes. "Humph. They just got here. They're unpackin'. You stay here. I'll check."

She pointedly shut the door in his face. "Felonious disposition," he heard her grumble.

A moment later, the door swung open again, and Serena stood before him, smiling widely. Hutch's heart did an illicit little tap dance.

Serena was long-legged and willowy, with dark hair, smoky green eyes and a bewitching sprinkling of freckles. She was one of the most beautiful women Hutch knew, and there was something intriguingly mysterious about her.

She always had a glow about her when Cal was near. But sometimes, without him, she looked pensive, locked in a solitary world. She made Hutch think of somebody poised on the edge of a great, secret sorrow.

But today, Serena didn't merely glow, she radiated. *My God,* thought Hutch, *no wonder Cal tumbled for her—who wouldn't?*

She threw open the door and flung herself into his arms, hugging him. "Hutch!" she cried happily, and kissed his cheek. "You found us. Come in."

She seized his hand and led him inside. Cal appeared in the kitchen doorway, stepped up to him and shook his hand. "You nearly beat us," he said with a grin. "We stopped in Crystal Creek. You drivin'?"

"Hitchin'," Hutch said. "The van broke down just north of Austin. You look like the cat that ate the canary. That business deal come through?"

"Smooth as silk." Cal nodded. "And we aim to invest the profits right here. In my brother's winery. No place like home. Right, darlin'?"

He put one arm around Serena, and she smiled at him. He smiled back, and the kitchen practically vibrated with the happiness and sexiness they gave off.

Hutch's brow furrowed thoughtfully. They were glad about more than money, that was clear. What? Not a kid—they weren't ever having kids. They'd made that clear to everyone long ago. They kept their reasons private.

So what accounted for such euphoria? Cal had something up his sleeve, Hutch could tell.

The black woman entered the kitchen, and Cal reached out, wrapping his free arm around her waist and pulling her to his side. "Did you meet Lettie Mae? Lettie Mae, this is Hutch. He's considerin' settlin' in Crystal Creek. Openin' up a chili joint."

"I've always admired ambition," Lettie Mae said, her nostrils pinched sarcastically.

"You evil-minded woman," Cal teased. "I read your brain. You think I'm gonna bankroll him, right? Wrong. He's a man of independent means."

Lettie Mae gave Hutch a long, measuring look that clearly said she didn't think he had the wherewithal to open a sardine can, let alone a business.

Hutch didn't mind. "Pleased to meet you," he said and tilted his hat brim higher in salute.

"Stop glowerin'," Cal ordered Lettie Mae, hugging her tighter. "You're gonna love this guy. I promise."

Lettie Mae seemed to soften a bit. Like most women, she found Cal hard to resist.

Cal was thirty-two, a year older than Hutch. He topped Hutch's height of six feet by two inches, and he was extraordinarily handsome, with strong, even features and hazel eyes with dark lashes and brows. The joke in the rodeo circuit, Hutch had heard, was that Cal had married Serena because she was the only woman he ever found prettier than he was.

Lettie Mae beamed up at him. "Scamp," she said and swatted his chest playfully. "Do your daddy and Cynthia even know you're comin'?"

"Nope," Cal said with his most reckless grin. "The whim took us, and we were gone with the whim."

He kissed Lettie Mae's cheek.

"Scamp," she said again, but she obviously enjoyed it.

"Where's Daddy and Cynthia?" Cal asked. "And Tyler and Ruth?"

"Your daddy had to go into Crystal Creek early this morning," Lettie Mae said. "Miss C. went in later. To shop. She's meeting him at the country club. At one o'clock."

Cal glanced at his watch. "Good," he said. "We can catch 'em. We'll stash Hutch in the guest house, let him get settled. What about Tyler and Ruth? Will they be there, too?"

Lettie May shook her head, and her expression clouded. "Ruth drove into Austin to pick up her cousin. I haven't seen much of her lately. She's keepin' to herself. And your brother? That boy is workin' himself to death. They're puttin' up those winery buildings now. That's all he does—"

"We'll catch them later," Cal said, drawing Serena to him more closely. He nodded at a key hanging on a hook next to the back door. "This still the key to the guest house?"

"Yes, but—" Lettie Mae said.

"Nobody's got it reserved or anything?" he asked.

"Not that I know. But—"

"Good." Cal released Serena, took the keys and tossed them to Hutch, who made a neat one-handed catch.

"Come on, Hoss," Cal said to Hutch. "I'll show you where to bunk."

"I don't need a whole guest house," Hutch protested.

"Too late," Cal said with a shrug. "You got one. And Lettie Mae, could you feed this desperado, once he gets settled in?"

"I suppose," Lettie Mae said. Then she thrust her chin up, as in challenge. "And I'll be makin' chili for tonight. If you're such a hotshot, you can earn your keep and help. Maybe I can teach you a thing or two."

"It'd be an honor, ma'am," Hutch said.

Cal shouldered into a sheepskin jacket and put on his Stetson at a cocky angle. Hutch followed him outside.

"I don't think that woman much likes me," he said, shaking his head. "Sorry."

"Lettie Mae?" Cal said. "Don't worry. She'll be eatin' out of your hand by the end of the day. Cook up some chili with her, tell her a few stories, and she'll be yours for life. I know you."

"And I know you," Hutch said evenly. "What you so happy about? It's more than that boot deal with Amarillo Tex, isn't it?"

Cal clapped him on the shoulder and gave him a conspiratorial smile. "Yeah. A lot more. But I ain't sayin' yet. Gotta tell my daddy and stepmama first. Tonight, come out with us. I want to talk to my brother about business. I'll tell you all then."

"I don't want to intrude on your family affairs," Hutch said.

"You aren't intrudin'," Cal said. "This is something I want the world to know."

He gazed up at the sky with the mysterious air of a man who saw angels dancing there, where others saw only emptiness.

"Yes sir," he said with satisfaction, "I want the whole world to know."

THE DALLAS AIRPORT made Betsy Holden think of some futuristic city in a science fiction movie. Huge, hyper-modern, it teemed with people moving mechanically toward their destinations.

Betsy was small and slender with straight auburn hair that hung to her shoulders. The haircut was expensive, as was everything else about her, from her Spanish leather pumps to her diamond earrings.

She was extremely pretty, with delicate features and large hazel eyes, but she carried herself with a cultivated aloofness that she used to disguise her shyness.

She hurried toward the gate where her plane—the last, thank God, in this hopscotch journey—would depart. She was amazed when she heard her name announced over the public address system.

"Paging Am-Air passenger Betsy Holden. Paging Am-Air passenger Betsy Holden. Please pick up the nearest white courtesy telephone."

She stopped so abruptly that a stocky business man bumped into her. He apologized and hurried on. Betsy stood, looking about the endless concourse, wondering if she'd had an auditory hallucination.

But then the amplified, tinny voice echoed through the air again. "Paging Am-Air passenger Betsy Holden..."

Her first thought was that something was wrong at home—Betsy was in a worrisome mood. Her second thought was that something was wrong at the Double C, and her cousin, Ruth, wouldn't be able to pick her up at the Austin airport.

She hugged her shoulder bag more tightly against her body, gripped her carry-on more securely and looked down the concourse.

Sure enough, there *was* a white courtesy phone, only twenty or so feet away. It was as if it had just appeared there, by magic.

Betsy made her way to it, set down her carry-on and picked up the receiver. She identified herself.

"You have a call," the operator said. She had a thick Texas accent that sounded alien to Betsy's ears.

There was whirring and humming on the line, as if complex connections were taking place. Then a familiar voice. "Hello, Betsy? Is that you?"

She drew in her breath sharply. The voice was Michael's, but Michael was in London.

"Michael?" she said a little breathlessly. "What's the matter?"

There was an instant of silence.

"Nothing's wrong," Michael said. "I wanted to surprise you. I got your flight times from your mother. I didn't know if it'd work—but it did. Hello, sweets."

Betsy stiffened in surprise. Michael was doing graduate work at the London School of Economics. He was three thousand miles away, the last person she'd expected to hear from.

"Nobody ever paged me in an airport before," she said, her heart still drumming. "I thought there'd been some disaster..."

"That's not like you," Michael said. "You're always so levelheaded. I've never paged anybody, either. The logistics were challenging."

Betsy sighed. Michael loved challenging logistics. Betsy was supposed to love Michael. She imagined that she probably did, as much as she could love any man.

"I was going to call you on your plane," he said. "It's not possible. It's just not technically possible on a commercial flight. Did you know that?"

"No," Betsy said, rather blankly.

"So I hit on this instead," he said. "Happy anniversary. I thought this would be an interesting way to say it."

Betsy flinched, feeling guilty. It *was* their anniversary; their first date had been exactly a year ago today. He'd remembered. But she'd been too caught up in her own concerns.

"Happy anniversary," she said softly. She and Michael were engaged to be engaged. Whenever she thought of it, she envisioned the two of them as lifeless plastic bride and groom dolls atop an enormous cake.

They *were* like two dolls, her brother Mitchell had told her. Betsy was only five foot two and weighed slightly less than a hundred pounds. Michael was five foot six—not tall enough to be intimidating to her—but he was well-built and muscular. In college he had been a champion wrestler in his weight class.

Her mother insisted that she and Michael were an "adorable couple." Michael was so handsome that people on the street would actually stare at him. He had thick dark hair and black eyes, and everyone always said he looked like a smaller version of John F. Kennedy, Jr.

Michael was brilliant, sensitive, polite and richer even than Betsy would someday be. Her mother kept telling her how lucky she was. "Don't let him get away," her mother had said frankly. "Don't louse up this one."

Betsy swallowed. Until Michael, she had never allowed a relationship with a man to last for more than three or four dates. But to all outward appearances, Michael seemed flawless—and she felt safe with him.

"How's London?" she asked, trying to sound bright and chipper.

"Cold. Damp. But the theater's great. I'm going again tomorrow night. The Royal Shakespeare Company. Wish you could come. How's Texas so far?"

Betsy gazed out the nearest window. The tall buildings of Dallas stretched out forever, it seemed. "Cloudy. Not too cold."

"You really do sound edgy, sweets." His tone was indulgent. "You're not worried about the new job, are you?"

"Not at all," she said. In truth, thinking about it made her queasy. "Besides, it's only for a year."

"So's London," Michael said. "We'll be through at almost the same time. And I'll see you at Christmas. What do you want me to bring you from London, sweet Betsy?"

She smiled. He really could be darling and thoughtful, and she kept telling herself she was fortunate to have found him. "Just yourself," she said.

"My humble self is not enough. I saw a ring at Harrod's. It's beautiful. Would you take a ring? Or would that be pushy? Would you rather pick one out yourself?"

She was touched, but also terrified. *He seems so perfect,* she told herself. *Seems. And my parents approve of him.*

She took a deep breath. Her parents had been pressing her hard to get married, very hard. She felt like a woman about to step off the edge of a cliff. "I know anything you pick would be lovely," she said hesitantly.

She'd done it. She'd said it. She hadn't exactly said "yes," but she certainly hadn't said "no." She had the sensation of falling into something frightening and bottomless.

"I—I've talked to your father," Michael said, suddenly sounding almost shy. "He called the other night. We talked about the future. Your future."

Betsy came back to herself abruptly. What business did her father have calling Michael? To talk about *her* future?

"After Austin, he'd like you to keep your hand in the business. As much as possible."

Betsy knew that. "Yes?"

Her father had started out in television as a business manager and ended up buying the station. He now owned a string of small stations that he called, rather grandiosely, the Holden Broadcasting Network. He had four children, of whom Betsy was the youngest. He was not, he had declared, going to mollycoddle them.

If they were going to inherit this empire, they would by golly *understand* it, from the bottom up. They would learn it from the inside out. They would get their hands dirty, they would be in the trenches, work their way up, et cetera, blah-blah-blah.

Michael said, "Your father's still surprised you chose Austin. I am, too."

"Hey, I'm a Californian. I don't do winter. Austin's warmer," Betsy joked. But the familiar haunted, hollow feeling possessed her. A muscle twitched nervously in her cheek.

"Yes," Michael said. "Well." He hesitated. "If I go into investment management, I can start almost anywhere—as long as I start small. But the bigger the city, the better. Do you know what I mean?"

Betsy knew. She fought to keep from gritting her teeth. Her father specialized in small television stations in small cities. The only large towns in which he had holdings were Austin, Omaha and Reno.

"What your father wanted me to know—us to know—is that you can choose where you go next. So we should discuss this."

"I see," she said. Her father had told her the same thing: after Austin, she could pick whichever station and city she wanted—*if* she got married. Her father was not usually so generous. He had set ideas, and he was used to giving orders. But like her mother, he was anxious that she not let Michael escape.

"Betsy, I think your father's reasons for wanting you to know the business are sound," Michael said.

She repressed a sigh. "I know."

"I mean, the four of you will inherit the whole thing someday. The more you know about it, the better you can handle it. And the better you can work together."

"I know."

"I respect his reasoning. I know that television isn't your first love—"

It's not on my list of loves at all, thought Betsy. But that didn't matter. It was the family business, and it happened to be worth a fortune. The family was supposed to stick together and pursue its destiny—broadcasting.

"But you're a sensible woman," Michael said. "And a responsible one. Your father didn't want to raise a lot of spoiled rich kids—and he hasn't. He wants you to appreciate what you'll have. And I think you do."

"I'm trying," she said. She shut her eyes and put her fingertips to her forehead.

"And you want a career," he said. "You've always said that. So we'll have to decide what's best for both of us."

She squeezed her eyes more tightly shut. "Yes."

"I want you to be as happy as possible," he said. "You know that. I think we'll be very content. Don't you?"

"Yes," she said. Her head throbbed, and her chest suddenly ached so hard it threatened to choke off her breath.

"We're alike, you and I. We fit well together."

"Yes."

The voice on the PA system was paging someone else now. She heard the ding-ding of a passenger cart approaching. Michael started talking about his thesis.

Betsy listened and made the appropriate sounds at the appropriate times. She didn't understand what he was saying and wasn't really listening. She opened her eyes and stared about the concourse blindly. Its details seemed insubstantial, meaningless and dreamlike. Her head throbbed more madly.

At last he sighed and accused himself of babbling. He said, "You're a good listener, Betsy. You always have been."

She thought, *No, I'm a good pretender. I've had so much practice.*

"We'll have a lot to talk about at Christmas," he said. "I'll call you at your cousin's. Let me know when you have your own place and get a phone."

"Yes," she said mechanically. "Of course."

"And Betsy—" he hesitated, his voice suddenly earnest "—it goes without saying too often. I love you."

"I love you, too," she said. The ache in her chest grew more painful, almost knifelike. She *did* love him in a way. He was steady and sweet and bright and undemanding.

He made a kissing sound from his end of the line.

Although she felt foolish, she made a smacking little air kiss next to the receiver.

"Goodbye—sweetheart," he said in the sentimental tone that always surprised her.

"Goodbye," she said numbly and hung up.

She wondered how she could deceive him so glibly, so constantly. *Because I've been trained to deceive everyone, including myself.*

When her father had given her a choice between New Hampshire or Texas in serving her company apprenticeship, she'd known she should go to New Hampshire. In the name of all that was holy, she should stay away from Texas.

But without hesitation, she had opened her mouth and said, "Austin." It didn't matter that she had never been to Texas in her life.

Her father had looked at her oddly, staring into her eyes. She'd been careful to let him see nothing.

"Texas it is," he'd said without a glimmer of suspicion.

He had no idea why she wanted to go to Austin. In his stubborn mind-set, what was over was over. And if you didn't talk about something, then it ceased to exist, perhaps had never existed.

She picked up her carry-on and hitched her shoulder bag more firmly into place. Then she strode toward her gate with a confidence she did not feel in the least. The floor didn't seem quite solid beneath her feet, her knees felt strange, and her heart beat wildly, as if in panic.

No one in her family suspected Gary Dean Echtenkamp was in Texas. None of them even knew his name. But she did, because she'd found an agency that specialized in such matters. Unknown to her family, she'd had him traced.

Michael didn't even imagine such a person as Gary Echtenkamp existed.

But he did exist. And he lived in Fredericksburg, Texas, barely a hundred miles from Austin.

She would see him as soon as she was brave enough.

Then she would decide if there should be a next move or not. Would she, should she contrive to meet him, talk to him? Such thoughts both fascinated and terrified her.

He was a little boy, almost eight years old now. She had glimpsed him, barely, just once. She had been just sixteen.

He was her family's most scrupulously kept and shameful secret—her illegitimate child. And after all these years she was going to see if she had the courage to find him.

CHAPTER TWO

BETSY FELT almost light-headed when she got off the plane. When she set foot in the Austin airport, a ghostly tremble ran through her. *My child is here, only a few hours away.*

The thought frightened her, yet paradoxically, it didn't seem quite real. She was filled with fear that it was wrong, immoral, for her to have come to Texas to try to see him.

But fear evaporated when she saw her cousin, Ruth, waiting at the arrival gate. Ruth was as pretty as ever, creamy-skinned with a cloud of soft, dark hair and large brown eyes.

She was so slender that it didn't seem possible she was seven months pregnant. Her coat was open, and the blue silk of her maternity blouse showed only the faintest bulge.

The two women hugged fiercely, and questions and answers about their families flew back and forth.

Yes, Betsy admitted with a slightly shaky smile, what her mother had written to Ruth and told her on the phone was absolutely true. Betsy really was dating a young man who looked remarkably like John F. Kennedy, Jr.

"Are you going to marry him?" Ruth asked. Affectionately she stroked Betsy's straight hair back from her shoulder.

Betsy's smile faded. She supposed she should marry Michael—she almost *wanted* to. But so much depended on what happened here in Texas. Yet nothing might happen; she might decide not to see the child. Perhaps that would be best. She no longer knew.

She took a deep breath and said, "Time will tell. Enough about me. How about you and Junior? Or is it Junioretta? Everything going all right?"

Ruth hesitated a moment. A strange, haunted look crossed her face so fleetingly that Betsy wondered if she'd imagined it.

Ruth put her hand gently on the small rise of her abdomen. "Everything's fine, just fine," she said. "We don't know if it's a boy or a girl. We want to be surprised."

She looked up at Betsy, something eager in her eyes. "I felt it kick this morning," she said. "My—my doctor says everything's right on schedule."

"Is this the same doctor you had? Mom said you had one you didn't like," Betsy continued. She made such conversation only out of politeness. Pregnancy was a painful subject to discuss; it held shameful memories for her.

Ruth gave a stiff little shrug. "Oh, no. The first doctor was this old man, Nate Purdy. Everybody in Crystal Creek thinks he's God. But he's—he's opinionated and old-fashioned, and he probably hasn't read a medical article for thirty years. I found a doctor of alternative medicine in Austin."

Betsy gave her cousin a sidewise look. "Alternative medicine?"

"*Natural* medicine," Ruth said with conviction. "I take a lot of vitamins—natural vitamins. No red meats or poultry. Herb teas and exercise. Positive thinking. That sort of thing."

Betsy said nothing. Her uneasiness stirred back to life. Ruth seemed not at all her usual self and had an odd, distracted air.

Something's wrong, Betsy thought with a wave of foreboding.

And although they talked with their old familiarity all the way to Crystal Creek, Betsy couldn't shake the sense that Ruth was troubled. She looked healthy enough—and prosperous. The car she drove was a Cadillac, with an interior of flawless plush and leather.

"How's the wine business?" Betsy asked, stroking the velvety seat. "You're not actually making any yet, are you?"

The question, innocent as it was meant to be, seemed to put Ruth on edge. She set her expression into determined pleasantness.

"Oh, no. It takes three years for the vines to mature. We're still in the early stages. You don't start a winery overnight. Sometimes Tyler...has to be reminded of that."

She turned to Betsy, smiled and changed the subject. "God, Bets, you don't know how good it is to see you, you really don't. Somebody from home. Somebody from way back when—and without a Texas accent. I mean, I love Texas, but sometimes it's overwhelming. It's so *Texan,* you know?"

Betsy didn't know, but she nodded politely.

Ruth turned her gaze back to the road. "I love Tyler and his family, I really do. But sometimes they're a bit much. All this family loyalty—McKinney this, McKinney that. Don't get me wrong. It's just nice to have one

of my own around for a change. I hope you'll stay a long
time."

"We'll see," Betsy said noncommittally. So that was
it, she thought. Ruth was homesick and probably frightened about having a baby so far from home.

*It's scary having a baby a long way from home when
you're all alone. It's terrifying. It's hell.* She tried to push
the memory away. Suddenly, staying near someone
pregnant while she did her house-hunting didn't seem like
such a good idea to Betsy.

"I hope I can find someplace to live soon," she said as
lightly as she could. "Dad wants me to buy a condo. He
hates the idea of renting. The whole family's like that.
They have a rent phobia. I've never understood it."

"Maybe you're adopted," Ruth joked. "And they
never told you."

Betsy stiffened at the word *adopted,* but forced herself to smile. "Maybe I was," she said and stared out the
window at the hills.

Ruth reached over and gave her thigh a pat. "I'm
sorry. I shouldn't make fun. It's just that I'm glad to see
you. I hope you'll like Texas. It's wonderful, really."

Betsy shook her head. "I have misgivings about moving in right on top of you. I mean, I could stay in a hotel
until I find a place."

"Nonsense," Ruth said. "You won't be on top of us.
You'll be in the guest house. It's off by itself. I stayed
there myself when I first came here."

Then Ruth went strangely quiet. Perhaps she was
thinking of her earliest days with Tyler. She remained silent until they reached the lane that led to the ranch.

"We're here," Ruth said, snapping back to present
reality. She seemed all brightness and cheer.

Almost mechanically, she pointed out the sights of the Double C. First the hay fields and the pasture, where a few horses grazed. Then, at last, the impressive ranch house of white frame and native stone, where the senior McKinneys lived, Tyler's father and stepmother.

With an equally abstracted air, she pointed out the foreman's two-story white house. It had a porch swing and a trellis covered with winter-dead roses. The bunkhouse and stable lay beyond it.

A cozy-looking guest house was at the third corner of a triangle formed by itself, the foreman's home and the main house. A small winter garden of pansies and dusty miller grew around its front door. It must have rained recently; the leaves and flowers glistened wetly.

"This is it," Ruth said. She stopped the car, then frowned. From behind the guest house, as if he'd been lurking there, a horseman appeared. He was a tall man on a bay horse. He wore a leather jacket and a cowboy hat pulled low over his eyes.

"Tyler," Ruth breathed and rolled down the window.

Ah—so this was Tyler. Betsy observed him carefully. He was a handsome man in a hard-jawed way, with sculpted cheekbones and black brows. But the brows were drawn together, and the dark eyes had a disgruntled expression.

He dismounted, ground-reined the bay and strolled to the Cadillac. Bending, he peered into the window on the driver's side. He eyed Betsy and gave her a smile that didn't reach his eyes. He tipped his hat slightly. His hair was crisp and dark, almost black.

"Tyler, my cousin, Betsy," Ruth said with a tight little nod in Betsy's direction. "Betsy, Tyler—my husband."

"Pleased to meet you," Tyler said, but he didn't look particularly pleased.

He leaned his crossed arms on Ruth's window. "We got us a complication."

Ruth looked at him warily.

Tyler jerked his thumb toward the guest house. "It's occupied," he said from between his teeth.

"Occupied?" Ruth said. "But I thought—"

"Yeah. So did I," Tyler said.

"Who's there? Did somebody bring a visitor?"

"Yeah, somebody did," Tyler muttered, shooting the house a resentful glance. "Cal. Some saddlebum friend of his. Cal promised him he could stay here while he gets his act together."

"Cal's home?" Ruth said in apparent surprise. "Serena, too? And they didn't tell us?"

"Oh, hell," Tyler said, "when did Cal ever think ahead ten minutes? Anyway, he came in dragging this friend of his—named Mutt or Hump or some damn thing, and before I could do anything about it, the guy's camped in the guest house like he owns it."

Ruth didn't miss a beat. She turned to Betsy and gave her a slightly strained smile. "Cal's Tyler's younger brother. We—didn't know he and his wife were coming this weekend. Or that they'd be bringing anybody."

She took Betsy's hand. "It's no big deal. You'll stay with us. We don't have all the tile down in the guest bedrooms yet, but if you're willing to rough it, well, I wanted you to stay *with* us from the start."

Betsy felt a frisson of foreboding. She sensed tensions between Ruth and Tyler, between Tyler and his brother.

I shouldn't have come here. I shouldn't be in Texas at all. I'm being given omens—warnings.

But she was trapped, at least temporarily. She didn't even have a car, and she couldn't ask Ruth to turn around and drive her all the way back to the city.

Tomorrow, Betsy vowed, she would find someone to take her back to Austin. She would rent a car, take a room at the Hyatt and retreat to the safety of solitude.

"Just for the night," Betsy said, giving Ruth's hand a nervous squeeze.

"Nonsense," Ruth insisted. "We've got this huge house. I rattle around in it all by myself. Tyler's hardly ever home."

"Ruth could use the company," Tyler said shortly, as if that settled it. "You stay with us."

Betsy smiled noncommittally. Tyler's invitation sounded more lordly than friendly, but she sensed a certain grudging guilt in it, as well. What was going on?

"Why are Cal and Serena home?" Ruth asked Tyler, looking puzzled. "I thought they were going to Wolverton."

"Hell, I don't know," Tyler said. "Cal says he had a change of plans. He wants to take us to Zack's tonight. He says he's got news. I told him no."

"But Tyler," Ruth protested, "I'd love to. We haven't been out for—I don't know how long. And Betsy should see Zack's. A real Texas honky-tonk. She'd love it."

"I'm too busy," Tyler said, "and you're supposed to take it easy."

"You're always busy," Ruth countered. "And I don't need to take it easy. I'm fine. I *like* being with Cal and Serena. They're fun."

Tyler gave his wife a piercing, dark-eyed glance. "If I take you, would you eat a steak instead of rabbit food—"

"I have a diet to stick to. I'm sticking to it," Ruth said. "Please, Tyler. If Cal says he has news, maybe it's something important. We can't just ignore—"

"All right," Tyler said, throwing up his hands in surrender. "All right. We'll go. I'll call him and tell him."

He straightened up, hooked his thumbs into his belt. "I'll be home about six. You girls have fun."

He walked back to the horse, picked up the reins and vaulted easily into the saddle. After he turned the bay around, he kicked it into a canter. He didn't look back.

Ruth put the Cadillac in gear. "You'll have to excuse him," she said, not looking at Betsy. "He's been working too hard. He really has."

Ruth turned the car around and headed in the same direction that Tyler had taken.

"It must be a huge job," Betsy said as tactfully as possible. "Starting a winery from scratch."

"It is," Ruth agreed. "And he's—we're learning as we go. We have some big decisions ahead."

You mean you have some big arguments ahead, Betsy thought, studying her cousin's profile. She felt a tug of sympathy for Ruth. It could not be easy, disagreeing with a man like Tyler McKinney.

"The brother," Betsy said hesitantly, "he's the one who's into boot making or something?"

She sensed a story in the relationship between the two brothers, and wondered if Ruth would speak of it.

Ruth gave an ironic smile. "Cal and Serena just may end up *being* boot making in Texas. They've been...very lucky." She quickly added, "Not that they haven't worked hard. Extremely hard. Cal's a competitor, no doubt about it."

A wistful look crossed Ruth's face. "But Cal's always had the golden touch, you know? I don't know how else to describe it. Just a golden touch."

But Tyler doesn't, Betsy thought, understanding intuitively.

The Cadillac had taken a turn and now passed between the young vineyards. In the distance, Betsy saw a house built into the hillside, a beautiful house of reddish gray stone.

As they drew nearer, she saw its wet, sloping lawn was strewed with stacks of building material that signaled construction was still in progress.

"It looks a bigger mess than it is," Ruth said as they drew into the driveway.

She stopped the car. She suddenly reached over, seized Betsy's hand again and looked into her eyes. "I'm glad it happened this way," she said. "I'm so glad you're here. Don't go back to Austin. I need you here, Bets."

Betsy smiled as warmly as she could, but inwardly had a sinking feeling. Ruth's lovely face was full of naked need. *She's scared. She's unhappy,* Betsy thought. *More than she'd ever admit.*

She glanced up at the imposing house that overlooked the vineyards. It struck her that although it was a new house, not even finished, it was already full of conflicts.

A black-and-tan hound suddenly lunged out of the shadow of a bush where it had been digging a hole. Lean and gleaming, it seemed all long legs and large, muddy paws.

The dog acted as if the sight of the Cadillac had driven it slightly mad. It yowled, it whined, it barked and wagged its tail wildly. Although it was chained to a mesquite tree, it dashed toward the car so heedlessly that the chain caught it up short, and it was thrown on its back, paws waving foolishly in the air.

Undeterred, the hound leapt up and hurled itself toward the car once more, only to have its chain jerk it back again. It kept straining toward the Cadillac, choking and coughing.

"What's *that?*" Betsy asked.

Ruth cast an unfriendly glance at the dog. Its legs flailed, churning up the earth. It took turns barking and choking, but its tail never stopped its insane wagging.

"That," Ruth said, "is Bogus. It's a—a possum hound or something. Tyler's dog-sitting it. For a friend. It's the silliest dog on the face of the earth."

Ruth insisted on helping Betsy carry her suitcases into the house. Betsy followed and paused momentarily at the threshold. Again she had an eerie sense of being surrounded by relationships gone awry: *This isn't a happy house. It's keeping secrets from the outside world.*

She entered, giving no hint that she, too, had secrets.

TYLER HAD RIDDEN BACK to the building site. He had taken to riding horseback a lot lately; it helped ease the tension always tightening his body.

Part of the tension was sexual. Both Nate Purdy and Ruth's crazy doctor said it was okay to have sex as long as it wasn't too athletic. But sex made Ruth so nervous about the baby that she'd lie beneath Tyler unmoving and stiff.

The last time they'd made love, she'd gritted her teeth, as if forcing herself to tolerate him. It had struck him to the heart. He hadn't tried to touch her since.

He was used to Ruth being warm, eager, playful and passionate. He was used to her being funny and sensible and—well—being *Ruth*. She was like the other half of him.

He stopped the bay at the perimeter of the winery area because he didn't want to have to mingle with the workers just yet. He was in no mood to talk. *Damn!* he thought, frowning. He knew what was eating Ruth. It ate at him, too.

But they didn't talk about it. She wouldn't. And when she wouldn't, he found he couldn't. He didn't know what to say without sounding harsh and heartless.

She was scared to death of losing this baby. In a move completely unlike her, she'd scrounged up her damned "alternative" doctor. She'd gone Californian on him—all herbs and yogurt and vitamins and dogged optimism.

Nate had told them the child had a fifty-fifty chance of surviving—and even then there might be complicated surgery ahead. There was an irregularity in the baby's heartbeat, Nate said. A serious one. Tyler had tried to take the news like a man.

He was still trying. He did not count on the baby making it. Ruth did. That difference in attitude was like a chasm in the earth that had opened between them.

It seemed to affect everything they said and did. And they were having major disagreements—like how in hell were they going to finance this winery? They desperately needed more money.

Tyler wanted the ownership to stay as it was—a partnership between himself and Ruth, his father and stepmother. Ruth wanted to go public, sell stock. But then it would no longer be theirs. This was his dream. He didn't want to sell it to strangers, even in part.

He shook his head. He shouldn't be lollygagging around, getting introspective like some fool neurotic. He had a job to do. And his complicated family life to juggle—which included Cal.

He nudged the horse into a walk. He'd call Cal from the foreman's trailer. He loved his brother, but right now Cal was the last person he wanted to see. And God only knew what sort of character he'd dragged home this time.

IN THE KITCHEN of the ranch house, Lettie Mae was laughing so hard that she had to wipe her eyes on her apron. "Stop," she begged Hutch. "Don't say more. Quit."

Somehow, as Hutch and she worked together, they'd starting trading stories about Cal.

Hutch had been recounting a certain misadventure he and Cal had once had in a bar in Bandera that, unfortunately, had involved Cal's setting a piano on fire.

"I never did understand what was goin' through his mind that night," Hutch said, shaking his head. "He kept talkin' about Scarlett O'Hara and the burning of Atlanta. But how he got the piano mixed up in it, I don't know."

"That boy," Lettie Mae said, still wiping her eyes. "Thank God his mama never knew half the things he did. *Or* his daddy. Oh, me, oh, my. I shouldn't laugh about it. But I can't help it."

"Well, he's reformed now. But Bandera won't ever be the same." Hutch stirred the chili, tasted it critically, then offered the spoon to Lettie Mae. "Here. Try this. See what you think."

She took a sampling taste, savored it, then looked at him, one eyebrow cocked. "It's good. I wouldn't have believed it. Now how'd you ever come to try vinegar in chili, you rascal? That's a new one on me."

Hutch took another taste and shrugged. "I don't know. I was campin' out one night in Montana, alone, starin' up at the stars, and it suddenly came to me. It's like this mystical voice whispers, 'Vinegar. Use vinegar.'"

"Divine inspiration?" she asked wryly.

He gave her a solemn nod. "Possibly. What do you think? More salt?"

"Maybe you're right," she said thoughtfully. "But only a pinch."

The kitchen door swung open, and Cal and Serena came in, laughing, their arms around each other. "Hello, troops," Cal said. "How's it goin'?"

"Calvin," Lettie Mae said, "come taste this chili. You, too, Serena. I made a little change in my recipe."

Cal's eyebrow rose in disbelief. "*You* made a change in your recipe?"

"An improvement," Lettie Mae said firmly. "Come try."

Cal and Serena exchanged glances. Then Cal gave Lettie Mae a sly smile. "Be careful, Lettie Mae," he said. "You let this guy in your kitchen, and the next thing you know, he sweet-talks you into changin' your chili. He's exertin' undue influence over you. Mose is gonna be jealous."

"And you," he said to Hutch, "watch it. She's got a boyfriend. A big, possessive boyfriend."

"Oh, *you*," said Lettie Mae, and poked Cal's arm.

"It's all right," Cal said, shrugging. "We'll take him out of temptation's way, you heartbreaker. We got him a date for tonight."

"A date?" Hutch said dubiously.

"Kind of," Cal said. "Ruth's cousin. She's an heiress. Her daddy owns a bunch of television stations or something."

"Yeah?" Hutch returned. "Well, my daddy owned a gas station, and only one of 'em."

"See," Cal said with his careless grin. "You already got something in common. Both your daddies own stations. Besides, it ain't really a date. You'll just both be there."

"An *heiress?*" Hutch said ruefully. It occurred to him that this night could be as big a disaster as the one in Bandero.

He shrugged. At least it would be an experience. And maybe he'd get a story out of it, a funny one. For an experience or a story, he'd chance anything once. Even an heiress.

CHAPTER THREE

BETSY BARELY NOTICED the man at first. She was too fascinated by the contrasts between the McKinney brothers and their wives. Everyone had gathered in Ruth's living room before leaving for Zack's.

Tyler was handsome in his dark and dour way, but Cal was better-looking, and *he* was friendly. Tyler stayed tight-lipped, but Cal laughed and gave off charm as naturally as the sun gave off light.

Serena was beautiful, with long dark hair and gray-green eyes. She looked up at Cal as if she were making love to him with her gaze, the same way he looked at her. When Ruth and Tyler exchanged glances, it was almost warily, as if each found the other a troubling puzzle.

No, the McKinneys were so interesting, that Betsy at first was hardly aware of the third man in Ruth and Tyler's living room. He stayed in the background and called no attention to himself.

It was Cal who dragged him forward, flinging one arm around the man's neck.

"What you hangin' back there like that for, like you're shy?" Cal asked his friend. "This is my brother, Tyler. Tyler, how come lately you always look like you're suckin' on a pickle?"

Tyler grunted something unintelligible.

"This is my friend Hutch Hutchison," Cal said. "He's played a little baseball, done a little rodeo, done a little everything."

Hutchison and Tyler shook hands. Hutchison was shorter than Tyler, perhaps six feet even. His tight, low-slung jeans were clean but worn, his brown plaid flannel shirt faded from too many washings.

"And this is Ruthie," Cal said to Hutch. "She's way too sweet for ol' Tyler, but she took him anyway."

Hutch pumped Ruth's hand, and she smiled as if she didn't quite know what to make of him.

"And this," Cal said, putting his free hand on Betsy's shoulder, "is Cousin Betsy from California. Tyler kept tellin' me she went to Stanford. The college. Cousin Betsy, this is Hutch. He went to Harvard. The college."

Hutch extended his hand, took hers and shook it. Betsy stared at him in disbelief. *Harvard?* Tyler had said the man was in town to open a greasy-spoon café.

Hutch seemed to read her mind. "I didn't go long," he said. He gave her a lazy smile.

Betsy smiled automatically, but found herself reevaluating him. At first glance, she'd thought him plain, unremarkable, even lanky.

But he wasn't lanky at all, only lean. Despite his worn clothes, his body was spare and graceful. He had overly long hair, brown, thick and unruly with waves.

His brows were thick and dark, and a sly intelligence shone in his eyes. They were clear, blue-green eyes, quite beautiful, really, and made his gaunt face handsome. The slant of his mouth was full of self mockery and easy merriment.

Betsy was so taken aback that she forgot to draw her hand from his. "Pleased to meet you," she said automatically.

"Pleased to meet *you*," he answered. His mobile mouth crooked a fraction more with amusement.

Tyler frowned. "You went to Harvard?" he said dubiously.

Hutch released Betsy's hand and hooked his thumbs into the back pockets of his jeans. He gave Tyler an easy, lopsided grin. "Baseball scholarship. But I quit."

"Why?" asked Ruth, clearly puzzled.

He shrugged. "Harvard's baseball stinks. I transferred to Arkansas."

Betsy was intrigued, but Tyler frowned harder. "You left Harvard for the University of Arkansas?" he asked.

"Better baseball," Hutch said.

"Arkansas's a party school," Tyler said, and Betsy detected scorn in his voice.

"Don't much go by labels, myself," Hutch replied mildly. "And they've done some good work in cold fusion physics."

Cold fusion physics, Betsy thought, more intrigued than before. Tyler's head snapped back a fraction of an inch, as if he'd been tricked.

Cal darted his brother a sidelong look of satisfaction. "Are we gonna stand around talkin' about school days, or are we gonna to eat?"

"To eat," Ruth said with conviction. "I'm ready to go *out.*" She reached into the coat closet, withdrew a baby-blue suede jacket and handed it to Tyler.

"Come on, sugar lump," Cal said to Serena, winding his arm around her. He and she led the way to the door. Tyler, his back stiff, followed with Ruth.

"We'll take a separate car," Tyler said. "In case Ruth gets tired and wants to leave early."

"I won't get tired," said Ruth.

"Betsy? Hutch?" Serena said. "Won't you ride with us?"

Betsy reached into the closet and took out her car coat.

"Ma'am?" the Hutchison man said. He took the coat and held it so that she might slip into it more easily. "May I?"

She smiled at his unexpected courtliness.

Why, he must be an eccentric, she thought, pleased to find a distraction. *A real Texas eccentric. Wait till I tell people about this.*

Michael, in particular, would find it funny. Michael liked harmless, offbeat people who were down-to-earth and outspoken. His parents' gardener, for instance, Geraldo. Geraldo was such a character that—

But when Hutch, adjusting her collar, accidentally brushed his hand against the edge of her jaw, all thought of Geraldo and Michael evaporated. His work-hardened fingers seemed to sear her skin, sending flickers of intense, painless fire running beneath it.

Startled, she turned, looking up into his eyes. They were so clear, so alert, that for a moment she forgot he was merely a harmless oddity. She saw him as a man, unconventionally handsome, who was studying her as if *she* were the oddity.

There was something else in his gaze, the slightest spark of sexual interest. It startled her, chilled her, drove her into herself.

She gave a forced smile and took a step away from him. "Well, I guess you and I are stuck together." Her tone, unnecessarily frosty, was meant to keep him at a distance.

But he merely shrugged again, as if nothing of consequence had happened. She wondered if she had only imagined the hint of sexuality in his eyes.

MALCOLM "HUTCH" Hutchison was seldom bored. His mind was a nimble one, always observing. What he saw this evening interested him.

Cousin Betsy, for instance. She was mighty pretty, with her big hazel eyes and smooth auburn hair. But she was an icy little number, and he was trying to figure why. She'd seemed friendly enough at first. Then he'd accidentally touched her. Boom—she'd turned into the Snow Queen.

Interesting.

She wasn't really getting caught up in the conversation around the table. She also observed everything—almost as closely as he did.

There was plenty to watch, Hutch thought. Simply put, Cal and Serena were happy. Cal's brother and his wife were not.

Hutch could see that Tyler's stoniness irked Cal. That was why, Hutch figured, Cal had let the cat out of the bag about Harvard.

Tyler must have needled his brother about the Snow Queen and Stanford. So Cal had slam-dunked Harvard on him. He hadn't done it with malice—there was no malice in Cal—but he'd done it.

Hutch wasn't particularly proud of having gone to Harvard. Neither was he ashamed. Such things didn't impress him. He'd been born for experience, not classrooms.

Experience told him complicated things were happening in this little steakhouse adjoining Zack's. Ruth, for instance, tried to act cheerful, but seemed troubled.

As for Tyler, Hutch reckoned his mood could make any woman uneasy. Hutch didn't think there was innate meanness in Tyler. Rather, he seemed like somebody about to crack under too many pressures.

Cal teased his brother, trying to get Tyler to lighten up. Tyler did a fair job of pretending to. Cal didn't see it was only pretending—he was too damn happy to notice.

Serena, too. Hutch's heart tightened when he looked at Serena. He was in love with her, he supposed, just a little and harmlessly. Lord, he thought, she was beautiful.

But she was crazy over her husband. She treated Hutch as if he were an old teddy bear who always amused her. He didn't mind. He'd made a habit of settling his affections on unattainable women. It kept life simple.

"Oh, Hutch," Serena said, suddenly smiling at him. "Tell everybody the story about the snake charmer who retired to Lewisville Lake."

"Oh, God, that's funny," Cal said. "Yeah, tell it."

Hutch looked into Serena's green eyes and felt like a jester infatuated with his princess. He gave everyone at the table his best aw-shucks smile.

Telling a story, Hutch knew, was an art much like seduction. You kept drawing an audience farther into your web of wiles until finally they were yours, begging for more.

He decided to direct the tale mainly toward Ruth, partly because he saw sadness in her eyes. It would be good to make her laugh. He began the snake charmer story the way he always did.

"One summer, I traveled with a carnival. It seemed like a good idea at the time...."

By the story's end he was rewarded by Ruth's bubbling laughter. For a change, the Snow Queen smiled almost naturally. Even Tyler gave a grudging grin.

Then Serena begged for another story, and Hutch could not deny her. Maybe she sensed the uneasiness in the air and wanted him to put people at ease. For her—and for Cal—he'd do his best.

When the meal was almost over, Ruth swore she couldn't remember the last time she'd had so much fun. Even Tyler had loosened up a little. But not the Snow Queen. Hutch didn't mind. The night was young.

Cal ordered a bottle of champagne, and said it was time for the news, at least the first part. The waiter filled the glasses. Ruth asked for ginger ale instead. So did Serena.

Cal looked around the table, then raised his glass. The others raised theirs, too, and waited.

Strangely, for once Cal seemed at a loss for words. He glanced at Serena. He swallowed. He took her free hand in his. He set his jaw at a determined angle.

"Things change," he said and looked at Serena again. "Thank God things change. Wish us luck. We're gonna make a baby."

Then he squeezed Serena's hand, and he and she smiled at each other.

Surprise swept over Hutch. "I'll be damned," he said with a slow grin. "Congratulations." He clinked his glass against Cal's and Serena's. They hardly seemed to notice.

But in that split second, Hutch noticed plenty. Tyler looked stunned, somehow pained, as if he'd lost something.

All laughter vanished from Ruth's eyes. She blinked once, very hard. Quickly her hand moved to her stomach, as if to protect it.

Hutch knew then. *They're worried about the baby. They haven't told anybody. Cal and Serena have no idea.*

Tyler snapped back to normal first. He touched his glass first to his brother's, then to his sister-in-law's. Ruth followed suit and tried to smile.

And something—briefly—had happened to the Snow Queen. For an instant, Betsy Holden no longer seemed regal. She looked like a dismayed child, lost and alone in the cold.

But then she smiled more widely than either Ruth or Tyler, and clinked her glass against the others. "Congratulations," she said, and seemed to mean it.

She and Hutch were the first to drink to them. Tyler raised his glass and took a hard gulp, as if he were downing a shot of whiskey. Ruth cast her eyes down and took a small taste. She moved her hand away from her stomach, and set her clenched fist next to her water glass.

A muscle twitched in Tyler's cheek. He watched Cal and Serena sip at their drinks as if they'd forgotten the others were there.

"I thought you weren't going—" Tyler began, then paused. "I thought you weren't."

"This is a wonderful surprise," Ruth said, barely audible. "I wish you the best."

Tyler kept staring at his brother. "I thought you weren't," he repeated. "Having kids, I mean."

Cal kissed Serena's hand on the knuckles. "Things change," he said again. Then he looked around the table. "This is hard to say. Serena had—a condition. She was at risk for a certain . . . disease."

Cal was obviously still having trouble talking. Serena held his hand more tightly. She tried to look cool, but Hutch knew she felt as strongly as Cal did. She was better at disguising her feelings, that was all.

"I was at risk for a hereditary disorder," she said in a controlled voice. "Huntington's chorea. If I had it, I could pass it on to our children. For years there was no way for me to know. It was impossible. Then, just recently, they announced they *could* tell. They discovered something called a marker gene. If you have the marker, you'll have the disease. If you don't, y-y-you won't.''

That was the only time her voice faltered, just that once. Hutch felt an ache in his throat. *Serena? At risk for something god-awful?*

"She doesn't have it," Cal said, looking at her again. "She—doesn't. She's fine."

Tyler looked stunned and a little blank, as if he'd never heard of the disease. "That's—great," he said. He darted a glance at Ruth, putting his hand over hers protectively.

"It took me four months to work up the nerve to take the test," Serena said, talking more swiftly now. Her voice trembled, but she seemed to want to get it all out. "I mean, you think, 'Well, what if I have it? What do we do then?'"

She set down her glass. She took Cal's hand between both of hers. "But he was with me all the way. I mean he was there for me—all the time."

She took a deep breath. "So I took the test. And we found out I was all right, and then I—I cried a lot and stuff—and it took us another four months to decide about children. I mean I'd never thought I should, and—and—"

Hutch was afraid she was going to cry. Hell, he was afraid *Cal* was going to cry. So he rose and quickly went to Serena.

He stood behind her, put his hands on her shoulders, bent and kissed her cheek. "Oh, hush up now," he said gruffly. "That baboon you married's gettin' emotional."

Serena smiled shakily. "Thanks, Hutch," she said. "You're right. I don't want to say any more about it— ever. It's over. Everything's different now. It's fine."

Hutch released Serena and gave Cal a contemptuous swat across the shoulder. "And you, you ugly booger. You sure picked yourself a tough job. Makin' babies with the prettiest girl in Texas. Just don't make one that looks like *you*, hear?"

Cal swallowed again, but managed a mock glare. "Look like me? You seen a mirror lately? Lord God!"

"Well, that's great, just great," Tyler said with a heartiness that didn't quite ring true.

"Yes, it really is," Ruth said, smiling a strained little smile at both Cal and Serena. "I had no idea—none of us had any idea—"

"Well, hell," Cal said, clearly embarrassed by his own feelings, "let's not get all mushy. Let's go to Zack's and party. I want to celebrate. And this meal's on me."

He stood, slapped Hutch on the back and gave everybody a crooked smile. He drew back Serena's chair and when she stood, wound his arm around her waist and kissed her, long and hungrily, where her throat joined her shoulder.

"Cal!" she admonished, laughing.

"I'm gonna celebrate like a crazy man," he said, "then I'm gonna take you home, sugar, and get to work. A man's gotta do what a man's gotta do." He kissed her again and growled, deep in his throat.

Hutch watched.

THE HONKY-TONK was crowded, noisy, and the air smoky. Betsy felt dislocated in time and space. She'd never been one for crowds or loud music, and Zack's struck her as the country and western version of hell.

Her mind spun like the dancers whirling around the dimly lit room. Something had gone awry with the evening, and the relationships among the McKinneys seemed complicated and emotionally loaded.

And since she'd arrived this afternoon, the idea of babies seemed to be closing in on her from every side. For years she'd hardened herself not to think about babies or to wince when they were mentioned. Suddenly she felt sickeningly vulnerable again.

Oh, God, I won't drive myself crazy with this. She fought to keep her facade cool and uncracked. *It's too confusing—I won't think about it at all.*

But she couldn't help it. She kept thinking about the little boy in Fredericksburg.

Earlier, Cal, in high spirits, had insisted on signing them all up for something called a "chili-off" at the park the next weekend. He, Serena, Ruth and Hutch acted as if it was the funniest thing they'd ever heard. Tyler wasn't amused, and Betsy was apprehensive.

She tried to make small talk with Ruth and Serena while Cal and Hutch laughed and cracked jokes. Tyler was withdrawn, closed off in his world.

Once in a while, she would catch Hutch eyeing her, and it always gave her an unpleasant start. Pointedly, she would look away from him.

The band started playing a song she vaguely recognized, "Dream Baby." Hutch rose, came to her side, bent and spoke low in her ear. "Want to dance? I think these people have family matters to discuss."

She would have liked to refuse, because the man unnerved her. But when he put it as he did, she couldn't say no.

She stood and didn't resist when he drew her onto the dance floor. His hand was hard and rough to the touch, a laborer's hand. It made odd sensations swarm up her arm.

"I don't know anything about this kind of dancing," she said. She made her voice cold, even distasteful.

"Don't worry," he said and took her into his arms. "I'll lead. Just follow. Or is it against your principles?"

She gritted her teeth. He was too tall; he loomed over her. He didn't smell like cologne or after-shave lotion or anything artificial. Michael lived in a perpetual cloud of the scent of bay rum. For her, it had become the safe, acceptable scent for a male.

Hutch smelled like soap and warmth and human flesh. The worn flannel of his shirt was soft beneath her fingers, but under the cloth, his muscles were iron-hard.

He held her with more authority and confidence than he ought to. "I can follow," she said tightly. Her hand was tense on his shoulder.

"Good," he said and swept her away.

Great heavens, Betsy thought, gliding to his complex signals, the man could *dance*. She was an excellent dancer by nature, and her parents had seen she had the best lessons. Never in her life had she met a man who was better than she. Until now.

He seemed to sense he was getting too complicated too fast and slowed his pace to accommodate her. "You're very good," he said without emotion.

"Thanks. So are you," she said in the same tone.

"So what do you make of it?" he asked. "What's goin' on in that family—between the lines?"

"I haven't the faintest idea what you're talking about," she said.

She glanced up at his shadowy face. She wished she hadn't. He wasn't nearly as handsome as Michael, but there was something arresting in his looks—the only word she could think of was *character*.

"You're lying," he said genially, and led her into a series of spins that left her dizzy. "Your cousin's worried about her baby, isn't she?"

Betsy blinked up at him in surprise. "I don't know."

"No." He bent nearer. "But you guessed. So did I. Things aren't right between her and Tyler, are they?"

"I haven't any notion," she said, discomfited by his insight.

"Oh, you got notions aplenty," he said. "You watch and watch. You don't miss a trick. Cal and Serena are too wrapped up in each other to catch on as fast as you did. Tyler's jealous of Cal, isn't he?"

Betsy was certain what he said was true, but she didn't want to validate it. "It's none of my business—or yours."

"Cal's my friend," he said and once more swept her through a series of whirls that left her breathless. "So's Serena. I think Cal's going to make Tyler a business offer. I hope it doesn't blow up in his face."

"Is that why you asked me to dance? So they could talk?"

"Yes. Partly."

She knew she shouldn't rise to the bait, but she did. "Partly?"

"I wanted to see if you felt as cold as you acted."

Damn him! she thought. "I assume I do," she said as aloofly as possible.

"You assume wrong," he said and held her more tightly.

Her muscles stiffened. "I thought Serena'd be the one you'd ask to dance," she said. "I thought I saw a gleam in your eye when you looked at her." *There,* she thought. *That'll put him in his place.*

It didn't. "That's right. So I never ask her to dance."

"You said Cal's your friend," she challenged. "Do you always covet your friends' wives?"

"On occasion. But that's all I do, covet a little."

"Well," she said, tilting her head spitefully, "what a wonderful friend you must be. Does Cal know you harbor carnal thoughts about his wife?"

He gripped her hand more firmly, tightened his hold on her waist. "They're not carnal. Carnality you can always get. What's hard is findin' a woman to admire. Besides, he's so in love with her, he expects everybody else to be. Hell, I wouldn't cross him. He's my friend."

"I see," she said. "You're a medieval sort—what you feel for her is 'courtly love.' You admire her from afar, but your love is pure, so to speak. Sheer fantasy."

"Courtly love. Exactly. It's a shame it went out of style. Keeps a guy out of trouble."

He drew her into a corner more shadowy than the rest of the floor. His dancing style had changed. They were slow-dancing now, and somehow he made it seem casual and intense at once.

She glanced over his shoulder. Most of the other couples were no longer dancing singly. They were linking together, arms around one another's waists, doing complicated steps in unison.

"We're not dancing like everybody else," she said, watching them so she didn't have to look at him. The group movements looked strange to her, almost ritualistic.

"That's line dancing. I don't line dance. It's sort of a variation of the concept of marchin' to a different drummer."

"And you dance to your own beat," she said. "Quite the character, aren't you?"

"Some would say I got no character at all. Why are you so tense? Is this slummin' for you? To be with somebody like me?"

"Oh, don't be ridiculous," she said. He made her angry at both him and herself. She supposed she did sound like a snob. She didn't care. He was too male and too unpredictable. Everyone else this evening seemed to view him as the classic good ol' boy, but to her he exuded danger, and it was real, not subtle in the least.

"The McKinneys 're talkin' pretty intense over there," he said, looking over her head. "I think we should keep at this for a while. Should we try to make conversation? Or should I just shut up?"

His frankness confounded her. "I—I'm perfectly capable of civilized conversation. I—I—why did you leave Harvard? Most people would kill to get in."

"Told you," he said, turning her round and round, "Arkansas had better ball. *Damn* fine ball."

"Did you finish school there?"

"No," he said. The music changed again, and he caught her up once again in more complex rhythms and moves. "I went pro. Got drafted by the New York Yankees—minor league. First Double-A, then Triple-A."

Betsy knew little about baseball and cared less. But she knew at least that the Yankees were a prestigious team, so he must have been good.

"Why'd you quit?"

He swooped her off in an unexpected direction to avoid colliding with a couple dancing blindly into their path.

"Had to. Broke my wrist. It stiffed up on me. Not bad. But too bad to pitch."

"You sound very philosophical about it."

"How else should I sound?"

She shrugged. If he went into another one of his whirling phases, she would be so giddy she'd have to lean against him for support. The thought of laying her head against his chest both unsettled and appealed to her.

"You could sound regretful," she suggested.

"I don't believe in regret. It probably happened for the best. Those guys that go up to the majors—and I was going up—they don't have real lives anymore. Too much money, too much pressure, too much everything."

"But you," she said, trying to sound cool and in control, "you've had a real life?"

"Yes," he murmured, pulling her closer. "Have you?"

The question caught her off guard, as usual. "Of course I've had a real life."

"Then relax and just dance, will you? Put your cheek against mine."

"Why?" She heard the tension in her voice.

"Because we'll feel closer, move better. You're good, really good. I never found anybody as good. So let's do it right, okay?"

His reasoning made a mad sort of sense, and Betsy felt unreal, dreamlike, like a person caught in a spell.

She laid her cheek against his. His jaw was hard, warm and freshly shaved. He held her hand against his chest "Better," he said in her ear. "Much better."

He was right. They were moving almost perfectly together. And now that she was getting used to him, she wondered if she could match anything he did.

It seemed he wondered, too. He began moving across the floor in a way that seemed almost supernatural in its intricacy and rightness. She closed her eyes to concentrate on following perfectly.

"What—what—" she managed to say, "did you do after you left baseball?"

"This. That. Everything," he said. His voice was low, his breath warm on her throat. "Bummed around. I wanted to see the world. I saw it. I wanted to do everything. Damn near did it. God, you're good. You're really good."

She took a deep breath and didn't trust herself to speak. She no longer felt merely human. She could be dancing on a moon-silvered cloud, no longer attached to the dull, constraining earth.

They could move together as one person. Such a thing had never happened to her before. It was eerie, but enchanting.

"I used to want to be a ballerina," she found herself saying. She had no idea why she'd said it. She hadn't thought of it for years.

"Why didn't you do it?"

She couldn't answer.

He asked an unexpected question. "Do you have a guy?"

Her eyes flew open. "Yes. I do."

"Shh." He nuzzled her ear slightly. "You're goin' tense on me again. Relax. Go with the flow."

She relaxed. She went with the flow. She closed her eyes again.

"So where is he?" Hutch asked, spinning them in large, complicated circles. "Your boyfriend?"

"London," she said, squeezing her eyes more tightly shut. "He's in London."

"Why's he clear over there while you're here?" he asked. "Is he a damn fool?"

"He's at the London School of Economics."

"Good for him," Hutch said. He kissed her, just under the ear. His lips were surprisingly gentle.

She pulled away from him abruptly. She stopped so quickly that it dizzied her worse than moving had done. He kept one arm around her waist, her hand captured in his.

He stared down at her, his lips slightly parted in a rueful smile.

Her pulses drummed crazily and her face was hot with anger. "Are you coming on to me?" she demanded in disbelief. "Making a pass? You *kissed* me."

"Hey," he said in his easy way. "It was like joinin' the carnival. Seemed like a good idea at the time."

She shook her head furiously. "You have no right—"

"When you dance like that, I got the right," he said.

"What a crazy, male chauvinist...sexist thing to say," she fumed. "Nothing gives you the right—"

He sighed. "I never did get the political correctness thing down. Okay. I'm sorry. It won't happen again."

"I want to go back to the table," she said.

"No. The talk looks strained. Let's stay here. Unless you want to go outside."

"It's raining outside," Betsy objected. But she could see the McKinneys' table from where they stood, see it quite clearly, in fact.

Cal was leaning across it, talking earnestly, and Tyler looked displeased, close to anger. Ruth stared at Tyler with disapproval, and Serena seemed embarrassed.

"Oh," Betsy said in resignation, "I should have stayed in California." She surrendered herself unwillingly to Hutch's arms again, but this time she kept her distance.

"California," he joked, ignoring her coldness. "Where everything's perfect, like a Hollywood movie?"

"Yes," she said derisively. "It *is* perfect. And tell me, please, what is this 'chili-off' thing Cal signed us up for? And how do I get out of it?"

He smiled in his lackadaisical way. "A chili-off is a chili-cookin' contest. Which Cal figures we'll win, 'cause he's got me on his side."

"A person could say you were conceited."

"Or realistic. Hell, he's doin' it as a favor, I know that. He figures it'll help me out. He's a generous guy."

"I don't want to cook chili," she said from between her teeth. "He should *ask* people first."

"Give him a break. He's ridin' high—he's happy. Or is that a foreign concept to you?"

"I know what happiness is, thank you."

"Yeah? You don't look like it. You don't act like it. Back out of it if you want to. He didn't mean any harm. Just tryin' to make you feel at home, is all."

"I *will* back out," she said stubbornly. But even as she said it, she knew she sounded querulous and childish. But why had he gone and kissed her that way? The evening had become ruinous. The kiss had triggered a hoard of memories and thoughts she didn't want.

He shrugged and started making his hypnotically smooth and complicated moves again. Ironically, her body moved with his in flawless harmony, no matter how intricate his steps.

She allowed herself the pleasure of giving herself to the music, hoping it would sweep her away from her inner conflicts.

But she refused to dance close to him again. Dancing close had been lovely in its crazy way, she admitted against her will—quite lovely. But how could she feel that way, she wondered in confusion. And then the memories began to swarm again, tormenting her.

Then, suddenly, Cal was beside them, his hand on Hutch's shoulder. They stopped dancing. He looked atypically solemn as he handed Hutch a set of keys.

"Ruth doesn't feel so well, and Tyler and I, we need to talk something out," Cal said. "So if you don't mind takin' Betsy home—"

"'Course not," Hutch said easily and shoved the keys into the back pocket of his jeans.

Cal gripped his shoulder more tightly. "Thanks." He nodded at Betsy. "Sorry. A sort of—family matter came up. You're in good hands. See you next week at the chili-off."

Betsy nodded numbly and said nothing.

Cal turned and threaded his way across the crowded floor. Betsy looked at the table. Even in the shadowy gloom of the dance hall, she could see that Tyler looked grim.

She was so distracted that she allowed Hutch to pull her a fraction of an inch closer. "Well," he said, his tone mocking, "it's like you said at the start, Cousin Betsy. You and I are stuck together."

She turned her gaze to him and fought the absurd urge to cry. She didn't want to be in his arms. She didn't want to be with him at all.

Somehow she had blundered into Ruth's unhappy household where no outsider was needed. Worse, much of Ruth's unhappiness stemmed from her desire for a child. Tonight, her first night in Texas, Betsy found that the mere word *child* bewildered her, filling her with a dull ache. Her emotions were exhausting her.

"What's wrong?" Hutch asked unexpectedly. She was surprised at the concern in his face and his voice.

"Nothing," she lied, and wondered what on earth she was doing in a stranger's arms.

Her throat was tight, her heart was starting its panicky rate again, and she knew it now for a certainty: she should never have come here.

CHAPTER FOUR

CAL WAS SITTING in the chair by his old desk when Serena came out of the bathroom. He was bare-chested and barefoot, clad only in his jeans. She came floating out with her hair down, wearing something long, wispy and lavender.

He seized her by the hand and pulled her onto his lap. She settled there happily, putting her arms around his neck.

Then he leaned his forehead against hers and put one hand under the silky strap of her nightgown. "How come you always go puttin' these things on?" he asked her, slipping the strap down. "When you know I'm just gonna have to take it off you?"

"Maybe," she said, "it's because you're so good at taking it off."

He slid the other strap down, and he started to bend to kiss the dusky valley between her breasts. But she caught his face between her hands and tilted it up to hers.

"Wait," she said softly. "Let's talk first. You're worried about Tyler, aren't you?"

"Not *that* worried," he said. "I can still do my husbandly duty."

Her green eyes were smoky with desire, but he could tell that she was bothered and that she was the one who needed to talk.

"Cal, I think we—we got carried away. Maybe we shouldn't have sprung everything on Ruth and Tyler so fast. It never occurred to me that Tyler might—well—resent our offering to invest in the winery. I thought he really needed the money. He didn't act happy at all."

Cal touched her face, ran his finger over her lower lip. "He's just bein' Tyler, is all. He's got too much on his mind lately. He'll come around."

She stroked his jaw softly with her thumbs. "I'm still worried. They didn't act like themselves tonight. Ruth, either. And they're so closemouthed about their baby, too. You don't suppose there's anything wrong, do you?"

He frowned and twined a strand of her dark hair around his finger. "Wrong? What makes you think that?"

Serena shrugged one shoulder. She had beautiful, pale shoulders with freckles scattered across them like constellations. He loved her shoulders.

"I don't know," she said. "For one thing, she really didn't feel well tonight. And she seems troubled. I mean, I'd hate for them to be worried, then we go carrying on about having a baby—like we're gloating, or something."

He put his hands on her shoulders to enjoy their satiny smoothness. But he could feel his face going serious. "Honey, after what you went through for all those years, you shouldn't ever have to be ashamed of bein' happy. Ever."

"We went through a lot this past eight months," she said, laying her hands against his bare chest. "I was all over the place emotionally—up—down—back—forth. I don't see how you stood me."

"I guess 'cause I was mostly goin' up and down and back and forth with you."

He gazed at her, drinking her in. Once he'd lived in fear that at any time, the disease might set in, take her from him. But she was safe, and that struck him, every time he looked at her, as a miracle.

She shook her head and gave him a shy smile. "I never thought you'd get so excited about having a child. You always talked like it didn't matter."

He laughed. "Back then, it wasn't an option. Now that it is, seems like a pretty damn nice one."

"Yes," she breathed. "It does."

He could tell how happy she was, and it made his heart do sweet, crazy things. They'd talked a lot about children after she'd gotten her test results, those blessed test results.

Sometimes it had seemed to him that all they talked about was kids—kids and business. But he wanted it to be her call, because she'd lived her life thinking she would never have children. He didn't want to force her decision, hurry it.

Yesterday, her period had ended, and he'd been thinking all day about making love to her. She'd been brushing her teeth before going to bed. He'd been standing beside her, brushing his. Suddenly she'd looked over at him with those big green eyes, and said, "Calvin, I want a baby. I really, really do."

She'd sounded so positive, so confident, so satisfied, he'd stared at her in amazement.

"I threw my pills away this morning," she'd said, nodding.

He'd been wearing only his jockey shorts and had a mouthful of foaming toothpaste, and like a fool he could only keep staring at her. But tears had sprung to his eyes.

She'd been wearing a pale green nightgown that swirled around her knees. Carefully, she'd set her toothbrush back in the holder, then looked him up and down.

"So will you spit that out and make love to me?" she'd asked.

He'd spit out the toothpaste, rinsed out his mouth and started kissing her up and down. They'd almost not made it back into the bedroom, and once they were in bed, he'd made love to her as he never had before.

This morning they'd woken up and made love again, languorously and tenderly, taking their own sweet time. By the time they'd gotten out of bed, it was as if they were both hungover with love, and Cal kept grinning idiotically and said he wanted to go to Crystal Creek and tell his family.

His sister and her husband and kids were in Hot Springs this weekend. But everybody else was at the Double C, and besides, they'd been planning on going soon to make their offer about investing in the winery. They could do everything at once. He felt happy and lucky, and wanted the whole world to feel the same way, especially Tyler, who'd been down in the mouth lately.

They were supposed to have been at home for Hutch, who would stay with them before he went on to Crystal Creek. But Cal was so overflowing with good spirits by then, he'd just left a note for Hutch to join them.

Now he studied Serena's face. "Hutch has got a crush on you," he said meditatively. "Maybe it'll stop once you're a pregnant lady."

She rubbed her forehead against his. "Liar. He's never had a crush on anybody. He's too footloose."

"I know him," he assured her. "He always does it. He only sets his heart on what he can't have, and that way he never gets tied down. 'Course in your case, he can't hardly help himself, but—"

"You don't have to flatter," she said, her lips almost touching his. "You know you're going to get exactly what you want from me."

"Will I?"

"Yes," she said and kissed him, but not nearly long enough.

"Are you still worried about Tyler and Ruth?" he asked.

She grew more solemn, and she drew back from him slightly. "A little. Everything's gone our way lately. But things have been harder on Tyler. And Ruth seems . . . I don't know."

"Look, sugar," he said, pushing her straps down farther, "give him time to get used to the idea. He'll be fine. Money worries must've got him down worse than I thought. Him and Ruth are probably goin' through a little rough patch, is all."

Her hands rose to frame his face. "You think so?"

"I hope so," he said. He took one of her hands and kissed it. "So why don't you concentrate on bein' happy yourself for a change?"

He wound his arms around her and brought his lips close to hers. Her nearly bare breasts were soft against his chest.

"I am happy," she said.

"Then be prepared," he whispered as seductively as he could, "because I am about to try to upgrade you to outright ecstatic."

BETSY AND HUTCH DANCED almost until closing time. Their dancing was odd, because while their bodies moved in perfect unison, they hardly spoke. Since he'd been audacious enough to steal the kiss, she'd frozen him out, lost in her own troubling thoughts.

She glanced at her watch, relieved when she saw how late it was. "I should go back," she said. "They've had plenty of time to talk by now."

He slowed, then stopped and gazed down at her, his arm around her waist, his hand still holding hers. "Yeah," he said absently. "I suppose they have."

He dropped her hand, withdrew his arm, stepped back from her. Then he looked her up and down in a measuring look. "It was a pleasure," he said. "In a peculiar way."

She gave him a controlled smile that she knew looked haughty, but she no longer cared what he thought of her. She wanted only to escape and be alone.

He led her back to their table without trying to touch her. "Your boyfriend," he asked, as he helped her with her coat. "Does he dance?"

"Yes," Betsy said. "Some." Michael was an adequate dancer, but conservative. He never took chances or tried anything new or difficult. *Michael,* she thought, her temples pounding. *What will I do about Michael?*

Hutch shrugged into his worn denim jacket. "You gonna marry him?"

The smoky air suddenly seemed to smother her, the crowd around them to press too near. "Yes," she said, raising her chin. "I suppose."

He started toward the door that led outside. She followed closely and carefully, not wanting to lose him in the crowd. Her ears, she realized, were ringing from the loudness of the band, and although she should have been tired, her blood was racing strangely.

He held the big exit door open for her. The rain had stopped, but the air was cool and misty, the night black.

The silence sounded monumental after the din of the music.

"You don't have an engagement ring," Hutch said, throwing her a sideways look.

"I'll probably get one at Christmas," she said. She lifted her hair from beneath her coat collar, smoothed it into place.

She studied him as he unlocked the door on the passenger's side of Cal's Jeep. "What about you?" she asked, trying to steer the conversation away from herself. "Never been married, I suppose."

"Nope. Don't believe in it."

He opened the door and she slid inside. He walked to the other side, got in beside her.

She paused a moment, then decided to ask a question. She didn't like him, she hadn't forgiven him for the kiss, but anything was better than being alone with her thoughts. "Why did you think Cal was going to make Tyler some kind of business offer?"

He merely shrugged as he started the Jeep and put it into gear. "He mentioned it. Cal's got more money than he needs. Tyler's startin' a business. To start a business, you gotta have money."

She settled against her seat. "And why does Cal have so much money? Just from making boots?"

Hutch eased the Jeep out of the parking lot and onto the street. "He had the right connections at the right time. He got Serena to tie in with a guy he knew named Amarillo Tex."

"I never heard of Amarillo Tex," she said loftily and stared off into the darkness.

"Hasn't slowed him down," Hutch said sardonically. "At any rate, this singer came along, and he liked Serena's boots. He had her custom-design him a pair. Real famous singer."

"Who?" Betsy asked, not really caring.

When Hutch mentioned the name, she didn't recognize it, either, and said so.

Hutch frowned in disbelief. "Everybody's heard of him. Every time he breathes in or out, another million records are sellin'."

"Not to me and my friends," she said. She didn't mind sounding contrary. She supposed she was punishing him because his kiss had opened up such a Pandora's box of memory and conflict in her.

He shook his head. "You have to know him. A big guy. Tall. Chubby, kinda. Wears a great big hat. If he does anything—even goes on a diet, those supermarket papers have him all over the covers."

"I," Betsy said firmly, "don't read those supermarket papers."

"No," he muttered. "I don't suppose you do. Well, anyway, he liked these boots, and he ordered four more pairs just like 'em."

"Why?" Betsy demanded. "Why would anybody need five identical pairs of cowboy boots?"

"Because he's a star is why," Hutch said impatiently. "He wore 'em on this tour he just finished. He wore 'em on the cover of his last album. They're distinctive-like. They got like a flame design up the side."

"Why do country singers always have to dress up like that, anyway?" Betsy said.

Hutch flexed his fingers on the wheel. "Look—you asked. I'm tryin' to explain."

"Then explain," she said, buttoning her coat more tightly. "I'm not stopping you."

"All right," he said. "So Cal comes up with this idea that Amarillo Tex turns out these boots in big numbers, and that the singer endorses 'em and gets a cut of the profits."

"You mean everybody will run out and buy these things just because this singer wears them?"

"Yes," Hutch said. "That's exactly what I mean. This guy wears a big hat, men all over the West go out and buy a big hat. He wears a shirt with big old checks, they go out and buy a shirt with big old checks."

"I thought the true Western soul was independent," Betsy countered. "Not a slave to fashion."

"The kind of true Western sole I'm talkin' about is on the bottom of a boot, and these boots are on the market for Christmas, and they're already sold out, and they're back-ordered like crazy, and Cal and Serena have a big piece of the contract money. A *great* big piece."

"Oh," Betsy said, nodding. "I see. Which is going to be like this huge profit they should offset. So if they invest in the winery, they're basically pumping money from one family business into another, but at this stage of the game, it'll be a tax write-off."

He gave her a skeptical look. "Well, you don't understand the music part or the fashion part, but you got the money part down, sure enough."

"Well, I should. I majored in business."

"Sounds like a million laughs."

"Well, what did you major in?" she challenged. "Anything?"

"Yeah," he said, cocking his head at a satiric angle. "Philosophy. I suppose you're kinda taken aback that I can read."

"Not at all," she said, but she was surprised that he'd majored in philosophy, of all things. "Why'd you quit?

You could have gone back after you broke your wrist. You could be—a professor or something."

"Teach?" he said in disbelief. "Me? Give lectures and grade papers and sit in a stuffy office?"

"Well," she answered, "you might have gone back just for the intellectual stimulation. A good education—you know."

"Hell," he said, "I can read a book on my own. I don't need to get a grade for it. Jeez, there's more than one way to get an education. I don't have to sit in a class and have somebody spoon it out to me."

"Look," she said, turning to him, "I'm not trying to insult you, all right? It's simply that you're obviously a bright man. You could do better for yourself than opening a—a chili parlor, or whatever you call it."

"And I'm not tryin' to insult you," he said emphatically, "but you don't get it. I *want* to open a chili parlor. It may seem lowly to you, but it's what I *want*."

"But why?" she asked, truly puzzled. "I mean, once in a great while a restaurant does really well and can franchise, but that's very rare, so..."

"I don't want to franchise," he said from between his teeth. "I'm not doin' it for money. I like to make chili. I want a place, not fancy, where folks feel at home. Come in for a beer, a bowl of red, some conversation, a good time—"

"Conversation and a good time won't pay bills."

He sighed with exaggerated weariness. "I'm not worried about bills. I'm seekin' a certain quality of life, is what. Doin' what I like. Friends. Talkin' sports, talkin' politics, talkin' ideas."

"We're just not on the same wavelength," Betsy said and stared out at the night again.

"You can say that again," he agreed. "You belong with somebody from the London School of Economics. You can sit around talkin' profit-and-loss margins."

"I'm not a crass materialist," she returned. "I was just trying to be practical. I mean, what does your family think of this?"

The headlights caught the sign, far down the highway, that marked the entrance to the Double C. Betsy stifled a sigh of relief. The whole evening had been insane; she was desperately anxious for it to end.

"My family," Hutch said, "thinks it's fine. They accept me for exactly what I am. If I'm happy, they're happy. Which seems to me just how a family should be. But I suppose you've got different ideas on that, too."

The remark stung her. "My family," she said tightly, "is fine. We just—all pull together. We have common goals. It's different. That's all."

"Different is fine," he said. *"Vive la différence."*

She didn't answer. They reached the lane that led to the Double C. They passed the ranch house; it was completely dark. Cal and Serena were in bed, she supposed, and realized that they had probably made love—because they obviously so wanted to have a child. The thought intensified her empty, haunted, bewildered feeling.

She was a stranger in a strange land, worn out in heart and spirit from thinking about the child being so close. But suddenly she didn't want the night with Hutch to end on a bitter note. She knew she'd taken too much of her fear and confusion out on him.

She tried to change the subject again, to sound a little more human. "That must have been terrible for Serena," she said. "I've read about Huntington's disease. To have that hanging over her head? It must be like being born again, finding out she's safe."

"Yeah," Hutch said quietly. "Well, she never let on. Her or Cal, either. Yeah, I'm glad for them."

"Yes," she said. "And I hope things work out for Ruth and Tyler. And you, too," she added. "I mean with your chili business. I probably won't see you again, so, well, good luck."

He frowned slightly. "I thought you were stayin' with Ruth. We're both gonna be around. But if you don't want to see me, don't worry. I won't try—"

"No," she interrupted. "I didn't mean it like that. I think it'd be better if Ruth and Tyler had their privacy. There's obviously a strain there, and I don't need to add to it. It's silly for me to drive all the way into Austin to house-hunt, anyway."

"Oh," he said. They were approaching Ruth and Tyler's house. It, too, was mostly dark, but a few lights shone within, left on for Betsy's benefit. The yellow porch light gleamed, lighting the stairs.

Oddly, the foolish dog didn't bark at their approach. Betsy couldn't even see it stirring. It probably barked at everything *except* strangers, she thought, which almost made sense, as topsy-turvy as she felt.

Hutch brought the Jeep to a stop. "I'll walk you to the door."

"No," she said. "Let's just say goodbye here. Thanks for everything. I know we're—very different, but it's been interesting. And I do mean it. Good luck with the chili thing."

He smiled rather ruefully. "The same to you. And you're a good dancer. The best I ever found."

She was touched that he would compliment her, as prickly as she'd been. "You're good, too. The best *I* ever met. It must run in your family. Being athletic, dancing, things like that?"

His smile grew more musing, more crooked. "I don't know."

She looked at him curiously. In the dim glow that fell through the windshield from the porch light, he looked unexpectedly handsome. His lean face, she realized vaguely, grew more interesting the longer she looked at it.

"I just meant," she said, "are there any other athletes in your family?"

Why am I asking these things about family and heredity? What's wrong with me? Why did I bring this up?

"No. Just me."

"Dancers? There must be."

"No. Just me."

"That's strange. My brothers like to dance. But not as much as I do. Heredity's weird."

I shouldn't say that, she thought with a painful twinge. *I'm talking like that because all I can do is wonder if the little boy... I've got to stop. I have to. I need to go in the house, get some sleep, start over in the morning, try to think straight....*

He smiled and extended his hand to her for a goodbye shake. She accepted it.

"Don't know much about heredity," he said, still smiling his crooked half smile. "I'm adopted. Well, take it easy. Good luck apartment-hunting or whatever."

The word *adopted* stabbed through her like a knife.

The casual way he'd said it stunned her. A strange feeling, partly chilly, partly scalding, washed over her.

"What?" She clutched his hand more tightly. "What?"

"Good luck apartment-hunting," he repeated, studying her face. His smile faded, and he drew one eyebrow down in a curious frown.

"No," she said, her voice unsteady. "Before that. You're—adopted?"

"Yeah. It's no big deal."

He'd caught her off guard when she was least prepared and most vulnerable. She stared at him helplessly.

"What's wrong?" he asked.

She prayed he wouldn't see the need, naked and shamed, that must be in her eyes.

"Sometime—sometime," she stammered, "would you tell me what it's like? Would you tell me—please? I have to know. I need to—to—to—"

She didn't quite know what she was saying. She couldn't finish the sentence. She stared at him more helplessly than before.

He looked back with those clear, intent eyes that seemed to see everything and now were seeing her, as if for the first time.

And, she realized, with a sickening start, he *knew*. Just as he'd guessed so many things tonight, he now guessed the truth about her.

CHAPTER FIVE

It FELL INTO PLACE for Hutch at that moment. He'd been trying to figure her out all night. So *that* was it.

Somewhere she had a kid she'd given up for adoption. He didn't know how he knew, he just did.

Her hand had tightened around his, and he was sure that she'd done it without thinking. And her request—blurted out so spontaneously—had something desperate in it. So did her voice.

He wondered if she had any idea about the expression on her face. She looked both stricken and hopeful. The aloof mask had fallen. He saw a young woman who was quietly frantic.

So he kept hold of her hand, and when he spoke, he tried to make his voice as kind and convincing as possible. "It was great," he said. "Being adopted was great. I had a happy family. A very happy life."

She nodded distractedly. She seemed embarrassed by her outburst. She gazed at the porch, bathed in its glow of yellow. "I didn't mean to sound as if you were some sort of—of curiosity or something."

"That's all right," he said. "Ask anything you want." *My God,* he thought, *she doesn't realize I've still got her hand.*

"I never knew anybody who was adopted," she said, not looking at him. Her voice was shaking. "Except this one girl at college, but that was different. She was Vietnamese. She'd lost her family in the war, and—"

Her voice trailed off. She shrugged.

"Did that make her so different?" he asked. He watched her struggling hard to control her expression. She was almost succeeding.

She gave a rueful little laugh that had no mirth in it. "Of course not. In lots of ways, she was more American than me. I mean, she was this fiend for rock and roll. She was a cheerleader, for heaven's sake."

"She was happy?"

"She seemed happy," Betsy almost whispered. "I never asked."

"Did you want to?"

"Yes," she said, her voice even lower. She swallowed.

"Were you afraid you'd embarrass her?" he asked.

She licked her lips. "Yes. Partly."

"You won't embarrass me. I promise. Ask anything."

She seemed to think hard. Still, she didn't look at him, and still didn't seem to realize her hand clutched his.

"Did you ever wonder about—your real parents?" she asked at last.

"I think of the people who raised me as my real parents. They did the real parentin'."

She ducked her head. "About your biological parents, then. Didn't you wonder?"

"Some. Not much."

"You didn't wonder why she—they gave you away?"

"I figured they had their reasons."

She seemed to mull this over. "I see," she said. "But I don't suppose you're typical. You're this...I don't know, freewheeling type."

"Betsy," he said quietly, "there's probably no such thing as typical. Now me, I always reckoned it didn't matter that much who brought me into the world. I'm here, and I'm me. For my brother, it was different. He wondered a lot. It was important to him."

Oh, God, he thought with a sinking heart, she was crying. Silently, and without almost any physical indication, except the tears themselves. They glinted in the light from the porch.

He held her hand more tightly. He unsnapped his seat belt and bent nearer to her. "But he and I were different, see? It wasn't that he wasn't happy. It's just he had to know. And I didn't. And our sister was different, still. She didn't *want* to know. She resented that somebody gave her away."

Betsy sat staring at the porch, the tears running slowly and steadily.

"There were three of us," he said. "We were all adopted, and we all turned out okay. Now maybe you think I'm not so okay, but I'm a satisfied man. I've lived life absolutely on my own terms. My brother, he's different, a settled guy. He's an electrician down in Hondo. Married. Got two children of his own now."

He clenched his teeth because he wasn't sure he was saying the right things.

"My brother's name is Harry. Now, Harry pretty much had to meet his birth parents. That's how it was for him. And my folks, they felt kind of threatened by that. My mother especially. But they told him."

He reached into his jacket pocket with his free hand. He gave her a clean bandanna handkerchief. She took it wordlessly and tried to blot away the tears. He didn't understand how she could cry like that and not make a sound.

He wrapped both his hands around hers. "When Harry was eighteen, he looked them up—found his birth

mother first. And she was happy to see him, glad to see
he turned out so well. His birth father, that was dicier.
But they finally worked things out. So now Harry's got
two sets of parents. That's fine. That's how he wants it."

She took a deep breath but made no other movement.
He felt she wanted him to keep talking, so he did. "Then,
Marliss—that's my sister—Marliss's mother showed up
one day, wantin' to meet her. Marliss didn't want anything to do with her. But she did, at last. Turned out they
didn't have much in common. It's just they know each
other. It's fine."

He, too, took a deep breath, exhaled it from between
his teeth. "Now Marliss knows who her birth father is,
but she's never looked him up. She's got some health information on him, that's all, for her own sake and her
kids when she has 'em. Marliss is a nurse in Waco. She's
gonna have a baby next March. She's happy, Betsy. She's
happy—truly."

He shook his head. He supposed this was happening
because he was a stranger, and she never had to see him
again. For some reason, she felt near the end of her rope
and had to let the tears out.

"Now, me, I was different yet," he said. "After
Harry—he was the oldest kid—wanted to know, my folks
thought we should all know. So I know who my birth
mother is, and father, too. I know she was from Dallas."

Betsy tried to rub the tears away again. He was starting to wonder if she had an unlimited supply. "Once,"
he said, "when I was rodeoin', I got busted up in Dallas.
I was hangin' around while my arm mended, and I decided to check her out, just for the hell of it, you know.
The curiosity. But when I tracked her down and phoned
her, she didn't want to see me. She didn't want to talk to

me. She told me never to call again. She wanted to forget I ever existed."

He gave a ragged sigh. "I know you think I'm way too laid-back about things. You probably think that it didn't bother me. It did—that's a fact. It made me feel right odd for a time."

Did she grip his hand a fraction more tightly, or did he imagine it? He studied her profile. If it weren't for the tears, she might have been staring calmly at a scene from a play instead of at the darkness.

"But it didn't kill me or even come close," he said. "You've got to understand that. See, I must have represented a real sad, bad time in her life. She didn't want to remember, she didn't want people to know. She must have been hurt a lot by it. I didn't need to hurt her more."

Betsy made a tiny sound between a gasp and a sigh. She held her chin higher.

Hutch said, "My father, I never knew. I never will. I checked on him, more out of curiosity than anything. He died in Vietnam. His name is on that black wall. I went to see it once."

He paused. He had never talked this frankly about his past to anyone, ever. But he had a compulsion to tell her, because somehow it seemed she needed to hear what he had to say.

"I—I'm thirty-one years old now," he said. "That's eleven years older than he was when he died. So he never seems quite real. He was married, I know that. To somebody else, not my birth mother. She's got a son by him. I don't figure she needs to know about me. It'd just hurt her. My half brother, maybe someday I'll look him up. Maybe."

Betsy put her hand, shaking badly, to her forehead. "I'm sorry," she managed to say. "I know you think I'm probably crazy—"

"No," he said and bent nearer. "I think I understand. Yeah. I think I do. Now. You want to talk to me about it?"

She seemed to draw further into herself. She shook her head and quickly wiped her eyes, then held the bandanna clenched in her lap. "No," she said. "No. Thank you."

He swallowed, surprised she didn't draw her hand away from his. Maybe she needed somebody to hold on to. Well, hell, he thought, he could do that much for her.

"I think maybe it'd help," he said. "'Cause it seems you're holding things inside till you're about to explode. It's okay to tell me. How old were you?"

She bit her lip. He thought she wasn't going to answer. "Fifteen," she said at last, in a tight voice. "But sixteen when I had it. Him."

He nodded. "Okay," he said. "Your family. They probably took it hard. You bein' so young. They probably thought they should keep it quiet."

She ducked her head. "Yes."

"Did they send you away?"

She lifted her chin again. "Yes. To this—this place in Utah. They said I was spending half a year with my oldest brother and his wife. He—they were in London. He was studying film and video there."

Hutch frowned and patted her hand awkwardly. "I think you should blow your nose. You sound all stuffed up."

She complied. He watched her struggle to keep more tears from coming. They'd slowed, at least.

"I don't know why I'm telling you this," she said in her choked voice. "I don't understand at all."

"It's because I'm nobody important," he said. "You never have to see me again. And don't worry. I won't talk about this to anybody. It's nobody's business."

"It's not," she said, clearly miserable, "and I don't know why I'm inflicting it on you. I'm upset. I never should have come here."

He touched her chin, just barely, so she wouldn't be startled or draw away. "Look at me. It's okay. Tell me why. You need to tell somebody, Betsy, because you're *mighty* on edge."

She flinched slightly at his touch, but let him turn her face to his. The features he'd thought so aristocratic and aloof were smeared with her tears, now, and the once-cool hazel eyes swam with them.

But she met his gaze. "Nobody knows. He's here. My s-s-son. He's here. In F-F-Fredericksburg."

"Okay," he said encouragingly. He let his hand rest lightly on her wet cheek. "Go on. It's all right."

"Nobody knows," she repeated. "My family. They don't suspect. Ruth doesn't even know there is a—a child. Nobody outside my immediate family knows. Except for agency people. And the other g-girls. Who were in that place. In Utah."

She spoke with the broken rhythm of someone who has run a long way and cannot get her breath.

"All right," he said, laying his hand more firmly against her cheek. "Okay. So your boyfriend, he doesn't know, either?"

She closed her eyes and swallowed. "No. Michael doesn't know. He has no idea." She made that small, pained sound again, half gasp, half sob.

"Shh," he said. "You don't have to close your eyes. I think you're a nice woman. Look at me."

Slowly, her eyes fluttered open. Her mouth twitched. "I'm *not* nice. I've lied to a man who wants to marry me."

Her shining hair spilled over the shoulders of her coat. Hutch had the absurd desire to smooth it into place so it hung down her back. He resisted.

"Maybe it's for the best," he said as levelly as he could. "Or maybe you'll change your mind and tell him. That could happen."

"I shouldn't have come here," she said, looking into his eyes as if searching for the answers she needed.

"You came because of the boy? To find the boy?"

Her mouth twitched again. "Yes. No. I don't know. I—just don't know."

"Are you going to see him? Make contact with his parents?"

She shook her head so that her hair fell over the lapels of her coat. "I don't know. I don't know what's the right thing to do."

Oh, God, Hutch thought, breathing hard. He was starting to be overly aware of her as a woman again, which was the last thing he should do. He knew she must be scared to death of sex because of the kid.

He took his fingers away from her face. He loosened his grip on her hand. He drew back from her a bit, but probably not enough.

"I can't tell you what to do," he said.

But still she was gazing up at him as if he held keys to all the mysteries that plagued her. Her chin quivered slightly. "You could take me away," she said.

The way she put it startled him, as if she were asking him to run off with her. "What?"

She nodded and bit her lower lip. It was a full, delicately shaped lip and looked incredibly soft. "You could take me back to Austin. Now. Tonight. I could go in the house right now, get my things, leave a note for Ruth. You could drive me to the airport. I'll go home. There's another job I can take in New Hampshire—"

"Whoa," he said. He raised his hand to settle it on her shoulder, to steady her, then knew he shouldn't touch her again. "No. Slow down. You don't want to do that. It's too—"

"I know this is Cal's Jeep," she said. "I know you don't have your own car. I heard you say so at supper. But Cal's your friend. You could explain. I'll make something up. I'll pay for the gas. I'll pay you for your time—"

He held up his hand for her to stop. Her tears had finally ceased, and he didn't want to set her off again. But he didn't want her grasping at straws, either.

"It's not the time," he said as earnestly as he could. "Or the money. It's too sudden. Everybody'll know something's wrong. Don't run scared. Stay. Think it through. You just got here."

She turned from him again and withdrew her hand from his. She laced her fingers together in her lap around the crumpled bandanna. Her shoulders sagged slightly.

"I shouldn't have done this to you. I shouldn't have told you."

"Hey," he said, trying to sound like a friendly old uncle. "You needed to talk. Sometimes it happens."

She shook her head as if trying to clear it. "I didn't even have to tell you, did I? You guessed. You're right. I was close to the edge. Was I that transparent about what happened?"

He sighed. The yellow glow of the porch light shone on her silky hair. "No," he told her truthfully. "I've got instincts. I read people pretty well."

"You've read me like a book," she said almost bitterly. "A very easy-to-read book."

"No. Just instincts. And practice. I used to be a blackjack dealer in Vegas. Part of my checkered past. For that kind of job, you gotta read people."

"Well," she said, sadness in her voice, "you're good at it. And good at listening. I didn't mean to unload all my shameful secrets on you. I guess I should say thanks."

His hand felt strangely empty without hers, so he made a meaningless gesture. "Hey. Listenin's been my job, too. I was a bartender in Reno. Your secrets aren't so shameful. Trust me. A bartender in Reno hears everything."

She turned. Amazingly, she almost managed to smile. "You really are something, you know?"

"No," he said, "*you're* something. You're strong, Betsy. You'll get through this."

He leaned back against his seat, clamped one hand safely on the steering wheel. He supposed there were all kinds of things he should say to make her feel better, but he didn't know what they were.

She was silent a moment, and he was surprised she didn't try to say goodbye and escape. For how long had this small, delicately made woman needed to talk so badly to somebody, anybody?

"It was a closed adoption," she said softly. "That's what makes it hard to decide. I signed these papers never to see him, never to try to be in touch—I signed whatever they told me to. I don't even know if the boy knows he's adopted. Or if I did see him, what I'd feel."

Hutch nodded, sensing she wanted to go on. Her face was slightly swollen, but he thought she looked prettier than when she'd been all perfect and cold.

"I—" She paused and turned to face him again. "I—don't even know what he looks like. I keep wondering if he looks like me."

He shook his head philosophically. "He might look like his father. Would it matter? Would it bother you?"

"I think it might," she said. "Can I tell you something? That's a stupid question, because I've already told you things I never told anybody."

"Hey," he said gruffly, "a bartender in Reno, remember?" He had the uneasy conviction that she was fighting back tears again. "Say whatever you want."

She laced her fingers more tightly together, and squared her shoulders. God, he thought, she looked so little and prim sitting there.

"It's not like I was involved with the father," she said, her jaw held rigidly. "It was my first date with him. A party. I wasn't drinking, or anything like that. But he was. Things were getting wild. I started getting scared. I should have called for somebody to come get me."

No, he thought, *don't blame yourself. You were a kid, a child.*

"But he said he'd take me home. He was mad at me. Because I wouldn't—you know."

"Yeah," he said quietly. "I know."

"So he and two of his friends were supposed to drive me home. But they didn't. They took me to a—a park instead. It was dark. It was really dark. And they were still drinking. And—"

"If you don't want to say it, don't," he told her. "Say only what you want to."

"All right," she said, squeezing the handkerchief harder. She held her shoulders more stiffly. "They raped me. All three. They said if I ever told, they'd say I'd let them. I was scared. So I didn't tell—until—"

"Oh," he said. "I see. God."

She hunched slightly, as if at the memory of a blow. "I don't know which one is the father," she said.

There was nothing he could say. He'd have taken her into his arms, but he knew she didn't want that.

Finally he said, "That's why you don't like being touched much? Because of that?"

She nodded.

"But you still dance. You let me hold you when we danced. You even let me hold you close. For a while."

"That's different," she said and looked away.

"Why?"

She shook her head as if in sad wonder. "It's funny," she said. "It's the one time I can really like my body. Maybe the only time. Can you understand that?"

He understood. But it made something wrench inside him. "Let's keep talking," he said.

And they did. For the next four hours they sat and talked and talked.

WHEN BETSY ROSE the next morning, she wondered if guilt and degradation were visible, like a brand upon her forehead. She'd done the unthinkable, the absolutely forbidden. She'd *told* somebody.

She didn't understand her own feelings and didn't expect to. When she went into Ruth's kitchen, she felt like an actress on a stage, acting a role that had nothing to do with her real life.

"I was starting to get worried about you," Ruth joked as she set down Betsy's coffee. "I thought maybe you were so taken with Hutch, you'd run off with him. Your mother'd kill me if that happened."

Long ago, Betsy had perfected the art of not flinching. "We got to talking, that's all," she said lightly.

"You were quite an item on the dance floor," Ruth said, sitting down across from her. "I thought maybe he'd just—swept you away."

"I'm not the sort that gets swept away," Betsy said and began to spread jam on a piece of wheat toast.

Ruth smiled a bit stiffly. "I didn't think so. But you know your mother. She said I'm supposed to keep my eye on you. I'm not supposed to let you get involved with anybody down here. She considers you taken, you know."

Betsy glanced at her cousin. She had the sudden sensation of being cornered, almost trapped. "What?"

Ruth cocked her head and smiled again. "Oh, you know. She seems to think that the sun rises and sets on this Michael. And she worries that you'll find an excuse to break off with him. She says that you have a habit of finding these wonderful men, and then rejecting them."

Betsy fought down a surge of resentment. But what her mother had said was true. Betsy had never allowed a relationship to last beyond a few dates. Except for Michael.

Ruth seemed to understand. She looked apologetic. "I'm sorry. It's just that your mother worries about you. And she thinks that this Michael is almost perfect for you."

"Yes," Betsy said without emotion. "Almost perfect."

Ruth stirred her herb tea and gave a careless shrug. "So, I was concerned when you stayed out late. I mean, he's charming. He tells wonderful stories. He's very amusing. And a great dancer. But he's just a guy who wants to open a chili joint.''

"Don't be silly," Betsy said with a smile she didn't feel. "I have nothing in common with the man. We're from different worlds."

"That's an understatement," Ruth said. "He's quite a character, isn't he? Imagine—working with a carnival. Knowing snake charmers."

Betsy suppressed the desire to say she'd like nothing better than to run off with the carnival and know snake charmers and sword swallowers and exotic dancers and barkers. Sometimes, like now, her tight, proper, planned life seemed to stifle her.

Instead she said as brightly as possible, "I doubt if I'll see much of him. I've been thinking, Ruth. It's silly for me to drive back and forth to Austin to look for a place. And I don't feel right moving in on you and Tyler like this. I think it'd be best for everybody if I take a room at the Hyatt."

Betsy was surprised to see disappointment and something like alarm in Ruth's face. "Betsy, no. Please. I *want* you here. I can't tell you how much."

Betsy squirmed slightly. "It'd just be more convenient, I think..."

Ruth pushed away her tea, untasted. "But you don't know how much I've looked forward to this, Bets. And Tyler wants you here, too. He knows I need somebody right now. We both want you here—really."

Betsy shook her head. "You're still newlyweds—almost. I feel out of place. I—"

Ruth reached out and grasped Betsy's hand. "Can I be honest with you?"

Oh, God, Betsy thought, trying mightily not to flinch. *I thought I wanted honesty, and now I'm going to get it, and it's going to be painful.*

"Of course," she said, feeling like a hypocrite. Last night she had cried like a child on Hutch's shoulder. Ruth so obviously needed to talk to someone—how could Betsy deny her?

Ruth rose and paced to the counter. She cast an unhappy look at Betsy. "Tyler and I," she said slowly, "aren't getting along very well just now. We argued last night. And then again this morning."

Ruth shook her head. "I snapped at Tyler, and I shouldn't have. He's—he's making a lot of compromises for my sake. About financing the winery. It's a family matter, really. I won't bore you with it."

So, Betsy thought. Hutch had been right about the money and winery. He *did* read people and situations well. Impressively so.

Ruth crossed her arms over the small bulge of her pregnancy. "I haven't been easy to get along with lately. Part of it's being so far away from everything familiar. You don't know how scary it is."

Betsy wanted to cry, *Yes, I do know. I understand better than you'll ever know.*

"Oh," Ruth said with a disgusted expression, "I shouldn't dump on you like this. It isn't fair. I love Tyler, and he loves me. But we're both under so much pressure that when we're alone we always end up disagreeing."

"But I..." Betsy hesitated. "Wouldn't I just make things worse? Shouldn't you have privacy to—"

"No," Ruth said, almost pleading. "It's better when someone else is there. It defuses the situation. And if I only had someone to talk with, really talk with. He's gone so much."

Ruth glanced at the window, and Betsy thought she saw the flash of unshed tears in her eyes. "Oh, Bets, it's complicated. I don't have any right to drag you into it. But I feel so cut off from who I used to be. I need you. Just for a week or two? Don't leave yet. Please."

Once Betsy had been an affectionate, even a demonstrative person. She had suppressed that part of her personality for eight and a half years. But she knew what she needed to do, and she did it.

She rose, went to Ruth and hugged her. She didn't want to make the promise, but felt she must. She tried to keep her voice kind and comforting, the way Hutch's had been. She didn't think she was nearly as good at it as he was.

"I'll stay," she said. "At least until I find a place. Don't feel bad, Ruth. It'll be fine. You're just going through a lot of changes, that's all."

Ruth held her tight, so that Betsy could feel the swell of her cousin's stomach. "Gee," Ruth said, trying to laugh, "you'd think I'd handle this better. I mean, I'm over thirty. Maybe it's hard at any age."

The words went straight through Betsy's heart. She found she was holding on to Ruth harder than she had held anyone in years.

CHAPTER SIX

"WE GOT US a vehicular crisis," Cal told Hutch.

Cal lounged against the fireplace of the guest house. He looked like a working cowboy today—faded jeans, old plaid jacket and black hat pulled down low. Only his boots, plain but elegant, gave any hint he was a young man on his way up in the world.

Hutch nodded at the boots. "Serena made those for you, didn't she?"

Cal smiled smugly. "My birthday present."

Hutch shook his head in mock disgust. "You are the luckiest bastard in the universe. Why?"

"Just born that way," Cal said. "But I'm tellin' you, we got a shortage of wheels just now. I need a favor from you. And a promise."

"Sure," Hutch said. "Just don't give me any details on the baby-makin' business. I don't think I can stand it. The smile on your face is bad enough."

Cal smiled more broadly. "Old bachelor like you shouldn't think of it. You could experience a major sperm backup and explode."

"So what's the favor?" Hutch snorted. "And what's the problem?"

He stood in the bathroom doorway, tucking a green flannel shirt into his jeans. It was his newest shirt and his most respectable-looking pair of jeans; today he was going to inspect real estate.

"Ruth's car won't start," Cal said. "Cynthia took off in hers, and yesterday Daddy left his truck in town to get new shocks. He and Ken got the ranch truck. Tyler's usin' his to haul gravel. I'm gonna join him. We hafta talk. That leaves only the Jeep for you."

Hutch tried to comb his unruly waves into place. "Some Texas ranchers. You can only scrape up six cars and trucks between you?"

"We've fallen on hard times. In the meantime, I got one Jeep and two people needin' it. You got a real estate appointment in Crystal Creek. Ruth's cousin's got one in Austin. Can you share the Jeep? That's the favor."

Betsy. Hutch's insides gave a funny twist at the thought of her name. "Hell," he said. "No problem. I'll drive her in. I can put my appointment back. No big deal."

"Naw," Cal said. "You drive to Crystal Creek, let her take it on to Austin. She can pick you up on the way back."

Hutch put down his comb and leaned both hands on the sink. He stared out the door, narrowing his eyes at Cal. "Comin' back? She's not comin' back. She's gonna stay in Austin. It'll be easier. She told me last night."

Cal pulled his hat brim down a notch. "Been a change of plans. She's stayin'. So can you work out something with her about the Jeep?"

She's staying. Hutch didn't know what he thought of that. "Sure," he said easily, turning back to the mirror. "We'll work something out. No problem."

"Good," Cal said with an approving nod. "Now I need a promise. Keep your hands off her."

Hutch set down his comb a second time. *"What?"*

Cal hooked his thumbs into the back pockets of his jeans. "Keep your hands off her. My sister-in-law thinks you got a gleam in your eye."

Hutch's mouth took on a sardonic slant. "Your sister-in-law's wrong. I'm gleamless. Pretty much."

"It's the 'pretty much' that has her worried. You danced up a storm with that gal last night."

Hutch tried to make his face as expressionless as possible. "She's a good dancer, is all."

"You stayed out with her mighty late."

Hutch frowned in disbelief. "How do you know? Did you sit up and wait on me?"

"No," Cal said. "I got up because my back was achin'. Heard the Jeep. Looked out the window, saw you. It was four o'clock, old son."

"We talked. That's all."

Hutch frowned. He was too independent to feel guilty, especially when he had nothing to be guilty about. Yet an unexpected twinge shot through him. *I only held her hand. I only touched her face.*

Cal sighed, a sound of frustration. "Look. I don't like sayin' such a thing to you, to leave her alone," he said. "What goes on between the two of you ought to be your business. But the point is that Ruth's in a delicate condition."

"I noticed."

"Yeah. Well, she gets upset easy these days. And she's real fond of this cousin. She worries about her."

"Why?" Hutch asked, looking Cal up and down. "Does she think I'm a fortune hunter or something?"

Cal gave a sardonic laugh. "Hell, I don't believe you're that smart. No. This girl's got a guy. Rich, handsome guy. He wants to marry her. Her mother's scared she won't."

"Her mother?" Hutch said, frowning. "The woman's twenty-four years old, for God's sake. What's her mother worryin' about her for?"

"Hell, Hutch, that's what mothers do. And this girl—"

"Her name's Betsy. You don't hafta call her 'this girl.'"

Cal's eyebrow rose a fraction of an inch. "I see. Well, Betsy's got a reputation. For droppin' beaux. Her mama don't want her droppin' *this* dude. She made Ruth promise to watch out. And Ruth's doin' it. Sorry, buddy."

Hutch pointed first at Cal, then at himself. "Surely to God, *you* don't think this woman would break off with some handsome rich guy 'cause of *me*."

Cal shook his head. "'Course not. It's just that Ruth feels responsible. And like I say, she's in a delicate condition. And nobody wants her worryin'. Especially Tyler. And I'm tryin' to keep Tyler happy."

Hutch shrugged grumpily and opened the coat closet. He threw his denim jacket onto the couch. He took out his gray hat, pinched the crease and adjusted the brim.

He looked at Cal. "I spent the summer at Lewisville helpin' a snake charmer build a house. Before that, I tended bar in Reno. Before that, I did carpenter work in Alaska. Your sister-in-law thinks some heiress is gonna fall for *me?*"

Cal eyed him meditatively. He kept his thumbs hooked in his pockets. "The problem with you, Hutch," he said with perfect seriousness, "is that you got this weird mongrel charm."

"Charm," Hutch said with contempt.

"Trust me," Cal said. "I got an eye for these things. I hate to say this, but in the old days, you could be competition."

"That's the first I heard tell."

"See? That's part of your appeal. You're modest."

"Well, you never were."

"True," Cal admitted. "But anyway, it's simple—just keep your hands off her. All right?"

Hutch shrugged. It would be easy as hell to say, "Yeah, sure."

He looked Cal in the eye. "She's not my type," he said. But he made no promises.

WHEN BETSY HEARD Hutch's voice on the phone, the experience had been strange—and electrifyingly pleasant. She accepted his offer to share the Jeep, eager and apprehensive at the same time.

She sensed that Ruth wasn't happy that she was spending more time with Hutch, but she thrust the thought from her mind. She was an adult, after all.

Hutch came to pick her up, and Betsy's heart leapt when she saw him. His clothes were only slightly more impressive than the night before, but the gray Stetson, pulled at a businesslike angle over his brow, emphasized how strong and interesting his features were. Again she was struck by the pure intelligence in his clear blue-green eyes.

In Ruth's presence, he treated Betsy as the most casual of acquaintances. He was his lackadaisical, gentlemanly self, and acted as if they'd never discussed anything more personal than the weather.

But once in the Jeep, he was different. He took on a quiet intensity that caught her unaware.

"I thought you were leavin'," he said.

He gave her a sidelong glance that unexpectedly shook her, so she looked out the window at the brown hills. "Ruth asked me to stay," she said. "It seems important to her. I couldn't say no."

He was silent a moment. She wondered if she should mention last night, if he was embarrassed by it.

But then he spoke. "Are you okay? I don't want you to have—well—regrets. Sometimes a person's got to talk."

She turned to study his profile. Complicated emotions filled her. Being with him made her feel somehow safer and more complete. She liked this effect he had on her, and at the same time, perversely, she resented it.

"What about you?" she asked. "Do you ever 'got to talk'?"

"I do my share," he said without looking at her.

"Most people don't," she said. "Talk, I mean. It's amazing, really. My cousin actually talked to me this morning. About feelings. I think maybe that's a first in my family."

"Feelin's are tricky," he said noncommittally.

"Yes," she said. "But I think I should get my own place as soon as possible. I love Ruth, but I shouldn't try to be a Band-Aid on her marriage. Band-Aids don't cure anything. They just cover it up."

"Probably right," he said. "Just grab yourself any old place for the time bein'. Don't be particular."

He said it matter-of-factly, his eyes on the road.

She smiled ironically. "In my family, we don't just 'grab' places. We're raised to be very particular. Especially where property's concerned."

He threw her a wry look. "Does that mean I should have you along to pick out my chili joint? I never bought real estate before."

Betsy realized they were on the frontier of flirting. Normally she refused to enter any sexually charged territory. Yet he was different. She didn't know why or how, just that he was, and she crossed the boundary boldly.

"You could do worse than have me along," she said, lifting her chin a bit.

He gave her another sideways glance. "I s'pose I could. Should I drive you into Austin and watch you operate?"

Yes. No. Yes. No. She wanted to be with him. She shouldn't want to be with him.

"Suit yourself," she said with a false airiness. "I thought you had business of your own."

"I could put it off till later. All it takes is a phone call. I could come with you. Then you could help me."

She shrugged, as if it made no difference. "Sure," she said. "I *love* real estate."

"We'll look like a couple of odd ducks," he said, keeping his eyes on the road. "You don't mind?"

I don't mind at all, she thought. She wore a gray pantsuit from the priciest women's shop in San Francisco and a politically correct fake fur jacket of gray and white.

She knew she radiated expensiveness and understated chic, but somehow she liked the way he looked better. He wore his clothes, undistinguished as they were, the way he did everything, with easy grace.

"I've spent too many years worrying what people think," she said. "They'll have to take us as we are."

But then, to defuse the situation and what she felt was starting to happen, she said, "If you'll drive, I'll spring for lunch. It's on me. And I won't take any argument."

She thought a muscle twitched in his cheek. "You can just consider me the hired man, then," he said. "Okay. Fine."

The hired man. Betsy ducked her head, her cheeks blazing. He'd seen through her—of course. She'd flirted a bit, then put him in his place.

She knew her family could buy him a thousand times over in terms of money. And she had reminded him of it. She was ashamed of herself and knew she should be.

"No," she said, lifting her chin again. "As my friend. Can I look on you that way? As a friend?"

He seemed to think it over for a moment. "Yeah," he said, not looking at her. "Sure."

OH, GOD, he was fun, Betsy thought helplessly. The realtor, a sophisticated woman in her forties, had looked at them strangely, at first. But Hutch shortly had her charmed within an inch of her life.

Betsy was usually nervous making decisions involving money, because her father was a perfectionist in all such matters. But Hutch somehow made the nervousness evaporate like mist.

Still, she could make no decision, and he teased her about it. He let her buy him lunch—but only a cheeseburger and Coke.

"Hey," he joked, "I'm a cheap date."

Then they'd both looked away from each other in embarrassment, because they weren't really having a date. Such a thing would be stupid, they were an impossible couple.

She'd looked at fifteen different condos and town houses in Austin, and the realtor told her that were another thirty she could show. Betsy didn't know how she'd ever decide.

In Crystal Creek however, Hutch didn't have much of a decision to make. He had his choice between a run-down bar off the town square or a nearly bankrupt café on the highway.

The bar had been closed for two years and the windows were boarded. Dust covered everything, the ceiling

was stained by leaks, and the stove in the small kitchen
was black with grease. Mice had gnawed the woodwork,
and in one corner lay a dead tarantula, its legs in the air.

Betsy stared at the dead spider in horror, so transfixed
she could see nothing else.

"It's what we call a handyman's special," said Vernon Trent, the realtor. He was a wide-shouldered, stur-
dily built man with graying hair and lively brown eyes.

"The handyman'd better be *real* handy," Hutch said
musingly. "Is that a bat hangin' from the ceiling?"

Vernon squinted thoughtfully up into the darkness.
"Yes," he said, "but he won't cost you any extra."

"A bat?" Betsy said in disbelief. "A tarantula and a
bat? All you need is a black cat, some pumpkins, and
you've got a haunted house. There's probably even a
ghost. Yuk."

Vernon nodded thoughtfully. "There is a ghost, matter of fact, so they say. Old Joe Hice used to hang out
here, drinking Lone Star. Drank enough to float a bat-
tleship. Always said he was gonna give it up."

Betsy looked from the bat to the spider and back at the
bat. She shuddered.

Hutch put his hand on her shoulder. "It's just a little
bitty bat," he said softly. His touch sent a shiver of another, more complicated sort through her, but his words
made her smile.

Vernon nodded to himself. "They say one night, about
twelve years ago, Joe stepped away from the bar. 'Boys,'
he says, looking around the room, 'I'm through for good
this time. Not gonna drink no more. No, sir. I'm givin'
it up.'"

Vernon lifted his brows, as if in wonder. "Then he fell
over on the spot. Dead as a doornail. And somebody

said, 'By, God, this time he was tellin' the truth. He *ain't* gonna drink no more.'"

"But that's awful," Betsy said. "And he's supposed to haunt this place?"

Vernon nodded again. "They say he wafts in to smell the fumes. Sometimes you can feel a cold spot in the room. That's old Joe Hice, drifting by."

Hutch squeezed her shoulder comfortingly. "Sounds almost poetical. He comes back where he was most at home."

She knew she should have stepped away from his touch, as casual and friendly and harmless as it seemed. But she couldn't.

"Joe was a good ol' boy," Vernon said philosophically. "You sort of have to take your ghosts as they come."

"Sure enough," Hutch agreed. His hand seemed to burn through her coat, her silk jacket, her blouse.

Why am I letting him touch me? she wondered, but still she did not move away.

THE CAFÉ ON THE HIGHWAY was larger, cleaner, newer, brighter. But it had a strange, lost air about it, a joyless atmosphere.

The only customer was one weary-faced trucker. The waitress seemed preoccupied and sad. The cook was a fat, silent man who pretended that Vernon, Hutch and Betsy were not there. Vernon had told them that he was the owner and so anxious to sell that he went nearly comatose whenever a prospective buyer appeared.

Vernon took it in stride. "The location's good," he said, nodding toward the highway. "Place seats sixty. The kitchen's almost new, redone just three years ago. No liquor licence, but you could get one to sell beer and wine.''

Hutch looked at the place meditatively, and Betsy tried to think as her father had instructed her, totting up the financial pros and cons of such a place.

Vernon showed them how commodious the refrigerators were, how solid the structure, how clean the rest rooms. The parking lot, he pointed out, was more than adequate.

He drove them back to his office, where the Jeep was parked. ''Louie moved here about three years ago,'' Vernon said. ''Sick of the city, thought he wanted small-town life. But his wife hates it, he hates it. He was happier running a doughnut shop in Galveston. He's motivated to sell, sure thing.''

They got out of his car, and Hutch thanked him. Vernon said, ''You think it over. Give me a call if you want to see either place again—or both.''

Betsy and Hutch stood by the Jeep and watched him drive away. The afternoon was growing long, the sky beginning to darken. ''So what do you think?'' she said to Hutch. ''I have too many choices. You hardly have any at all.''

''Let's take a walk,'' he said unexpectedly. ''I want to get a feel for the town. How about it?''

''Sure,'' she said. She was half relieved, half disappointed that he didn't take her arm. They set off toward the square at a leisurely pace. Once in a while their elbows brushed.

''How do you read it?'' he asked. ''You're the one with the business smarts.'' A chill was falling, and when he spoke, his breath drifted up in a silvery plume.

She buried her hands more deeply in her pockets, looked around at the low buildings, the streets lined with winter-bare trees. "It looks," she said carefully, "like you don't have a choice. The first place is a pit. The second place is sound, it's clean, the location'd draw travelers and truckers. The owner's motivated to sell, so he'd probably lower the price. You might get a bargain."

Hutch stared off into the distance, shrugged, and made a sound like *hmmm*.

A sudden, startling realization struck her. "Good grief!" she said. "You like the other one better—don't you? Bats and ghosts and all. I don't believe it."

He shrugged again and smiled, almost to himself. "It's only one bat, one ghost."

"Hutch," she said in disbelief, "it'd take you a month just to get the grease off the stove. If there *is* a stove under all that grease. The roof leaks. There's a *tarantula*."

"But he's dead. That improves a tarantula's nature something immense."

"Hutch!"

"Look," he said, nodding toward the town's carousel on the square. "That's something, isn't it?"

She gazed at the animals. Their glossy paint shone even in the fading light, and the horses seemed frozen in mid-run, carved manes and tails streaming.

Hutch stopped to admire them, and Betsy paused at his side. She studied him surreptitiously. His hat brim was pulled low, his collar turned up. He had a strange, musing half smile on his lips.

"Cal told me a story about this merry-go-round. About the guy who made it . . ."

"You really want that bar, don't you?" she challenged. "Why? Do you know how hard you'll have to work to get it in shape?"

He turned to her, his mysterious smile in place. "I don't mind hard work. Besides, you're only tellin' me what you think. How did you *feel* about that second place?"

"Feel?" she asked, puzzled. "At least I wasn't repulsed. It was clean, it was—"

"No," he said, "you said that. How did it feel to you? Gut level. Just tell me."

She shook her head. The wind rose slightly, fluttering her hair, and she pushed a strand away. "Feel? Well—it was sort of cold, I guess. Empty. Like it wasn't a very happy place. But you could change that—"

He pulled his hatbrim down to a more determined angle. "I don't think so. I'm not sure anybody could. How'd the other place feel?"

"Dirty!"

He laughed. "I know that, Miss Clean. You know what I mean. The ancient Greeks said every place has its 'genius,' its spirit. They were right. Places have personalities. They talk if you listen. What kind of personality does that bar have?"

Betsy pushed aside another fluttering strand of hair, "Personality? Well—quirky. And Vernon's right. It seems haunted, somehow. Like there are a lot of memories still clinging to it."

He had his hands in his jacket pockets. He started walking again. "Good memories or bad memories?"

She grimaced in bewilderment. "This is the weirdest conversation I've ever had. How can I say? I don't know."

He gave her a sidelong glance. "You don't have to know. You just have to feel. You said your family didn't like to talk about feelin's. But you would. So I'm askin'—did they feel like good memories or bad?"

She hesitated a moment, searching within. "I—I guess mostly good. Some sad. But mostly good."

"See," he said, gazing at the courthouse, "what I figure is, you got to go with your vibes. Your vibrations.
Every time I ever got in trouble, it was 'cause I didn't
trust my vibes. And my vibes say that second place is always gonna be a loser. There's no friendliness in it. It
practically sucks friendliness out of the air."

She laughed. "What is this? The mystical approach to
real estate? You don't want a realtor. You want a swami."

"Nope," he said amiably. "Nothin' mystical about it.
Places just have different vibes, that's all."

She walked beside him in silence for a moment, thinking. The practical part of her mind recoiled from the
disreputable old bar for a thousand good reasons. But he
was right. Even empty, it had a strange vitality the other
place lacked, an aura of life.

She remembered her reaction to Ruth's house, that *it*
was unhappy, and she'd been right—just as Hutch was
right about the café on the highway.

"So what do you think?" he asked, looking at the neat
buildings lining the square. "Does this look like a hometown? Or not?"

She smiled in spite of herself. "You mean does it *feel*
like a hometown? Yes, it sort of does."

His eyes met hers. He, too, smiled. "Yeah. Funny,
huh?"

Her heart did an odd, tumbling thing. His lips kept
smiling, but his eyes grew serious.

"You bought me lunch," he said quietly. "How about
I buy you supper? Fair's fair."

She swallowed. "I—suppose. But nothing fancy. Like
you said, fair's fair."

He glanced away, across the darkening square. The
only building bright with lights was the Longhorn Coffee Shop. But neither of them moved toward it.

"I've—been thinkin' about you," he said.

Her heart took another long, steep tumble. She could think of nothing to say.

He exhaled, his breath silvery on the air. "It looks like, well, you're gonna stay awhile," he said.

She nodded and stared down at the sidewalk. "I guess I am."

"Do you know what you'll do yet? About the boy in Fredericksburg? About your son?"

Betsy stiffened and kept staring down. Nobody, ever, in her family had ever said those words to her. *Your son.* The phrase seemed to linger on the chill air, echoing.

"No," she breathed. "I thought maybe, if I had the courage, I'd drive over someday. Not to talk to him—that wouldn't be right. I did make the promise, I did sign things. But just to catch a glimpse of him. If I ever have the courage. Maybe I won't."

The November wind moaned around them softly. "If you should need somebody," Hutch said, "somebody to go along, give you moral support, I'd be proud to go."

She looked up at him, touched, her heart so filled with gratitude that it made her throat ache.

"That's very kind," she said tightly. "*You're* very kind. Why? You don't have to be. I don't understand."

He tossed her the briefest of looks. It amazed her. He, the usually imperturbable Hutch, seemed almost troubled.

"I don't know," he said, looking off into the evening again. "It just seems right."

Then he held out his hand to her. He said nothing. He didn't have to.

Frightened and elated, her heart beating hard, she gave him her hand. Without speaking, they walked toward the light.

CHAPTER SEVEN

"OH, HONEY, oh, honey," Cal said on a groan. "More—please."

"Cal, I'm only human," Serena said. "Maybe I should go to chiropractic school."

They were in the bedroom, with Cal facedown and shirtless on the bed, his fists clenched. He'd thrown his back out helping Tyler load the damn gravel.

Serena, barefoot, in jeans and an oversize green shirt, straddled his upper legs. She kneaded his back muscles as hard as she could.

"Why did you have to go and shovel gravel?" she asked, her fingers working the hard muscles around his lower spine. "Why didn't you just throw around grand pianos and do yourself up really good?"

"It was a guy thing. I was attemptin' brotherly bondin'. Ouch. Oof. There. Oh, *yes*. There."

"Calvin, I swear if one more horse had tromped your spine, you'd be bent up like a pretzel. You should have quit that rodeo years before you did."

"Owrrrr," Cal said in a growl of pain and sensuality. "If I had, I wouldn't have met you, sugar. A couple vertebrae was a small price to pay—*ouch!*"

She sighed, and he felt her breath on his back. "I hope a couple more were a small price to pay for brotherly bonding. Did it work?"

He gave a grunt of pain. She bent so low over him that her hair brushed his shoulder blades. Her slim thighs straddling his were an excellent distraction from pain.

"Tyler's gonna be fine," he said, gritting his teeth. "He always did have a lot of pride. But we're only buying twenty-two percent, and, hell, I figure when he gets on his feet, he can buy our share back."

"I mean, how did he take it *exactly?*" Serena asked. She bent and kissed the back of his neck. "Do you think he's going to resent it?"

Cal took a deep breath. "There, sweet baby, there. Perfect. Yeah, he's gonna resent it. He'll get over it. We had lunch with Daddy and Cynthia."

"Shouldn't Ruth have been there?"

"She wasn't feelin' good. Heck, *you* should have been there."

"No. I feel like an outsider when Tyler freezes up that way. Did they talk sense into him?"

"Yeah. At least, Cynthia did. Daddy's bein' a little strange, but he went along with Cynthia. Ooh. Aah. God."

"I want you to go to a different doctor," she said. "You can't go on like this. When you're old you'll be all creaky and gimped up. The old rocking chair'll *have* you."

"Then I'll be givin' one pretty green-eyed old lady rockin' chair rides."

She gave him something resembling a series of soft karate chops up and down his backbone. It felt good, and it felt like hell.

"Why's your father's acting strange about it?" Serena asked, massaging his shoulders. "Sweetheart, all your muscles are tensed hard as rock. Is it because all this bothers you more than you're saying?"

"Arrgh," he muttered. "No. It's 'cause termites from hell are eatin' my spine. Daddy acts the way he does because he and Tyler are basically alike. They both got ideas on how things should be done. They're stubborn. And proud."

Her hands moved to his lower back again, squeezing and stroking. "I don't know why this hurts their pride," she said in a moody-sounding voice. "I thought they'd resent it if we had the money and *didn't* help out."

He grimaced. "I was the black sheep too long. Everybody thought I'd die drunk in the gutter or something. It's a switch, me bailin' anybody out."

He felt her hair brush his shoulder blades again. Once more she kissed the back of his neck. "Once you said you were the gray sheep, that they loved you too much to paint you all black."

He exhaled sharply. "Maybe I got darker in retrospect. Tyler's always been the straight arrow. It probably don't seem fair I got so lucky."

"Lucky?" Serena demanded, bearing down on his middle back. "You call *this* lucky? You're literally breaking your back to help him. *He's* the lucky one, with a brother like you."

"Yowtch. Honey, that's enough. Do a little bit more of that neck kissin'. I think that might do the trick."

She rubbed his shoulders and kissed him between the shoulder blades. "I mean it," she said loyally. "He's lucky to have you."

"Naw," he said. "I got everything. You're well. You're fine and you're mine. How could I get luckier than that?"

"You're a vile flatterer," she murmured and started kissing her way down his backbone. It sent tickles through his nervous system that met and frolicked in his groin.

"You're a vile temptress," he said. "Don't move. I'm gonna turn over."

"Cal—you're not feeling romantic. Not with your back like that. You can't."

He managed to roll over. She still straddled his thighs, resting her weight on her heels.

"Hold that position," he said, catching her hands. "It could lead to something interestin'."

"You'll hurt yourself." She shook her head, but he could tell she was tempted.

"Not if you was ever so gentle to me," he teased. He reached up and started unbuttoning her blouse. "I mean what if I've killed myself? Don't you want to make my last moments happy?"

"Five minutes ago you were immobile with pain," she said, but she let him unbutton the blouse. She put her hands on his pectoral muscles, and his heart quickened at her touch. "How can you think you can—"

"You've mobilized me. I'm gettin' mobilized like you wouldn't believe."

He pushed the blouse from her shoulders. He gazed up at her and smiled. His groin throbbed harder. "God," he said. "I love it when you wear those lacy things on your pretty things. And you do have pretty things."

"Are you just going to lie there and make me do all the work?" she asked, but her eyes were getting that dreamy look he loved.

"If I can." He laughed and pulled her closer.

TYLER WORKED LATE at the winery site, not wanting to go home. He loved Ruth. He just didn't want to go home to her.

He'd done what she wanted. He supposed there'd been no choice. But rightly or wrongly, he resented selling out to Cal.

But when night had almost fallen, he knew he had to return to the house. He drove back. When he pulled up to the house, it looked lonely, even with its windows shining in the darkness.

He knew Ruth didn't like staying home alone, but even her fool doctor had enough sense to forbid her to work. Taking care of herself, that was supposed to be her job. Such forced idleness was one of the things gnawing at her, he knew.

He parked the truck and got out. Bogus the hound began to bark and howl wildly. He raced toward Tyler, then was jerked up short by his chain. He landed with a thud on his back, then leapt up, yowling, and pulled the same dumb stunt again.

Tyler sighed. Ruth was right. He should foist the hound off on somebody else. He'd promised his friend Rydell he'd keep it until Christmas, because Rydell was going to New Zealand for two months. Tyler hadn't known a dog could be so useless. When it wasn't yowling or sleeping, it was digging. The goddamn lawn looked like an excavation site.

He entered the house. The lights were on, but he saw no sign of Ruth. Hagar, her cat, wandered in from the hall with a restless air. "Mrreoowrr," complained Hagar. "Mrre*owwrrr*."

Tyler went down the hall. The light was on in the room that was supposed to be the baby's. He gritted his teeth and went to the door. Hagar followed, waddling and grumbling.

Tyler stood in the doorway. Ruth looked up. He'd always liked her big, dark eyes, but these days they seemed so haunted it hurt him to look into them.

She was folding a pile of baby clothing. The clothes seemed impossibly small to Tyler: tiny white shirts, socks that looked like doll socks, little terry-cloth sleepers in yellow and green and white.

Ruth hadn't bought anything in pink or blue. She didn't want to know the baby's sex. She wanted to be surprised, she said. *Oh, Ruth,* he thought. *There may be a terrible surprise coming. Let's talk about the truth for once.*

"Hi," she said with false brightness. "I just thought I'd change the drawers around. I moved the changing table, and I thought it'd be more convenient...."

Her voice trailed off. She bent her head and smoothed out a minute crocheted bib.

Tyler looked around the room, his facial muscles tautening. A crib stood ready, made up with a sheet patterned with pastel teddy bears. In it, as if waiting for company, were two large, stuffed rabbits in denim overalls.

Hagar rubbed Tyler's ankles aggressively and kept up his growling meows. "What's wrong with this cat?"

Ruth glanced up, then took a stack of clothing and put it in the bureau drawer, turning her back to him. "The *dog* is what's wrong with the cat," she said. "Every time it goes crazy, it sets Hagar off. He hates it. He won't go out of the house anymore."

Tyler sighed wearily. "Look. It's only another couple of weeks. I promised Rydell. Give me a break, Ruth. I've done everything you wanted. Let up a little, will you?"

He saw her shoulders tense. She was silent a moment. "I'm sorry," she said.

"It's all set," he said. "Cal and Serena are in. We shook hands on it at lunch."

"I know," she said. "Cynthia called." She closed the drawer. She threw him the briefest of glances over her shoulder. "*You* might have called," she said. "You could have at least phoned."

"I didn't feel like talking about it," Tyler said. He felt angry and ashamed of his anger. At the same time, he was torn with concern for Ruth.

Stony-faced, he said, "How are you feeling?"

"I'm fine."

"You said you didn't feel well—"

"It was only a headache," she said, not looking at him. "It went away."

She was lying, and he knew it, but he didn't know how to deal with it. So he said, "Where's your cousin?"

"She's still out with that Hutch person," Ruth said. "She said they might be late. I don't know what's going on."

He walked to her side, and put one hand on her shoulder, but his own movement felt wooden to him. "Don't worry about her. She's all grown-up."

"I have to worry. I promised her mother—"

"Ruth, she's an adult. Her mother shouldn't—"

"You don't understand."

He closed his eyes a moment. He gripped her shoulder more tightly. "I don't understand. You're right."

He opened his eyes. She was looking up at him as if she was going to cry. "Betsy's—different," she said. "She has this thing about men. She just doesn't stay involved with them."

"I know. You told me."

"There was this boy, he was heir to a fortune. My aunt said he was a wonderful guy. He was crazy about Betsy.

But after four dates she dropped him. For no reason. She's afraid of commitment."

"Look," he said as gently as he could, "her problem shouldn't be yours. You've got enough on your mind."

"Tyler, this is my family," she said. "We're always caught up in your family's affairs. Can't you please listen about mine, for a change?"

He wondered how somebody as small as she was could simply open her mouth and make him feel he'd been hit in the stomach. "I'm listening," he said.

"She's gone with this Michael for a year," Ruth said, "longer than anybody else. Now I know Aunt Margaret's overprotective, but she's scared senseless that Betsy's going to back out of it. It'd be a huge mistake."

"Shouldn't Betsy be the judge of that?" he asked stiffly.

"Listen, please. No sooner does Betsy get here—and she admits she and Michael are talking marriage—than she takes up with this Hutch person."

"Last night you thought this Hutch person was the salt of the earth. Last night you thought he was Mr. Entertainment."

"Well, that's it," Ruth said, a bit desperately. "I mean, I can see where she'd enjoy his company. But to throw over this great guy in London? For somebody who wants to cook chili for a living? Tyler, that's self-destructive."

"Ruth," he said as patiently as he could, "don't read so much into this. She spent the day with him. So what?"

"Aunt Margaret called," Ruth said, her face stark with apprehension. "So did Michael, clear from London. Betsy was gone, both times. These people really care about her. So do I."

"Honey, don't get so involved. If Betsy's got a problem with commitments, it's Betsy's problem. If she
doesn't want to marry this other guy, then if it's not
Hutch, it'd be somebody else."

"Tyler, it's a family problem. I asked you to talk to Cal
about it. Didn't you? This shouldn't be happening."

His patience snapped. He'd talked to Cal, and he'd felt
like a jackass. Worse, Cal had razzed him about it when
they were shoveling gravel. Cal said *he'd* felt like a jackass, saying such a thing to Hutch. These people were
adults, for God's sake, he'd said.

Tyler took his hand from Ruth's shoulder. "I talked to
him," he said shortly. "And you and I had this conversation this morning. Ruth, get a grip. I feel like everything's spinning out of control here."

She looked at him as if he had betrayed her, tears in her
eyes. He had never felt so helpless in his life.

"I love her," she said. "I don't want her to make a
mistake."

AFTER SUPPER, Hutch and Betsy hadn't wanted to part.
And so, somehow, they'd ended up back at Zack's,
dancing again.

When Hutch danced with her, he got an eerie, other-
worldly feeling, as if they were bewitched. He also got
some far more earthy and familiar sensations.

My God, he'd thought. *What do you do when you're
crazy with desire for a woman who's scared to be de-
sired?*

His body, half enchanted, half human, burned, and his
mind told him, *You just keep dancing, you damn fool.*

He'd held her tight, kept dancing.

Then, in the middle of a song called "I Thought It Was You," he discovered that they'd stopped dancing and started kissing.

They'd moved more and more slowly. His cheek had been against hers, then almost imperceptibly his mouth moved to the corner of hers, not quite touching it.

He thought she would draw away from him. She did not. Ever so slightly she turned her face so that her lips were only a fraction of an inch from his.

It was almost as if she were offering her mouth to him, and the thought stabbed through him so sharply, he'd stopped dancing. They both went very still. A sizable piece of eternity seemed to pass. Then he kissed her.

They stood in the faint light, the other dancers swirling around them. He had one arm around her waist, and his other hand held hers against his heart. Dimly, he realized he was amazed at what was happening, but it felt so staggeringly right that he went with the flow.

Her lips were as soft as they looked, and they had a little tremble to them that rocked his heart. Still, she didn't draw away. He was pleased and excited to realize that she was standing on tiptoe, raising herself to be kissed more fully.

He wanted to part those soft lips with his tongue, taste her mouth as if it was nectar. But he knew better, knew that it would break the spell.

It was a spell, he was sure, because he couldn't stop kissing her, and the kiss itself was like a strange captivation. There was passion in it, but restrained to such gentleness that he ached. He'd never kissed a woman quite like this before. It made him dizzy and heated his blood.

He wanted her so much it frightened him. And it bewildered him as well, because this was a woman he couldn't have. It was a miracle she was allowing him this much intimacy.

And then, suddenly, she broke the kiss. She did not draw out of his arms, but she pulled back and turned her face from his.

"We should go home," she said, not looking at him.

He held her as carefully as he might hold some super-natural creature that had momentarily allowed itself to be embraced.

She stared off, expressionless, across the dance floor. Muted colored lights dappled it, playing tag with the shadows. Soft light, first blue, then gold, shone on her silky hair.

"I don't know how that happened," she said. He felt how tense her body had grown.

"It just happened," he said, studying her solemn pro-file. "Maybe it was supposed to happen."

"No," she said softly. She shook her head.

"Maybe," he said. Then he did something else he'd never done before to a woman. He lifted her hand and kissed it. "Maybe," he repeated.

THIS IS CRAZY, Betsy thought when Hutch pulled up in front of Ruth's house. It was half an hour from mid-night, and she'd spent almost fifteen straight hours with him.

She should be eager to flee from him after what had occurred on the dance floor, but she wasn't.

She shouldn't even be able to talk to him since that kiss, but she could. The surprising, dismaying thing was that it seemed so easy to talk to him, so natural.

Neither of them made a move to get out of the Jeep. She thought, rather giddily, that she wouldn't mind sitting and talking to him until four o'clock in the morning, just as they had done the night before.

"I hope your cousin doesn't mind," he said, looking at the shadowy house, the porch light shining out over the empty yard. "It's like I stole you from her."

Betsy followed his gaze and stared at the house. It still had its aura of unhappiness, and she was not anxious to enter it. "I know. She's lonely. I should be spending time with her. She needs somebody."

"Hey," he said gently. He touched the collar of her jacket with his forefinger, made the fur brush softly against her chin. "If you're gonna let yourself feel something, it shouldn't be guilt."

She smiled sadly. "Why not? I'm so good at it."

"If you've got it mastered, maybe you should move on to other things."

"Like what?"

"Whatever you want to move on to."

They were both silent a moment. He kept his finger resting at her collar, barely touching it. If another man had done such a thing, she would have recoiled from him. But from Hutch, she didn't. The realization filled her with reluctant wonder.

"I'm gonna give Cal back the key to the guest house," he said. "I'm movin' into town. There's a motel there."

Startled, she stared at him. "Into town? Why?"

His brow furrowed, and he shook his head. "He wanted me to promise to stay away from you. I wouldn't. He didn't want me to touch you. I have. If I can't respect his wishes, I got no right to his hospitality."

"Cal?" she said, not comprehending. "He hardly knows me. Why should he care?"

"It doesn't matter. What matters is he asked."

The unpleasant truth dawned on her. "Hutch, he didn't ask because of Ruth, did he?"

He didn't answer.

"Oh, he did, didn't he?" she said unhappily. "Why should *she* care, then? Oh, God, I know. It's my mother. She's been after poor Ruth with her 'Betsy can't make commitments' speech."

"What kind of speech is that?" he asked, tracing the edge of her collar.

She shook her head. "I haven't exactly been rushing into anybody's arms. She worries that I'm not normal. It really bothers her. Because nobody wants to admit there's any reason I might not be like everybody else. She thinks if I get married, it'll prove nothing bad ever happened."

She put her hand to her forehead, covered her eyes.

"Hey," he said softly. "Don't go cryin' on me again. I might not be able to stand it."

"I'm not going to cry," she said, but her voice was tight. "It's just I'm so tired of all the pretending. That was one thing I couldn't pretend. That I wanted a husband."

"Because of the rape," he said softly. "And the baby."

She let her hand drop to her lap. She bit her lip. "I'm going to tell you something terrible. You're the first man I ever liked kissing. Tonight. The first time, ever. I mean, since it happened."

"Then I'm a lucky guy," he said.

"It scares me."

"I know."

"What am I supposed to do?" she asked, turning to face him. "Just—trust my vibes?"

"I think maybe that's what we both should do."

She laced her fingers tightly together in her lap. "Your vibrations," she said. "What do they say about me?"

"I can't tell," he said, bending his face closer to hers. "They never said anything like this before."

"What's that mean?" she asked.

"I think it means I want to kiss you again. Would you let me?"

He bent nearer still. A hundred old emotions warred in her chest against a hundred new ones.

But she found herself raising her lips to him. "Yes," she whispered. "I think I would."

When his mouth touched hers, she thought, *This isn't possible. This is not possible.*

He showed her that it was. His touch made her half-faint with fear and happiness.

HUTCH PULLED the Jeep up in front of the main ranch house. The lights were still on. He climbed the porch stairs, carrying his worn duffel bag.

He was in luck. Cal answered the door. His shirt was half unbuttoned, and he was in his stocking feet. He carried himself as if he'd screwed up his back again.

"You got an odd notion of hours to come callin'," he said, but he grinned. "Come in. Want a beer?"

"No. I just wanted to talk to you. In private. Step outside a minute?"

"Man, it's cold and I'm near barefoot," Cal said, but gingerly he stepped outside. "Damn!" he said and started buttoning his shirt.

"Here," Hutch said, and handed him the keys to the Jeep and the guest house. "Thanks for everything. I'm headin' into town. I mean it—thanks."

"Town?" Cal scowled in disbelief. "You ain't even got a car, you fool. What are you, crazy?"

"Most likely," Hutch said, hiking the duffel bag onto his shoulder. "I also came to apologize. About Betsy. I touched her, after all."

Cal swore and looked heavenward. "You played hide-the-weasel with Cousin Betsy? Tyler'll kill you. Hell, he'll kill *me* on account of you."

Hutch bristled. "It's nothing like that. I kissed her, is all. But I'm likely to do it again, and I aim to keep seein' her. If you want to take a punch at me, take a punch. But don't talk about her like that. She's not that sort."

Cal swore again. "You just got home with her now? You were the one sayin' she wouldn't see anything in you. Why're you seducin' my Cousin Betsy that I hardly know?"

"I'm not seducin' her, and I don't know what she sees in me. But I thought I better tell you and turn in my keys."

"Hell, man," Cal said with concern. "You got no future with that sort of girl."

Hutch shrugged as if it didn't matter. "I know it better'n you."

"Listen, Tyler says this girl's supposed to get married."

"I reckon she should decide that, not Tyler."

"He also says she's got a problem settlin' on one guy. Maybe she's just usin' you so she don't have to marry this other guy, you think of that?"

Hutch had thought of it. He shrugged again. "It doesn't seem right to be talkin' about her like that behind her back."

Cal stared at him in exasperation. "Lord, Hutch. Why're you so protective? Look, you were ever the one for unattainable women, but this is a new extreme."

"Did I ever make cracks about your love life?"

"You never stopped. Climb down off that noble high horse."

Hutch smiled in spite of himself. Once Cal had been a gleeful Romeo with an infinite supply of Juliets, and Hutch had taunted him without mercy.

Cal narrowed his eyes and studied him a long moment. Then he clapped him on the shoulder. "Hey, man, if you and her got a thing for each other, that's it. You're right. It's nobody's business but yours."

Hutch's smile faded. He nodded. "Thanks," he said.

"Listen," Cal said earnestly, "it's no reason for you to go off. Stay. I mean it. If Tyler doesn't like it—"

"Tyler and Ruth," Hutch said. "Neither one's gonna like it."

"People don't always get what they like."

Hutch looked Cal up and down. "You're freezin'," he said. "Go back in. Give Serena my regards. It's not like I won't see you."

"Don't just walk off," Cal said from between teeth clenched against the cold. "Stay the night, you damn fool. We can drop you off tomorrow on our way back."

"I'll hitch. I've done it before."

"I'll drive you. Wait till I get my boots on."

"Nope," Hutch said. "I'd rather be alone. To think. Take care."

"*You* take care, hear?" Cal said.

"Always do," said Hutch.

He shouldered the duffel bag and gave Cal a mock salute. Once out of sight of the house, he set a brisk pace to make it to the highway. He might snag a ride, he might not, it didn't matter. He'd been truthful. He had thinking to do.

He had kissed Betsy Holden three times before she'd said she had to go inside. He'd touched her face, he'd touched her hair. That was all. No more. But he kept thinking about it, and it made the pit of his stomach feel as if he were in an elevator plunging down too fast.

Damned if he could figure it out. Cal was right. There was no future with this girl, no way.

But the present was interesting. The present was beguiling the very hell out of him.

Yesterday he'd been a little bit in love with Serena McKinney. Tonight, he told himself, he was a little bit in love with Betsy Holden. Very slightly, and nothing permanent. Next month he'd probably be a little bit in love with somebody else. That was the way it went, always had.

But he couldn't stop remembering how sweetly soft her lips felt or how there was something different about her. She made him think of some delicate, fairy-tale creature that couldn't be possessed.

And it was odd, in light of what had happened to her, but she seemed the most virginal woman he'd ever known. He wondered what would become of her.

Halfway to Crystal Creek, he thumbed a ride with a trucker hauling canned tamales. He earned his way as he usually did in such circumstances, by telling stories of places he'd been, things he'd seen.

"A ramblin' man, eh," the trucker said, smiling over a story.

"That's me," said Hutch.

CHAPTER EIGHT

BETSY SPENT the next day with Ruth, helping her repaint the trim in the nursery.

Subtly and more than once, Ruth warned her against getting involved with Hutch. "And if you do," she said at last with frankness, "please don't rush into breaking off with Michael. Your mother would kill me. Promise me that much."

Reluctantly, Betsy promised, and she felt guilty when a florist's truck arrived and the driver delivered a bouquet of roses from Michael with a teasing note about not running off with any "handsome cowboys."

But she went out with Hutch again that night. He had his van back, and a disreputable-looking van it was, but she didn't mind.

He took her to a small honky-tonk in the neighboring town of Blanco, claiming he needed to improve her education in country music.

The honky-tonk was small and only half-filled. Only a few dancers moved on the tiny floor, and they seemed complacent about letting Hutch feed the jukebox.

The floor was so small, he couldn't lead her into many fancy steps, but she didn't mind. Any sort of dancing with him was a marvel to her.

They moved together as if they had established some sort of telepathic connection. And she was amazed at how easily she could talk to him.

The only thing she didn't tell him was how Ruth felt about him. As usual, he seemed to know when she wasn't completely truthful. "Let's take a break," he said, and walked hand-in-hand with her to a booth. He ordered a Corona beer and she asked for a cola.

His beer mug came with salt around the rim and a thick wedge of lime. Betsy wrinkled her nose. "*Salt* with your beer?"

"That's the way it should be with Mexican beer," he said, twisting the lime into the mug. "So tell me. What did Cousin Ruth say about me? Not too happy, I suppose."

Betsy ducked her head, sipped from her straw.

"You might as well tell me," he said, pouring his beer. "It won't hurt my feelin's."

Betsy sighed and met his eyes. His beautiful, clear, blue-green eyes.

"She warned me," she admitted. "She said I shouldn't rush into anything. She's afraid I'm going to throw over my boyfriend. Michael."

"Are you?" he asked evenly.

"Oh, God," she said unhappily, "I don't know. I try not to think about it."

"You've been out with me three nights in a row," he said. "If you'll say yes, I'll make it four tomorrow. Will you? Say yes?"

She took a deep breath. Then she tried to mentally conjure up Michael's perfect face, the resonance of his voice. She could not. "Yes," she almost whispered. "Yes, I'll go."

"Do you want me to take you apartment huntin' tomorrow?"

She thought of his battered van, of jolting all the way to Austin and back. She knew he wouldn't be dressed up because he apparently had nothing to dress up in.

"Yes," she breathed.

"What else do you want from me?" he asked.

The question shook her. She looked at his lean face, his wide shoulders. *I don't know what I want from you. I don't even know why this is happening,* she wanted to say.

Instead she shrugged. She thought of why she had come to Texas. "I think—" she said "—I think I want you to take me to Fredericksburg."

He regarded her with a gaze so steady it made her feel shuddery and strange. "To see the boy?"

"Yes," she answered. "That's all. Just to see him. Nothing more. Just to see if he looks healthy and happy."

"When?"

"I don't know," she said. "Soon, I think."

He nodded. "All right. What else?" He took a sip of beer.

The shuddery feeling grew stronger, played up and down her spine. "I don't know what you mean."

"What else do you want from me?"

She shook her head helplessly, not knowing what to say.

"Your boyfriend," he said in a low voice. "You never talk about him. Why?"

Michael. The name tolled within her hollowly, like a bell of mourning. "I guess I don't want to talk about him."

"Why?"

She stared at her drink, twisted the straw. "Because I suppose I'll disappoint him. The way I have everybody else."

"Is that why you're with me? So you have an excuse to tell him goodbye?"

She shook her head. "No. I don't think so." And she didn't. Hutch seemed to have nothing to do with Michael. Or perhaps he had everything to do with Michael.

"So why're you with me?" he asked. "Tell me the truth."

The truth. She was always wanting the truth from others. Now he wanted it from her. She shifted nervously. "I suppose I'm with you because—because I want to be with you. Why are you with me?"

"Same reason," he said. "I want to."

She raised her eyes to his again. "I don't have designs on you," she said. "If that's what you mean. You're helping me through a rough time. But that doesn't mean I'm going to come to depend on you or anything. I wouldn't be possessive—anything like that."

"Good," he said. "I'm not possessable. I hear tell you're shy of commitments. I'm shy of 'em myself. We're two of a kind."

She should have been relieved to hear him say such a thing. Yet, for some reason, relief was not what she felt.

She searched his face. He was handsome in his strong-boned, lean way. He was smart and funny and kind and original. She wondered why some woman hadn't snapped him up years ago.

"You've never even been engaged?" she asked.

He paused, and arched one thick eyebrow meditatively. "Almost. Once."

Unaccountably, she felt a twinge of jealousy. "What happened?"

"It was when I was playin' ball. Right before I got hurt. There was this girl. I liked her a lot."

"Did you love her?"

"I suppose. But then I broke my wrist. She wanted me to stay there, get married and work for her daddy. Her daddy owned a ball bearing factory. Can you think of one thing more boring than a ball bearing? I said I had the urge to hit the road, think it over. There was a lot of world to see before I settled down to a life of ball bearings. I said if she'd wait, I'd be back."

"And?"

He sighed philosophically. "She wasn't a waitin' woman. She said if I hit the road, I could stay there. I hit the road. Been on it ever since."

"Until now," Betsy said, twisting her straw again.

"Come on," he said, offering her his hand. "Let's dance. I can't stand to watch you twist that straw. It's too damn Freudian."

"Freudian?" she said and dropped the straw in alarm. He laughed and took her hand. She blushed. Ordinarily such a remark would have offended her or made her fearful. But Hutch had taken her hand in his, and when he touched her everything was all right.

And when he took her in his arms, the enchantment returned. It was that simple.

But her feelings weren't simple. Not in the least. "After all these years," she said, "you decided to settle down. In Crystal Creek. Why now? Why there?"

"It felt right," he said. "Like this song? It's the man in the big hat singin'."

"It's fine," she said. She was starting to understand the country music, to yield to it. But she was more interested in Hutch.

"Why didn't you go home?" she asked. "To D'Hanis? Isn't that the town?"

"Too small. Besides, my folks are retirin' to San Antonio. I'm not a city sort. And I'm too independent. I

don't want my Aunt Dora gettin' in my face all the time
because she doesn't like my religion or politics.''

"I thought you got along with your family."

"I do. My immediate family. My Aunt Dora's a bat-
tle-ax from hell. And she's got a daughter just like her.
Darlene. Ga-awd." He gave a mock shudder.

Then, while they waltzed, he told her Dora and Darlene stories, each more outrageous than the last.

She looked up at him with shining eyes. She'd never
met anyone like him, even remotely.

"Now I have this great-aunt over in Uvalde," he said.
"Her name's Hazel. And Harry used to call her Witch
Hazel behind her back. But one day she heard him. . . ."

The tale rolled on to its absurd conclusion. She
laughed. He drew her closer, held her more tightly, laid
his cheek against hers.

The jukebox was playing "Gentle on My Mind." And
Betsy realized, with a start, that she was falling in love
with this man. Nothing could come of it, of course. But
it felt wonderful, quite wonderful.

"Yeah," he said, as if he could read her thoughts.
"Funny, isn't it?"

He kissed the corner of her mouth. Shyly, like someone doing something for the first time, she kissed him
back.

They parked in Ruth and Tyler's unfinished driveway
and necked like the youngest and most innocent of teenagers. Transported, Betsy found herself doing unthinkable things. She wrapped her arms around his neck. She
did not simply accept his kisses, resolutely and without
emotion. She shared them and returned them.

It was completely new to her, affection this intense.
Expressing it was exquisite, sweet and dreamlike. She
could have kissed and been kissed by him all night long.

For Hutch it was sweet, but a nightmare of self-control. He ached to do far more than kiss her, but he knew she wasn't ready. That she was this ready, this warm and caressable, made him ravenous for more ardent lovemaking. It made him crazy.

But he knew any real sexual aggression on his part would terrify her. It would break the spell that seemed to have bewitched them both. So he kissed her mouth, her extraordinarily adorable mouth, and he held her. That was all. It was intoxicating, it was addictive, it was maddening, and he thought it might kill him.

He was almost relieved when she murmured that she had to go in. He was bereaved, as well.

"No," he said and kissed her again, a more dizzying, headlong kiss than any of the others. She gave a tiny, pleased gasp that made him crazier still.

He seemed to take a long, slow tumble off the earth and through the outer reaches of the galaxy. He was lost, gone. He was also rent by desires so powerful he could no longer completely restrain them.

He took her face between his hands, which were tense. Her lips parted. *Her lips parted.* It was sheer miracle, nothing less. He thought he might start shaking from yearning.

But carefully, gently and with the utmost restraint, he ran the tip of his tongue over the curve of her lower lip, once, twice, three times.

She didn't flinch or wrench away from him. Another miracle. His forehead pounded. His heart pounded. Inside his jeans, other parts of him pounded, as well.

He let his tongue caress the undercurve of her upper lip.

"Ooh," she said softly, but she did not draw away. Instead, she pressed against him more tightly.

I'm gonna die, he thought. *This will kill me dead.*

Then he felt the delicate flicker of her tongue against his, so light it was like butterflies flirting. It was over almost instantaneously, but he took another long, slow tumble through the universe. A third miracle, he thought, and this time, he was the one who gasped.

He felt her tense in his arms. She had to know how much sexual hunger was in that gasp. "I should go in," she said, drawing back. But she was close enough that her breath was warm against his lips.

"No," he said and almost kissed her again. He stopped himself. "Yes. Maybe you should."

"Yes," she said, regret in her voice. "Don't walk me to the porch. Please. We'd just start this all over again. And I don't understand it yet."

"Yeah," Hutch said, trying to catch his breath. "Well. I don't understand it, either. That's understandable, I guess."

"That makes no sense." She laughed, a low, soft laugh, and he closed his eyes, because once again he felt her breath fan his lips.

"Sometimes good sense doesn't make sense," he said with resignation. "But good sense tells me you should go inside."

"Good night," she said and kissed him all too briefly on the lips.

"Good night," he breathed in return.

When he drove back to the motel, he'd exceeded the speed limit. He took the longest, coldest shower he'd ever taken in his life.

"SHE THINKS she's in love with him," Ruth announced to Tyler. It was five nights later. "She hasn't said so, but I can tell."

Tyler stood, undressing for bed. Ruth was already tucked tightly under the covers. She wore a long flannel nightgown with a high neck, and she was propped up in bed with an open book on her lap.

Tyler unbuttoned his shirt. "So she thinks she's in love." His voice was cynical. "She'll get over it."

"Of course she'll get over it," Ruth said. "The question is, what do I tell Aunt Margaret in the meantime?"

"Don't tell her anything." He shucked off the shirt, hung it on the back of a chair.

"What if she asks me?" Ruth demanded. "What then?"

"Lie," Tyler said from between his teeth. He unbuckled his belt.

"Tyler, this is my aunt. I love her."

"Then lie to her," he said.

"And there's Michael," Ruth said, smoothing the bedclothes over the swell of her belly. "I begged her not to tell Michael. To give this thing with Hutch two weeks, at least, before she said anything. But he phoned again yesterday morning. She was so stiff with him, he's got to suspect something."

"That's not your problem."

Tyler usually slept naked. He took off his jeans, pulled his T-shirt off over his head and stepped out of his shorts.

Pointedly, Ruth didn't look at him. He got into bed beside her. Gently, he put his hand over hers. "Ruthie," he said, "if Betsy's really in love with this Michael, she wouldn't be falling for somebody else. It's her life. Let her work it out."

Ruth tensed at his touch. "It's not that Hutch isn't a great guy," she said. "He is. It's just that he and Betsy are too different."

"Don't worry about it. Take care of yourself instead. How're you feeling?"

"I'm fine," she said impatiently. "But I can't imagine what Betsy's thinking. He's so footloose, and all he wants out of life is a chili parlor, for heaven's sake. Do you know how much Betsy's going to be worth someday? Millions, probably."

"Hey," Tyler joked, "a million dollars could buy a lot of chili powder. They could serve the stuff in golden bowls."

"It's not funny," Ruth said. "It's—"

But at that moment the baby kicked, hard. Tyler felt the impact, even through Ruth's hand, which seemed to leap beneath his.

He looked at her face. It was transformed, radiant.

"He kicked," she said in wonder. "He hasn't done that for a long time. I was worried that—"

She bit the words back, not finishing the sentence. But a small smile stayed on her lips and she stared in fascination at her stomach. "Did you feel it?" she asked. "He kicked *hard*."

He squeezed her hand. "Yes. This is the first time you ever called it *he*. Why?"

She met his gaze, almost shyly. "I don't know. Sometime this month, I started thinking of him as a *him*. Woman's intuition, maybe."

He saw the hope in her dark eyes, and he offered up a heartfelt, silent prayer that the child would be all right—for her sake.

He had the sudden desire to have her in his arms, to love her, protect her, possess her, to be as close to her as possible.

It must have shown in his face. She looked away from him.

"Ruth," he said as kindly as he could, "it's been a long time. I miss you. I'd—be gentle."

Her hand went still as death beneath his, and her face grew taut. She stared at her book and said nothing. She meant *no*.

He cursed silently. He took his hand away from hers. She was scared, he could tell. She pretended there was nothing wrong with the child, but she was terrified of hurting it. God, why couldn't she face facts? She was going to drive them both crazy. And he didn't know how many times he could take being pushed away from her.

"Forget it," he said and turned from her. He switched off the lamp on the stand at his side of the bed. He stared, unseeing, into the shadows.

Outside, the dog started to howl.

FOR FIVE DAYS and nights, Hutch and Betsy had been almost inseparable. She spent mornings with Ruth and had lunch with her.

But afternoons belonged to Hutch. He helped her hunt for her condo in Austin. She helped him pick restaurant equipment out of catalogs, and together they doodled, making up everything from alternate floor plans to menu designs.

After supper, they usually went dancing, but one night they went to a movie and shared an enormous box of popcorn. It was a terrible movie, and Hutch whispered such absurd comments in her ear that at one point she laughed so hard she choked on the popcorn, and he had to pound her back.

Tonight, however, was a special night. Hutch had made his bid on the bar, and Vernon Trent had managed to close the deal in record time. This morning, Hutch had signed the papers. The keys to the bar were his—along with its mortgage.

They'd celebrated by buying two bottles of champagne, putting on their oldest clothes and starting the formidable task of cleaning out the bar.

Betsy had never had to clean for herself except in college and graduate school, and she'd never been faced with cleaning anything as downright dirty as the bar.

But the first bottle of champagne made her giggly, and filled Hutch with inspired lunacy. They worked hard, but laughed just as hard.

The first place they tackled was a room in the back of the bar that had once served someone as a sleeping place. It had a tiny closet and a cramped bathroom with a battered metal shower stall. It was a bare, dreary little room with dust, grime and cobwebs for its only ornaments.

Hutch said he would live there. Betsy couldn't imagine having such a small room for one's only home, but she pitched in and helped him.

That single small section of the building took them almost four hours, but at last the bathroom fixtures were scrubbed clean, the room was swabbed out and smelling of pine soap.

Hutch and Betsy sat on the bare floor and leaned with satisfied weariness against one damp wall. He opened the remaining bottle of champagne.

"Happy housewarming," she said and clinked her glass against his.

"A man's home is his castle," Hutch said, clinking back.

He put one arm around her shoulders, drawing her closer. She nestled against him, looking toward the ceiling.

"My lord's castle's got a leak in its royal roof," she said, eyeing a suspicious stain.

"Not to worry, my lady. I've patched a roof or two."

"The royal shower's a scandal," she said, laying her head on his shoulder. "Even clean, it's nasty."

"I'll replace it with one more regal."

"Your Majesty's linoleum's seen better days."

"I'll exile it. I can tile in style."

"Your Worship's walls are squalid. They need paint."

"I'll give 'em a kingly coat."

"I don't know how to put this delicately, Your Highness," she said, "but I think your throne leaks."

He laughed. "Won't be the first throne His Highness has fixed. Maybe I'll use a plumber's friend for my scepter."

"Can you really fix almost anything?" she teased.

"Yup," he said with satisfaction. "Even your nose. It's besmudged, sweet drudge."

He dug into his pocket for his handkerchief, rubbed the tip of her nose and wiped her cheek clean. "Lawsy," he said, "I bet you've never been this dirty in your life. You've got spider goober in your hair. That web stuff."

He brushed away a broken veil of cobweb, then ran his hand over her hair, smoothing it back into place. "You work hard," he said. "If the television biz ever fails, you can hire out cleanin' bars. I'll give you the highest recommendation."

She sighed and snuggled closer to him. "Some days I wish it would fail. TV's crazy. The competition never stops. Neither does the pressure."

He nuzzled her hair. "Why do you do it?"

She shrugged. "It's what I know."

They were quiet a moment. They sipped at their champagne. Then Betsy set aside her glass, still half full.

"Hutch?" she said and put her hand on his chest.

"What, baby?" He kissed the tip of her ear. It tickled in the most marvelous way. And he was the only man in her life who'd ever called her "baby."

"I've been thinking. My father's always so dead set against renting. But I've looked at the real estate situation in Austin. I don't think this is the time to buy. I'm going to rent. I'm going to trust my judgment, follow my vibes."

"Good for you." He kissed her ear again.

"Besides," she said moodily, "I think I should leave Ruth and Tyler's. I love her, but I've imposed enough. And I don't think I'm helping things between them. Probably just the opposite."

"Because of me," he said. "Right?"

She took a deep breath. "She worries."

"About what?"

Betsy shook her head. "She keeps telling me that you and I have no future. I suppose we don't."

He touched his forefinger to her nose. "So what? We've got now. But if you move to Austin, it'll be harder for me to see you."

"I know," she said unhappily.

"I'll miss havin' you close," he said. "But we'll still see each other. Won't we?"

"I hope so," she said, catching his hand in hers. "I want to. But Hutch—"

"What, honey?"

She smiled slightly. Every time he called her by some endearment, it gave her a small, pleasant start. But the smile quickly faded. She looked at him searchingly. "I think I'm ready to go to Fredericksburg," she said.

He gazed down at their hands locked together. He held hers more tightly. "You're sure?"

She, too, stared at their hands. She nodded.

With his free hand, he stroked her hair again. "Okay. When?"

"As soon as possible," she said, shivering slightly. "Before I lose my nerve."

He nodded and appeared to think it over. "How about tomorrow then?" he asked.

She blinked in surprised wariness. "So soon?"

"You said soon as possible."

The possibilities of what might happen seem to crowd around her like a jostling mob. Tears rose in her eyes. "Maybe I won't even be able to see him. But I could see his house, at least. That'd be something. Not much, but something."

"Something," he agreed. He took her in his arms.

She clung to him. "I don't know if I could face this without you," she said in a choked voice.

His answer was to kiss her temple, her cheek, the corner of her mouth.

His touch made her tremble, not with fear, but with feeling for him. She turned her face slightly so that he could kiss her full on the lips.

"No," he whispered, his mouth provocatively close to hers. "You kiss me first this time. Can you?"

She put her hand to his face. She'd learned to love his mouth, both for the words it formed and the things it could tell her without words. Slowly she raised her lips to his and kissed him.

A sound between a sigh and a groan escaped him. "Betsy," he said and kissed the hollow of her throat. He drew her more closely to him.

He stared into her eyes, and gave her a small, enigmatic smile. "Would it scare you if I said I love you a little?"

I love you, he'd said. *I love you a little.*

Her heart leapt against her ribs. "Would it scare you if I told you the same thing?" Her voice shook when she said it.

He put one hand beneath her chin, looked solemnly into her eyes. "I don't think it'd hurt us to love each other—a little. We wouldn't say forever. We wouldn't make promises. We wouldn't pretend it was permanent."

"No," she said, and found she was fighting back tears again. "No promises. We'd never pretend."

"We'll take it a day at a time," he said. "We've got *now*. We'll make all we can of it—all right?"

He kissed her again, and she felt weak and hot with yearning for him, faint and frenzied at the same time.

He spoke the truth; they had no future, only this unexpected and wonderful gift of the present. But it was a complicated gift, as well.

Each night their lovemaking had become bolder, more intense. Each night carried them more irretrievably toward even greater intimacies. It was like being borne along by a river at flood stage, frightening and exhilarating at the same time.

Tonight when he unbuttoned her blouse, unfastened her bra, held her bare breasts and caressed, then kissed them, she was not shocked or threatened.

But when he gently put his hand between her thighs, it gave her a strong surge of physical response she neither expected nor understood. She tensed in his arms.

He'd taken off his shirt so that they were naked from the waist up. She loved the sensation of having her breasts pressed against the warm, delicious hardness of his chest. But he must have sensed her muscles stiffen in nervousness, and he withdrew his hand.

"We'll go only as far as you want," he promised. "We'll go at the pace you want. Tell me. Show me. Help me."

Love me, she wanted to say dazedly against his lips. *Love me all the way.*

Instead she said, "I'm still frightened. Will you hold me? Just hold me?"

She could only guess what it cost him each night to become so aroused—it was clear he was aroused—yet never be satisfied.

"I'm sorry," she said against his bare chest.

His arms tightened around her. "It's all right."

She wound her arms around his neck. She kissed his breastbone. He shuddered slightly, ground his teeth.

And she knew it would happen soon. They would make love. For the first time in her life, sex did not seem like a monster that picked you up, shook you viciously and tried to break you apart.

He was teaching her that it could be tender and giving. She was learning, and she loved him for it. The only thing she feared was that she loved him far more than just a little.

THE NEXT MORNING Hutch set off to pick up Betsy for the trip to Fredericksburg. It was going to be a hard day for her, a hard night for him. He'd taken enough cold showers that week to permanently deplete the Texas water supply.

He'd done everything in his power to hold back with her. But it was excruciating when he embraced her, touched her nakedness, wanting her so much that it literally hurt.

He'd tried to slow himself by reciting the multiplication tables in his head, and last night he'd made it clear through the twelves. Then he had forced himself half-way through the thirteens, no mean feat.

He'd also tried silently listing baseball statistics. He'd gone through five full years of New York Yankees' batting lineups, game by game. He'd even, God help him, conjugated Spanish verbs. He'd also ground his teeth so hard he thought he'd cracked a molar.

But she was worth waiting for.

He knew that they were going to make love eventually. He knew it. She knew it.

The first time would be difficult for her. He understood that, and wanted to make it as good for her as he could. But maybe he couldn't make it good enough. Maybe he was a fool to think he could.

Driving, he wondered moodily how he'd ever gotten caught up in this. He was a man who liked things nice and simple. How'd he get tangled up with such a complicated woman? It wasn't his style.

He parked the van and strode to the porch, brooding on why he'd let this little slip of a thing from California get such a hold on his heart. The reason, he told himself cynically, was that she was challenging, but safe. She could never really be his. He didn't want her to be.

But when she answered the door, he could tell how apprehensive she was about looking for the child. She smiled up at him, but the smile was shaky, and there was such a haunted look in her hazel eyes that it shook him deep inside.

At that moment, he would have walked through fire for her. Instead, he stood reading the apprehension in her face. He didn't speak and neither did she. So he simply took her hand and drew her to his side.

When the door closed behind her, he said, "Come on. Let's find your boy for you."

CHAPTER NINE

BETSY WAS SO NERVOUS that she felt cold inside and out.

She'd borrowed the keys to Ruth's gray Chevrolet. She'd wanted a car because the battered old van seemed too conspicuous. She asked Hutch to drive, telling him she was too edgy. He understood.

She sat in the passenger seat, staring at the country-side, haunted by unwanted memories. First of the party, that long-ago, stupid party when things started spiraling out of control, and she'd been too naive to understand.

She could remember the tiniest details. The color of the paper napkins—yellow. There was punch, pineapple-orange, and somebody'd spiked it, of course. She'd drunk cola out of a plastic glass. There'd been Madonna albums on the CD, and Michael Jackson, and U2.

There were cashews underfoot because somebody had thrown them, and somebody else had knocked over a lamp, breaking it. Couples kept disappearing into the bedrooms, and when Betsy's date had tried to pull her inside one, she'd pushed him away and demanded he take her home. Instead he'd driven her to the park, his two friends in the back seat.

His face was graven on her heart as if by a burning blade. Once she'd thought of him as handsome. He'd been a tall, blond, blue-eyed boy who played football. The Californian, all-American type.

His name was Denny. At the park, he'd hauled her out of the car and dragged her to the ground. While the other two boys pinned her down, he'd taken her first.

The other two were football players, too. She was so small that one of them laughed at how easy she was to hold down. He'd *laughed*.

Oh, God, she thought, putting her hand to her forehead. They'd been boys, only boys. Her date had been seventeen, the other two sixteen.

They'd been bestial, reckless children cruelly hurting another child. The boy who'd laughed at her powerlessness was a tall, dark, lean boy named Paul Simmons.

He'd been the one who'd hurt her most. She thought, in the moments that she allowed herself to think about it, that maybe Denny hadn't penetrated her completely, and it had been Paul who'd really torn away her virginity.

She remembered his weight crushing her, the tearing pain as he drove into her, his hands mauling her breasts. Afterward he'd lain on her a moment, panting, so heavy that she thought her ribs were breaking.

She'd panicked that she was suffocating because somebody had a hand tight over her mouth and nose. She couldn't scream or breathe. Then Paul had risen over her, laughed and raped her a second time, just as hard.

The third boy was Kevin. He was short, brown-haired and stocky. He'd taken her swiftly and without Paul's brutality. He used her and was through. Afterward, he'd helped her to her feet.

She was still ashamed to remember that she had felt so battered and helpless that she'd actually thanked him, genuinely grateful that he wasn't hurting her.

Denny said if she ever told, all of them would swear she'd let them, and it would be their word against hers, three against one. Nobody would believe her.

Beaten and humiliated, she'd agreed. All she wanted was to go home. She had a vague, terrifying suspicion that what had happened was her fault—she could not even say why. She felt dirty and ripped up and ruined forever.

Somehow she'd managed to slip into her house unseen. She supposed that some protective, primitive part of her mind had given her the animal wiles to escape detection. She'd kept taking bath after bath, because she thought she would never be clean again.

She cut up her underwear and dress into little pieces with scissors and hid them in a bag, planning to burn them as soon as possible. She was still too deep in shock to think of being pregnant.

When she began to suspect she was, it was like being trapped in a nightmare with no end. She finally summoned the courage to buy a home pregnancy test. She wept herself sick when it showed she was positive.

She thought about killing herself. She thought about running away forever. She did not have the chance. Every day at school at lunchtime, the smells of cafeteria food made her throw up. Once she almost fainted. The school nurse phoned her parents, who forced her to go to a doctor. When her parents learned—

Hutch reached over, took her hand. "I can turn around any time you want. You don't have to go through this."

She gave him a grateful look. He was, without question, the kindest man she'd ever known. "Yes. I do," she said. She laced her fingers through his and held on tight.

He watched the highway. "It might be better if you talked, got it off your chest," he said. "You're sittin' over there thinkin' so hard I can feel it. It doesn't do any good to keep it bottled up inside."

*Talk. Get it off your chest. Don't keep it bottled up. All
the things her family had never said to her.*

She shook her head. "I was thinking of my parents. I
had this dumb idea of running away. I made the mistake
of telling my brother. He told them. I wanted to die."

"You shouldn't have. It wasn't your fault."

"I'm not sure they ever believed that. I'm afraid they
thought I'd asked for it and wouldn't admit it. They
never tried to do anything about the boys. There was
never a word about taking them to court—that would
have been a scandal."

"Parents aren't perfect, honey. They might have been
scared as you."

"I know," she said, looking out at the barren hills.
"Maybe they did what they thought was best. But they
never wanted anybody to know, because it was so
shameful. So the lies started. And they never ended."

He squeezed her hand. "You've ended some."

"They lied to everybody about where I was when I was
in that place for unwed mothers. God, I hated it there."

She recoiled from memories of the home. She'd had a
roommate, Cindy, who was also sixteen and cried all the
time because she wanted to keep her baby. She said she
was in love with the child's father, but he, too, was only
sixteen. Their parents wouldn't let them marry. They
were sending him to military school and making her give
up the baby.

But Betsy had felt emotionless, like a zombie. Her
baby never seemed like a real, human child to her. She
thought of it as something alien planted within her, and
felt that she was forced to carry it like a penance.

"I didn't think twice when they had me sign the papers," she said, remembering. "I didn't think I'd ever
want to see the baby. It never occurred to me that he

might want to see *me* someday. I didn't think. I just signed him away—like he was nothing. A piece of unwanted property."

Hutch turned to her and for a moment let his clear eyes rest on her. "You were sixteen. You were scared. You did what you were told."

When he looked back at the road, so did she. It was an innocuous-looking stretch of highway, but it led to Fredericksburg. And the child.

"After I got back home," she said, "I always *tried* to do what I was told. I wanted to make it up to them, my parents. My father especially. He's never said one word about it. Do you know that? Never. My mother said he was too hurt. I tried to pretend it had never happened, and I tried to be perfect. But it hasn't worked. I can't marry Michael just to make them happy."

"I know," he said. "I knew that from the start. He's no good for you."

She looked at him in surprise. He kept his eyes on the road. "How do you know?" she asked.

"I just know."

She shook her head and swallowed. "And I can't go on pretending this child doesn't exist, that he never happened, and that he has nothing to do with me."

He nodded. "We're flying blind, you know. We may not see him at all. We may have to do this more than once."

She ran her hand over her hair in frustration. "I know. But maybe I shouldn't try more than once. It seems almost like stalking—you know?"

"Yeah," he said. "I know."

"I don't mean any harm to anybody," she said, looking at the weathered hills. "I know I promised not to try to see him, not to get in touch with him or his—his parents."

"You've got rights, too," he said. He pulled his hat brim down to a more determined angle. "I mean, if you wanted to, you could probably go to court, *make* them recognize you."

"I know," she said softly, still staring at the rolling countryside. *To my child, these are the hills of home,* she thought. *Except he may not know he's my child, may not even suspect he's adopted. Maybe I really shouldn't have any rights in the matter. I don't know.*

She saw a sign in the distance and closed her eyes so she couldn't read what it said.

Hutch squeezed her hand. "We're almost there. It's Fredericksburg. Are you all right?"

She kept her eyes closed. "Yes," she lied.

HUTCH LOOKED UP the Echtenkamps' address in a telephone book at an outdoor phone. Dazed, Betsy looked about at the buildings of Fredericksburg. Hutch had told her it was a German community, rich in German-American tradition.

Years ago, the wealthy farmers had built small weekend houses in the town, and many still stood, like lovely Victorian playhouses.

A nice place to grow up, she thought numbly. *A pretty place to grow up.*

Hutch climbed back into the car, pulled his hat brim lower. "Got it," he said. "I'll stop at a gas station and get a town map."

She nodded. They were on the main street. There were restaurants with German names, advertising German food. There were shops, and the sidewalks were surprisingly full of people, perhaps early Christmas shoppers.

Every time she saw a little boy among them, her heart gave a frightened jump. She might be looking at her son and not recognizing him.

Hutch stopped and got the map. They set off again. Her pulsed pounded, and her mouth was dry.

They came to a quiet street lined with big oak trees. The homes were older, but well maintained, mostly two-story, the yards large.

"This is the street," Hutch said. Betsy drew in her breath. One middle-aged man worked in his front yard, raking leaves. There was no sign of any children.

Hutch pulled to the curb, stopping. "That's the house," he said, nodding at a tall brick structure with a wide porch. He had parked a few houses away from it.

Betsy stared at it, and felt her spirits take an odd, shaking plunge. There was a sign before the house. It bore the name of a realty company and said in large letters SOLD.

She clutched Hutch's sleeve. "They're moving," she breathed, numb with disbelief.

He put his hand over hers. "They may just be movin' to another house in town, sugar. Don't let it throw you. Look at it. It's a nice house. He's got a real nice house."

Betsy could clearly see the front door and a section of the back yard. The back was fenced. There was a swing set, painted red, and a black Labrador dog stood by the gate, as if waiting.

"It's—it is a nice house," she managed to breathe. "Don't you think?"

"Mighty nice," he said, studying it.

"He's got a swing. And a dog."

"Got a tree house, too. Can you see it?"

"No," she said. "Where?"

"Look this way." He put his arm around her, pulled her closer to him so she could see out his side of the window. When she leaned against the solidness of his shoulder, she could see a large, bare tree, with a crude platform in it.

"A tree house," she said and almost smiled. "My brothers always wanted a tree house. But my mother was sure they'd break their necks. They never got one."

"Well," Hutch said with satisfaction, "*he's* got one. My dad built Harry and me a tree house. God, I loved it. A great place for dropping water balloons on girls. Just like 'Calvin and Hobbes.'"

She glanced at him worriedly. "We can't park here long. It'll seem suspicious. I don't want to alarm anybody."

"It's okay," he assured her. "I'll look at the map. Like we're lost, getting our bearings. That'll buy us a few minutes. We probably should have come on a school day. We'd have had a better chance to see him."

Betsy stared at the house, trying to memorize it, every brick and shutter of it, every tree and shrub in the yard.

I shouldn't come back here again, she thought guiltily. *I feel like a spy or a kidnapper or a Peeping Tom. Maybe this is all I'm supposed to see.*

But at that moment, a small miracle occurred. She sensed it even before Hutch spoke.

"Look behind you," he said quietly.

She whirled in her seat. A woman with two children, boys, had rounded the corner behind them. They walked down the side of the street on which Betsy and Hutch were parked.

The woman was about thirty-six, tall and plump, with a plain but good-natured face. She wore a green jacket and carried a stack of library books.

She held a small boy of about five by the hand. He
wore a yellow jacket with a hood and turquoise-blue
mittens. His round face and glasses made him look like
a small, chubby scholar. He looked up at the woman,
said something, and she laughed, throwing her head back
slightly.

Betsy took all this in instantaneously, almost sublimi-
nally. What truly riveted her attention was the older boy.

The second she saw him, she knew. Her breath seemed
knocked out of her, as if she'd been struck in the midsection, and at the same time, she had a sensation of
falling.

He looked nothing like her. He was tall for his age,
very lean and athletic looking. He wore a red jacket, his
hands jammed in his pockets, three library books
clamped under one arm. No hat.

His hair was thick and so dark it was nearly black. His
face was handsome, with regular features, and he had
thick, straight black eyebrows.

He was the image of Paul Simmons, the boy who had
laughed when he held her down, the one who had raped
her twice.

Oh, God, she thought in despair, *he's Paul's. I didn't
want him to be Paul's.*

Her emotions were intense, yet so tangled she couldn't
sort them. She felt frozen, knowing she shouldn't stare,
but unable to stop.

They drew closer. Betsy's heart beat so hard that her
body shook. She pretended to look into the back seat, as
if searching for something. It was an awkward charade,
and she was vaguely conscious it would fool no one who
looked at her closely.

But the threesome paid no attention to the parked car.
The older boy said something to the smaller one, who

giggled delightedly. The woman laughed, too, and the older boy smiled up at her.

He looks exactly like Paul, she thought in confusion. *It's like there's nothing there of me.*

She had carried him in her body for nine months. In fear and pain she had brought him into the world. But she could see no trace of herself in him.

The woman and two boys passed the car. Betsy stared at the older boy, and for the briefest moment his eyes met hers. Then he turned his attention back to the woman. It was as if he hadn't really seen Betsy at all.

But in that instant, Betsy saw something that shook her to her soul. He did not have the dark, almost coal-black eyes of Paul Simmons. The eyes that had looked back at her were large and hazel, identical to her own.

He really is part of me, she thought. *And I'm part of him.*

The trio walked about twenty yards farther. Betsy kept her gaze on the older boy's back. He carried himself straight and tall.

But then her heart dipped in disappointment. They turned and walked to the porch of the wrong house.

Dismay swept over her. Had she been wrong? He wasn't her child? It seemed impossible for him not to be. She'd been so certain....

But the woman didn't open the door, she rang the bell instead. An older woman with a cane answered the door. The younger woman handed her a library book. They stood talking.

Then the older boy did something that made tears spring to Betsy's eyes. He knelt beside the littler boy, took a handkerchief from his pocket and wiped the younger child's nose, gently but with adult thoroughness. Then he straightened the boy's collar and stood again.

He said something to the mother, and she nodded. He unzipped his red jacket slightly, ran down the walk, looked both ways, then raced across the street, across the lawn of the brick house, then up its porch stairs.

The tears in her eyes grew hotter, more painful to hold back. It *was* his house. He *was* her child. Gary.

He set his library books on the low brick wall around the porch. Then he ran to the gate of the fence. The dog was leaping with excitement, its tail wagging madly.

Gary Echtenkamp unlatched the gate and slipped into the backyard, shutting the gate firmly behind him. The dog jumped at him, putting its forepaws on his chest and licking his chin. He grabbed the dog and fell to his knees, petting it and rubbing its jaws.

It jumped at him again, knocking him backward into the leaves. He laughed and grabbed for the dog, which joyfully sprang atop him. They tussled, rolling in the leaves together.

Then the mother crossed the street, holding the smaller child by the hand. She called to the older one. He rose, brushing the leaves from his clothes. Carefully he opened the gate again, slipped out and reclosed it.

He ran up the porch stairs, took up his library books. His mother unlocked the door and ushered the littler boy in before her. Betsy watched the older child follow them inside. The door closed behind him, shutting off her view of his red jacket, his dark hair.

She stared at the door in silence, as if she could not quite believe what she'd seen.

"Now might be the time to go," Hutch said quietly. "This might be a good way to remember him."

She nodded mutely. But she kept staring, hoping the door would reopen, that she would catch another glimpse of the boy. But it did not. Hutch started the car, eased away from the curb. She watched the house, almost desperately, until it, too, disappeared from view.

She turned and gazed, unseeing, at a different street, a strange street. She couldn't speak, only numbly stare.

Hutch got back on Main Street, stopped at another public telephone. "Do you want me to see if I can find where they're movin'?" he asked, concern on his face. "Or do you want to know?"

She nodded, still feeling dazed and full of tumult.

He got out of the car, looked up the realtor's number in the phone book, dropped coins into the slot. The breeze stirred his thick hair. He talked for a few moments to someone, and he acted as if he were doing the most casual thing in the world.

He got back into the car, worry in his eyes. "They're goin' a long ways off, sugar," he said. "His father's a hospital administrator. He's taken a job in upstate New York. They leave in a couple of weeks."

"New York?" she said, disconcerted. "A couple of weeks? Oh, Hutch," she said, "I could have missed seeing him."

"Well, you didn't, sugar. You saw him. You all right?"

She nodded, but her thoughts were still muddled, her emotions dizzying.

Hutch started the car again. She could think of nothing to say.

"He seems healthy," he said at last, not looking at her. "And happy. He's a handsome kid."

"Yes," she said, her voice tightly controlled. "Did you see how fast he could run? He did look healthy—didn't he? And happy—didn't he? He did seem happy—didn't he?"

"Yeah. He sure loves that dog."

Betsy managed to blink back her tears. She sat rigidly, squaring her shoulders. "The mother," she said. "She looked like a nice woman, a good woman—didn't she? The way she held the little boy's hand? The way they laughed?"

Hutch nodded. "She'd taken them to the library. That's nice."

Betsy twisted the button of her jacket unconsciously. "Very nice. And she'd brought a book for her neighbor. That was kind of her. She looked like a really motherly sort of mother, didn't you think? The sort who bakes cookies and goes to the PTA?"

"Yeah," he agreed. "She does."

"Did you see how he wiped his little brother's nose?" she asked. "The way he knelt down and did that? He seemed so serious when he did it. Then he straightened his collar for him. And the way he petted the dog? He seems like a nice boy—don't you think?"

"Yeah," Hutch said. "He does."

"And he looked both ways before he crossed the street," she said, her voice still tight. "He set his books down carefully—did you notice? And he pulled the gate shut behind him, both times. He was really careful. They—they've taught him well."

She paused. She stared out at the gray November sky. "He had on a Cub Scout shirt under his jacket—did you notice?"

"I noticed."

"He's a Cub Scout. That's good—don't you think?"

"It's real good."

She was silent a moment, remembering. Her heart still pounded insanely. "He looked at us—just for a second. Did you see?"

"Yes."

"He—he has my eyes," she almost whispered.

"He has. Exactly. I noticed."

She twisted the button harder. It came off in her hand. She stared at it, hardly noticing what she'd done. "Otherwise," she said slowly, "I guess that he—he doesn't look like me at all."

"No." Hutch's voice was low and neutral. "He doesn't."

"In his looks," she said, her voice starting to shake in earnest, "he takes after his fa—fa—his biological fa—"

She couldn't get the word out. She simply couldn't.

"Father," Hutch said, his eyes trained on the street. "He takes after the biological father."

She couldn't speak. She remembered the child's face. And she remembered Paul Simmons's face. She remembered his laughter, his weight crushing her against the ground, everything. For a whirling moment she thought she would be ill.

Hutch was silent. He pulled onto the main highway, exceeded the speed limit slightly and got them quickly out of Fredericksburg. As soon as the town was out of sight, he pulled over to the side of the road.

He turned to her. "Okay," he said, his face somber. "You know who the father is now. Does it matter?"

Her face felt so stiff that it might break. She stared at Hutch, feeling naked. "It was the wrong one," she choked out. "Oh, any of them would have been wrong. But he was the worst. The one I hated most."

Then she was mortified to burst into tears. She covered her face with her hands.

Hutch pulled her into his arms and held her tight. "Hush, sugar, hush, love," he said against her ear. "It's all right. Lots of good children got bad daddies, through no fault of their own. This little boy, he's probably got a real good daddy now, set him a good example, bring him up right. It looks like they're bringing him up right. It really does."

She clung to him and cried until her tears were spent and she could only lie, exhausted, against his shoulder. He had to give her his handkerchief, and she was reminded of her son kneeling to wipe his brother's nose. That made her want to cry again, but no more tears would come.

"Hutch," she said, crumpling the handkerchief, "I know I feel something for that little boy. But I don't know exactly what it is I feel. And I didn't want him to be Paul's. When I saw his face, I thought I'd never be able to love him—"

"Shh, don't beat yourself up. How could you love him at first sight, Betsy? You don't even know him."

She took a long, ragged breath. "But then I looked into his eyes, and I felt something so strong for him, but complicated. Can I call that love?"

He took her face between his hands. He drew back so he could stare into her eyes. "Listen to me. You got the right to have complicated feelin's. What does it matter what you call it? You're concerned about him, that's what's important."

"He's got another mother now," Betsy said shakily.

"Yes. He does."

"She seems to love him. To be raising him right."

He nodded. "That's right."

"If I'd kept him—somehow—I couldn't have given him the kind of life he has."

"That's right, too."

She cast her eyes down, unable to meet his gaze. "I probably couldn't have given him the love she does."

He tilted her face up to his again. "Stop harpin' on love. You feel what you feel."

"I feel—I feel I should leave him alone," she said. "But that I should keep track of him. And someday, if he does come looking for me, I can say, 'Yes, I know about you. I've watched you from a distance. I've thought about you your whole life.'"

He nodded and bent closer to her. "And then? What then?"

She shook her head almost imperceptibly. "I guess then—if he wanted to—we'd get to know each other."

"Good," he said. "That sounds good, sugar. Then what?"

She thought. She'd been through a hundred alternatives a hundred times during the past months. But now she thought she might know the right one. "Then," she said, "if we were lucky, we might learn to—"

She couldn't finish.

"You might learn what?" he coaxed.

"Then we might learn—to love each other. And that would be nice."

"It would." He searched her face. "But if it never happened? If he never came looking for you?"

"I don't know," she said honestly. "I suppose I would try to understand. And accept it."

He bent nearer and kissed her. It was a short, gentle kiss, but it seemed impossibly sweet to her.

She kissed him back.

She wound her arms around his neck. She leaned her forehead against his. "I've thought about this a lot," she said. "I've thought about what you said about you and your brother and sister and your birth parents. What I did today? If I were that woman, I wouldn't want somebody doing what I did."

He clasped the back of her neck, his fingers tangling in her hair. "You got rights, too."

"Yes," Betsy said, struggling to control her voice. "That's what they kept telling me at the agency that traced him."

"Some'd say his parents don't have the right to keep him from knowin' you. That it's not fair to him, either."

"Your parents tried to keep it from you at first."

"Yeah," he said softly. "They did."

"Why?" she asked, looking into his eyes. "They weren't bad people. They weren't trying to hurt you."

He paused, putting his hands on her shoulders. "I think they were tryin' to protect us. They didn't want us to feel that somebody hadn't wanted us. But I think they were tryin' to protect themselves, too. They wanted us to be *their* children. Same as if we'd been born to them. It was only human of them."

"They felt threatened?"

"Yeah, sugar. I expect they did. And who knows? The birth parents can get in the picture, and maybe it's a good thing, maybe not. It depends on the people."

"Yes," she whispered. "It depends on the people."

"That woman might live in secret terror of you," he said, gripping her shoulders more tightly. "That's crossed your mind, hasn't it?"

She nodded sadly. "Yes. That I'd show up on her doorstep and say, 'He's mine. You took him when I was too young and stupid to know what I was doing, and now I want him back.' And that I'd rip all their lives apart."

"Yeah," he said. "You could, you know."

She rubbed her forehead against his. "I couldn't do that to them."

"I know you couldn't."

"Do you think he knows he's adopted?"

"Probably. I knew. Long before they ever told us. Harry did, too. So did my sister, though she never said anything."

"But how did you know? If nobody told you?"

"Nobody had to tell me. It was a feelin'."

"Feelings," she said, resting her fingertips against his cheekbone. "It's always about feelings, isn't it?"

"Pretty much, sugar."

"Do you suppose they've told him he's adopted, but I'm—I'm dead or something?"

"They might have told him something. Probably have."

"Lies again?" she asked unhappily. "Don't they ever end?"

"Betsy," he said, "you don't know. Whatever they've said, they probably thought they were sayin' it for the best. My folks did. But the truth came out. It usually does."

She drew back and managed to smile at him. "So someday, somebody may ring my doorbell, and I'll open the door, and I'll have a *son* standing there, a man. Eighteen years old or twenty-one or even older."

He gave her a one-cornered smile in return. "Could be."

She shook her head. "If that ever happens, I wonder what he'll think?"

"I think," he said, bending to take her lips, "that he'll get the sweetest, prettiest surprise of his life."

And when his mouth touched hers, Betsy knew that she wanted to make love with him. With him it would be right. It would be beautiful, not ugly. With him she would no longer feel broken. She would feel whole.

CHAPTER TEN

THEY HAD SUPPER at the bar, sitting in Hutch's bare little room. Fast food from the local drive-in, that was all. He thought Betsy would rather that they be alone and talk over all that had happened. He was right.

Then he thought maybe she'd like to go dancing at Zack's, but feared she'd be too tired. No, she said, she was still full of nervous energy, dancing sounded good.

But once they were in each other's arms, the chemistry between them started exerting itself more strongly than ever. At last he was so full of need for her that he had to warn her.

"Betsy," he breathed in her ear, his voice pained. "I think we'd better stop dancin' so close for a while."

"I want to dance close." She pressed nearer.

He exhaled sharply. "You're doin' things to me."

"Good," she said, and kissed him on the chest. The warmth of her lips seemed to burn through his shirt.

He drew back and forced himself to dance farther from her. He stared at her pretty face, upturned to his in the soft light. "Betsy," he said, "you know that I want to make love to you."

"Yes," she said, her eyes holding his. "I know."

"Then the question is, do *you* want to? You might think so. We might—get something started, then you could change your mind. For which I wouldn't blame you. But we both ought to be prepared, because—"

She gave him a shy but determined look. It made his heart roll over in his chest and heat swarm through his veins.

"I won't change my mind."

"Betsy," he said, gripping her hand more tightly, "you've gotta be sure. See, you've had a real emotional day. I wouldn't want this to happen, then for you to regret it. To feel you did it because you weren't thinkin' straight. I want it to happen. But not for the wrong reason."

"I love you," she said. "Is that the wrong reason?"

He couldn't stop himself. He bent and kissed her mouth. "No," he breathed. "It's the right reason."

She closed her eyes a moment, shook her head. Then her eyes opened again and she said earnestly, "I want it to be tonight. Because this day changed my life. I want to change it still more."

"Sugar," he said, "what happened in Fredericksburg is something you'll keep thinkin' on. It'll haunt you. It's not over."

"I know, Hutch. I understand that."

"I just want you to know what you're gettin' into."

She gave him that look again, and again it made his chest ache. "I know," she whispered. "No promises. We take it one day at a time. That's all. No more."

He hesitated. But he had to be honest with her. "I'm not good at commitments. I never have been. If I don't feel free to travel on, I feel trapped."

"You're free to travel on," she said. "Away from here or just away from me. Any time you want."

He stopped dancing. He took her by the upper arms, peered into her face. "There's other things. What if we made a mistake? What if we—well—accidentally made a baby?"

That stopped her momentarily. She blinked hard, but raised her chin higher. "I'd be very careful not to make such a mistake," she said. "But if it happened, I guess I'd have to—to follow my vibrations. I wouldn't expect you to do anything."

He gritted his teeth. "I didn't mean it that way. Not at all. I didn't mean I wouldn't feel responsible. I would. We'd both have to go with how we felt."

"Hutch?"

"Yes?"

"We'll both be very, very careful. We know the consequences. You and I should know them better than anybody."

He looked into her eyes for a long moment. Then he nodded and smiled a little sadly. She smiled back the same way.

"I love you," he said. He said it almost involuntarily, as if he couldn't help saying it.

"I know," she said. "You've shown me."

SHE HELD HIM tightly, her face against his bare chest. He sighed with satisfaction and tucked the sheet so that it covered her breasts more securely.

She smiled because he understood she was still shy about being naked. She kissed his collarbone.

"You awake?" he asked, running his hand gently up and down her arm.

She snuggled closer to him. "I dozed off for a little, I think."

He turned so he could lay his cheek against her hair. "Me, too. Nice to wake up like this."

"Nice," she breathed. She lay listening to the steady rhythm of his heart against her ear.

He continued to stroke her arm. The movement was sensuous, hypnotic. "I'm sorry it had to be in a motel room," he said. "I wish it hadn't."

"It doesn't matter where," she said, closing her eyes. "It only matters that it was you."

They lapsed into silence, and she gave herself up to savoring his nearness. He'd brought her to his motel, but only because they had nowhere else to go. His cubbyhole at the restaurant wasn't finished or furnished.

It was a Spartan room, but the walls had been freshly painted white, the drapes were white, and to Betsy's eyes, the place had a kind of purity.

Once they were inside the room, Hutch had kissed her, caressed her, kissed her more and slowly undressed her. He was patient, he was kind, he was tender, he was passionate.

At times, as they ventured further, she would feel a wave of fear. He always sensed it and soothed it away, guiding her toward pleasure instead. Nothing they did seemed wrong or ugly, because she loved him.

She felt shy, awkward with inexperience. But he smiled and told her that most people were shy at first.

He even showed her that sex could have its funny side. She couldn't believe that they could find themselves naked and tangled up in the sheets and laughing. But they did, and it was wonderful, because she'd never experienced such intimate laughter.

And when they finally did make love, Betsy was swept away, not simply by physical yearning, but by the force of her feeling for Hutch.

Afterward she had lain in his arms, aglow with the tingling knowledge that they had been as close as it was possible for human beings to be.

She'd cried a little. She'd had to, because it was as if she had passed over a bridge and left a haunted land. He dried her tears, made her smile.

She would never forget what the three drunken boys had done when she was fifteen. But what they'd done seemed different now, not canceled, but diminished. Their power over her had fallen away, and she had achieved a kind of victory over them.

She no longer felt forever ruined or so dirty that she could never again be clean. She'd been taught all too well that sex could be a violation. Now she knew it could be a gift as well, an expression of love.

She nuzzled Hutch's chest, and he gave a small, sexy groan of pleasure.

"I know," she said, "that I probably wasn't very good at that. And that you took a lot of trouble with me."

"It was no trouble," he said with conviction. "Feel free to give me that kind of trouble any time."

She laughed softly. "I'm just a beginner. I'll get better."

He drew her closer and kissed her ear. "If you get any better, it could kill me. Don't go strugglin' to improve."

She caressed his side. He had a hard, muscular body, nice to touch. "You know," she whispered, "that was, in a way, the first time for me, really."

He kissed her ear again. "I know. It *was* the first time—really. I'm lucky. Thank you."

"No," she said, her voice tight. "I'm the lucky one. Thank you."

He put his hand beneath her chin, lifted her face to his. "Maybe we're both lucky," he said.

He slipped his hand behind her neck, cradling her head. Then he lowered his lips to hers and kissed her. His mouth was subtly more questing this time. His other hand moved to cover her breast, caressing and teasing it. His touch was more ardent than before, and she was pleased that it excited, not frightened her.

She parted her lips, so he and she could taste and explore each other as intimately as possible. His tongue toyed and mated with hers.

Her hands roamed tentatively down over his ribs, his waist, his strong thighs. He gasped and twined his legs with hers.

His lips moved to her jawline, her throat, down to her breasts, kissing them, doing things to them with his mouth that made her tangle her fingers in his hair, not wanting him to stop.

I don't want him to stop. The thought was still so new that her desire was mixed with sheer wonder. She shivered as his lips moved lower still.

He touched her in a way that made her throb and go warm and liquid. He kissed her in a way that made her hold her breath in pure, shuddering pleasure.

He was making love to her more boldly this time, with less inhibition, and she could not resist him. He kept touching her, softly, slowly, with exquisite eroticism. Every atom of her body seemed to pulse with such sweet desire that she felt she was losing control of herself.

"I can't hold out as long this time, sugar," he said huskily. "I'm only human."

She gave herself to him, and just as he entered her, something overwhelming happened to her body. She was shaken by rhythmic, delirious waves that made her arch against him, holding him as tightly as he held her. It was as if he had seized her up in a storm of pleasure, and they were both completely swept away by it.

"Ohh," Betsy said against his lips. Trembling, she kissed him, as another surge overtook her, transported her. "Oh—my goodness," she half breathed, half panted. "My goodness!"

A few moments later, they lay weakly in each other's arms, breathing hard. Hutch stroked her cheek.

She sighed, still awed by what had happened between them. "I think this is the part where I'm supposed to say, 'I didn't know it could be like this,'" she said. "My *goodness*."

"Oh, Betsy," he said with a gentle laugh, "I bet you're the only woman in America who'd say, 'my goodness' at a time like that."

She blinked in dismay. She wondered if he was hurt that she hadn't screamed or groaned or cried out his name the way people did in movies. "What was I supposed to say?"

He kissed the tip of her nose. "Exactly what you did. 'My goodness. My sweet, sweet goodness.'"

HUTCH GOT BETSY to say "my goodness" quite a lot during the next week. He considered it nothing short of a miracle, and smiled every time he thought of it.

She had an innate shyness about sex that he found both endearing and exciting. Yet sometimes she asked surprisingly bold questions. They got caught up in conversations that were sexy and innocent at the same time.

She found a furnished apartment in Austin and moved into it in the middle of the week. And he found that although he kept his motel room in Crystal Creek, he somehow never seemed to sleep in it.

Betsy didn't have to start work at the television station for another week, so she went back to Crystal Creek with him every day and helped him work on the bar. It was hard, dirty work, but she was a trooper, and he admired her for it.

Evenings they drove back to Austin. There they usually started out doing something ordinary—making macaroni and cheese for supper, watching television, or dancing to music on the radio. But it hardly mattered what they started; what they ended up doing was making love.

Betsy would sometimes get embarrassed by how frequently they did, and he kept telling her she'd been holding back so long that what was happening was perfectly natural.

"There was a warm, affectionate person in there all along," he told her. "She was scared to come out, was all."

"You've created a monster," she said with mock darkness. He'd only grinned in return.

They did not talk about the future. Hutch knew the time would come when they would drift apart. She had to know, too. What she didn't suspect, he believed, was that she would be the one to move on, leaving him behind.

She'd find somebody of her own kind who could offer her everything he couldn't, because other than love he had not one thing to give her.

Someday, sooner than she might guess, she'd be ready for promises, and the kind of man who made them. But until then, he was deeply satisfied to be with her.

Sometimes, he saw the fugitive sadness in her eyes and knew she was thinking about the little boy in Fredericksburg. He knew she'd like to see the child again, probably yearned to talk to his parents.

They talked about it, but she stuck to her decision. She'd signed those papers years ago, and after that one long, stolen look at her child, she seemed determined to keep her word. And he loved her a little more for having the strength to do it.

FRIDAY NIGHT was the night before the chili-off in Crystal Creek. Hutch and Betsy had been assigned the task of doing the shopping. They were repacking the supplies so they could load the van and take off first thing in the morning.

The phone had just been connected that afternoon, and Betsy was startled when it rang. So far she had given the number only to Ruth, and Hutch had given it only to Cal.

"It's probably Cal," Hutch muttered. "He'd better've scrounged up that kettle and propane stove like he promised. I gotta get all this stuff. I gotta cook all this stuff. I can't do everything."

She gave him a rueful smile. Chili seemed the one thing about which he allowed himself to be temperamental.

She answered the phone.

"Betsy?" said her mother's voice.

Betsy's back stiffened. Although being with Hutch seemed gloriously right, she felt a sudden wave of guilt.

"Mother," she said with false heartiness.

"Ruth had to give me this number," Margaret Holden said, plainly displeased. "You didn't even tell us you'd moved."

"I just got the phone," Betsy said defensively. "I haven't had a chance."

"I asked Ruth if you'd found a place, and she was very vague. She seemed positively evasive. And when I asked what you bought, she got even more evasive. I finally pried it out of her—you're renting. You know how your father feels about renting."

"He hasn't seen the real estate picture here," Betsy said. "I've made the right decision. I'm sure of it."

"Betsy, Michael keeps calling here. He hasn't been able to get in touch with you. Almost every time he's called Ruth's, you were gone. He says you haven't called him at all. Why? Why are you treating him like this?"

"I've been busy."

"Busy at what?" her mother demanded. "I asked Ruth that question, and she wouldn't give me a straight answer. Are you purposely avoiding Michael? Just what are you up to? Do you mind telling me?"

Betsy was about to smooth the situation with a vague lie, but something in her rebelled. *We always hide the truth,* she thought grimly. *I'm tired of lies. Let her face facts, for a change.*

"I'm seeing somebody else," she said, "Another man."

Her mother's silence was long and ominous. When she finally spoke, her voice vibrated with disapproval. "Another man? Betsy, you've only been there two weeks. How can you be involved with another man?"

Betsy glanced at Hutch. He was bent over the counter, his back to her, measuring chili powder into a pint jar. But he was listening, she knew. He couldn't help but overhear.

"I met someone—special. I'm attracted to him. Far more than to Michael."

"Betsy," her mother said, clearly aghast, "how could you find any man more attractive than Michael?"

Betsy gripped the phone more tightly. "I just do."

"He can't be as handsome as Michael. That would be impossible. Is he? Is he just better-looking?"

Betsy stared at Hutch's almost too-lean body, his worn clothes, his thick hair in need of a trim. "No," she said, "he's not."

"Betsy, someone in your position has to be careful. Some gigolo could try to charm you for your money. Does this man have money? I mean the money to be in your league?"

My league, Betsy thought with distaste. "No," she said shortly. "He doesn't."

"Then what's his appeal? Is he better educated? Are his prospects better? I can hardly imagine how. Is he some sort of artist or intellectual—is that his charm?"

Betsy sighed. "No. None of those things."

"Why haven't you told Michael? This isn't fair to Michael. It's cruel, Betsy. You practically agreed to marry Michael. Now you're sneaking around with another man?"

"I like him better," Betsy said with feeling. "Can't you understand? That's how I *feel.* I haven't told Michael because I promised Ruth I'd see how serious this relationship was first."

Margaret Holden's voice took on a dangerous frostiness. "Serious? Are you talking marriage?"

"No. We aren't. And we won't."

"Then it's not serious," Margaret asserted. "It's a flirtation. Get it out of your system and come to your senses. In that case, it's best you haven't told Michael. I swear—"

Betsy drew in a long breath between her teeth. "It's serious. More serious than anything I ever had with Michael. More real."

This time Margaret's silence was even more ominous, and when she spoke, her tone went from frosty to polar. "Who is this man? What is this man?"

Here it comes, Betsy thought and closed her eyes. "He's opening a bar and chili restaurant in Crystal Creek," she said.

Margaret's voice rose half an octave. "Betsy, you can't be serious! You're throwing Michael over for a bartender? Are you insane? Oh, my God."

"He's not a bartender. He's buying a bar."

"Some small-town tavern owner?" Margaret asked in contempt. "That you hardly know? You say it's serious? But you won't marry him? What's going on?"

"My life," said Betsy. "My life is going on."

"Betsy," Margaret said, clearly horrified. "Ruth sounded almost—guilty. Are you doing something wrong? How deeply are you involved with this man?"

"Very deeply. All the way."

"All the way?" Margaret gasped. "In high school, when we said that, it meant people were having—were doing—were going as far—"

"I know," Betsy said.

"Betsy! How can you say such a thing?"

"Because it's the truth. For once in our lives, can we just calmly discuss the truth? I love Michael as a friend, but as something between a man and a woman—"

To her distress, her mother began to cry.

"How can you do this to us? Again? Didn't you learn your lesson the first time? Oh, Betsy, don't get pregnant again. I couldn't stand it a second time. And it'd kill your father."

Betsy felt as if she'd been slapped. "I—I—" she stammered.

"I've borne four children," continued Margaret, weeping, "but none's given me the heartbreak you have. Won't you ever learn? Do you like to hurt the people who love you? Do you?"

Betsy gritted her teeth. She'd thought she wanted the truth. Was this how her mother saw it? Betsy felt sick, as if she'd unwittingly loosed a swarm of ugliness and pain.

"I don't want to hurt anybody," she said.

"Your father and I stood by you through that first mess. You were so young we thought you didn't know what you were doing. But it nearly killed us. I can't tell you the toll it took on your father. I thought he'd die of shame."

Betsy felt backed against the wall, falsely accused and found guilty. "I couldn't help what happened to me—"

"That's not what the boys said," Margaret said bitterly. "Your poor father went and talked to them all and their parents. They all said the same thing. Well, you sowed your wild oats, but we all reaped the bitter harvest, didn't we?"

Betsy was stunned, disbelieving. "You never told me you'd talked to any of them. You never told me that you thought *I* was the one—"

"It's not the sort of thing one wants to talk about," Margaret snapped. "It's not the sort of thing one wants to dwell on. Well, we stood by you. We tried to put it behind us."

"Those boys raped me," Betsy said hotly. "What they did was terrible. *They* did it. Not me. I was the one who paid the price. You expected me to pretend it never happened—"

"We acted in your best interests."

"It *happened,*" Betsy argued, angry tears rising in her eyes. "I had a child. You have a grandchild. He's eight years old and you've never seen him, and you don't care a thing about him."

"Betsy," Margaret said icily, "that child is not my grandchild. I don't want to see him. He's not our concern. His existence has caused me so much pain—"

"You?" Betsy fairly exploded. "What about me? What about him?"

"I see," Margaret said in a broken voice. "I understand now. You're blaming us. You're punishing your father and me. You're trying to hurt us as much as you can."

"I'm not," Betsy said, horrified. "I told you—"

"You're hurting Michael, too. Why? Because he's so good to you? Because he made the mistake of caring for you? So you kick him in the teeth. Doing what you've always done to people."

"I never tried to hurt you," she almost pleaded.

"An affair," Margaret choked out. "You have the nerve to do this, then expect me not to be hurt? I can't excuse you this time, Betsy. You're not an adolescent now. This time will you please try not to bring another bastard into the world?"

Betsy was too stricken to speak.

She didn't have to. Her mother gave a hiccuping little sob and hung up. The line went dead.

She put down the receiver, then stared numbly at the phone.

Hutch came to her, drew her into his arms, held her tight.

"She hates me," she said, pressing her forehead against his chest. "Maybe all these years she's hated me. They never believed me. This whole time—never."

"I believe you," he said fiercely. "Don't mind her. It's herself she hates. She thinks she failed with you or something. She's wrong. She just can't see it."

She locked her arms around his waist. "Oh, Hutch, I didn't know she was capable of saying such things."

"I'm sorry she couldn't take it better," he said, kissing her hair. "But try to see it from her side. I sure can't sound like much of a bargain."

"I shouldn't have told her about us. It was stupid. I didn't want any more lies, but they're all she can accept. She doesn't want the truth and never has. She can't understand."

"She'd have found out. As soon as you tell Michael. 'Cause you're gonna tell him, aren't you?"

"Yes," she said sadly. "I should do it soon. I'll call tonight."

His hands moved across her back, soothing her, caressing her. "Once you tell him, then you've burnt another bridge. There may be no goin' back to bein' the old Betsy. You know that, don't you?"

"I don't want to be the old Betsy again," she said passionately. "Not ever."

Later that night she phoned Michael. He took the news like a perfect gentleman, of course.

"This may just be something you have to work out of your system, Betsy," he said. "We'll see. I'll wait for you. We'll talk about it at Christmas. Promise me that much, at least. That we can talk at Christmas."

"No, Michael," she said unhappily. "We've been living a lie. It should stop now. I won't make promises. I can't."

"I'll wait for you," he said with a gentle but chilling determination. "The thought of marriage scares you a little, that's all. But you know we're right for each other. We need each other."

"Michael," she said desperately, "no. We can't do this. Please—be honest."

"I'll wait for you," Michael said with the same eerie calm.

He refused to accept what she told him. When she hung up she was frustrated by his maddeningly polite stubbornness.

She wanted the relationship broken off, finished, for that part of her life to be over and done.

Yet he wasn't allowing it. It was not over. She hoped it wasn't some sort of sinister omen.

But what bothered her more was her conversation with her mother. For years she had done everything in her power to please her parents and to make up for the pain she'd caused them. Now she wondered if she'd ever really known them at all. Or if they had known her.

CHAPTER ELEVEN

THE CHILI COOK-OFF was at the park, set up in its two big pavilions. The morning was glorious, unseasonably warm, the sky a vibrant, cloudless blue.

Cal and Serena and Betsy and Hutch had rendezvoused at dawn in Austin and driven to Crystal Creek. Betsy was getting used to Hutch's jolting, lurching van, was becoming almost fond of the old thing.

Cal and Hutch set up the folding table and propane stove, and laid out a formidable array of cooking tools. They moved quickly and intently like the rodeo men they had once been, used to working against a clock.

There were twenty-four cooking teams in all, and Betsy recognized only a few people. But Serena knew most. She pointed out the foreman of the Double C, Ken Slattery, and his wife, Nora, coaching a team of Cub Scouts that included their boy, Rory. The Scouts had put up a big sign that said, BE PREPARED for the World's Greatest Chili!

The sheriff, Wayne Jackson, headed a team of determined-looking deputies. They'd hung a banner across the front of their table: Jailhouse Chili—The Specialists.

The Hole in the Wall Dude Ranch had a team, led by its owner, Scott Harris, and his wife, Valerie. They all wore jeans, bandits' masks and gun belts with cap pistols. They kept pretending to shoot at the deputies, who retaliated by handcuffing Scott and throwing the key in the lagoon.

Martin Avery, his wife Billie Jo and two other lawyers and their wives were set up with a large poster that read, Legal Eagle Chili (Not Made with Eagles, 'Cause It Wouldn't Be Legal).

The volunteer fire department had a crew touting what it called Twelve-Alarm Chili. The high school band was represented by a crew dressed as heavy-metal rockers, and the band instructor, Tap Hollister, his arms covered with fake tattoos, stood on the table playing guitar with an air of true madness. They'd dubbed their chili Beavis and Butthead's Cool Hot Stuff.

"Okay," Cal said, as he fired up the stove. "We're set. What's the competition look like?"

"A bunch of crazy people," Serena said. "Don't be so serious. This is supposed to be fun."

"I play to win," said Cal.

"Don't worry," Hutch said lackadaisically. "We'll win."

"How can you be so sure?" Betsy asked. She was starting to worry. Winning would be wonderful advance publicity for his bar. But losing might have a negative effect.

Cal gave her a stern glance. "Don't you know the absolutely A-1 most important ingredient in makin' chili?"

"No," Betsy said innocently. "I don't."

"Tell her, Hutch," Cal said.

"Arrogance," Hutch said. "The most important ingredient in chili is absolute, unmitigated arrogance."

"We'll win," Cal said confidently.

Serena laughed. "Well, if arrogance does it, the win's in your pocket. So who's the toughest competition?"

Cal tipped back his hat and narrowed his eyes, taking in the other tables. "Those deputies actually ain't too damn bad. They won last time."

"There's your cousin, Beverly," Serena told him. "With the hospital team. The ones dressed up like devils. Is that new doctor, the Indonesian one, giving her the eye?"

"Oh, hell," Cal said. "Everybody gives Beverly the eye. Where's my brother? We're gonna be short-handed."

Betsy glanced at her watch. It was five minutes until starting time. Ruth and Tyler were indeed late. She wondered if Tyler had balked at coming.

"Everybody else has a fancier setup than us," Serena said worriedly. "Shouldn't we have come up with decorations or a gimmick or costumes or something?"

"Naw," Cal said. "That stuff doesn't really count for anything. We'll stay inconspicuous, the dark horse."

"Doesn't your chili even have a name?" Betsy asked Hutch.

"Nope," he said. "It's too pure to sully with a name."

"You really are arrogant, aren't you?" she teased.

"We're bad," Cal said, pulling his hat down to a determined angle. "We're bad."

"Kiss me for luck," Hutch said.

Boldly, for all the world to see, Betsy threw her arms around his neck and kissed him on the mouth.

He drew her close, kissed her back. "Now," he said, smiling and looking into her eyes, "how can I lose? I feel inspired. Practically immortal."

TYLER AND RUTH ARRIVED just before the high school principal, Dr. Mongan, fired the starting gun that signaled the start of the cooking.

Tyler looked distant and slightly disgusted. But Ruth was excited and seemed glad to be there. She hugged Betsy and took her aside.

"Bets," Ruth said, taking her by the upper arms, "your mom called, and I gave her your new number. She really grilled me. I probably said too much. I'm sorry if I did."

Betsy managed a small, unhappy smile. "It's all right. Mother can be pretty relentless."

"I know," Ruth said. "But she loves you."

Betsy looked away. She doubted her mother's words had been spoken out of love. She was still hurt and wondered if she'd been so busy trying to please her parents that she'd never really questioned anything about them.

"You're the baby of the family," Ruth said. "They've always been overprotective of you."

Betsy shook her head. "They want to control my life. They want me to marry somebody I don't love. They don't care. They just want me married—at any cost."

"Listen," Ruth said softly, "I've been overprotective, too. I haven't really been myself lately. Forgive me?"

"Of course," Betsy said and meant it.

Ruth hugged her again. "I can tell you and Hutch really care for each other," she said. "It shows."

Betsy smiled shyly. "It does?"

"Yes," Ruth said. "It does. You two always look happy together." There was something slightly sad in her voice, like nostalgia or regret for something lost. She cast a look at Tyler, but he didn't look back.

BETSY HADN'T REALIZED that making several gallons of chili could be such hard work. The morning passed in a blur. Serena and Cal slivered what seemed like an infinite number of garlic cloves and laughed at the odor.

At one point, when Cal thought nobody was looking, he reached over and patted Serena's stomach. "What do you think, little mama," he asked her in a low voice. "You think I planted anybody in there last night?"

Serena shook her head so that her long, dark hair swung. "If you didn't, it wasn't for lack of trying."

He bent and kissed her lightly on the lips. "I'm glad we're in this garlic together. Nobody'll come near us. You're all mine."

"Besides that," Serena said, "we're safe from vampires."

"Good. Don't want nobody nibblin' your neck but me."

Betsy turned from them, trying to suppress a smile. But the smile died a quick enough death when she saw Ruth trying to talk to Tyler as she measured out salt.

Tyler stood apart, leaning against a pillar of the pavilion. His arms were crossed, his expression stolid. He barely replied to Ruth's remarks. At last, looking hurt, she went silent and didn't try to speak to him again.

Betsy was cutting onions, and they were starting to make her cry. Tears welled in her eyes.

"Okay," Hutch said, when he caught sight of her. "That's enough of that. Go wash your face and hands. Woman, don't you weep for me."

"This isn't cooking," Betsy sniffled. "It's an exercise in masochism."

"Gotta be mucho macho," he said. "Stand back and let me do my manly thing."

"Gladly," she said, and went to find the rest room before she was onioned to death.

She had to wash repeatedly and was patting her face dry when Ruth came in, leaned against the wall and covered her eyes with her hand as if she was trying not to cry.

"Ruth," Betsy said in alarm. "What's wrong? Did the onions get you, too?"

Ruth shook her head. "No. It's nothing."

"It must be something," Betsy said, concerned. "Can I help?"

Ruth dropped her hand away. She stared at the ceiling, obviously warring to keep control of her emotions. "It's nothing," she said, as if trying to convince herself. "I'm being stupid. I'll be fine."

"Do you want to be alone? Or should I stay?"

"Yes. No. I don't know," Ruth said and swallowed. "Wait. Give me a minute, then we'll go back. Oh, God, I'm so emotional these days. Hormones run riot. You're lucky never to have gone through it."

Betsy tensed. She thought of the little dark-haired boy and wondered if she'd ever see him again.

"I guess I am," she said tonelessly.

Ruth moved to the sink, examined her makeup, opened her purse and made a slight repair on her eyeliner. "Forgive me," she said. "I really was being stupid. That meddler Nate Purdy came by from the hospital team."

Betsy watched her. "Nate Purdy? The doctor?"

"Yes," Ruth said, retouching her lipstick. "He started asking how I felt. As if it's any of his business. I'm not his patient anymore."

Betsy nodded mutely.

"Then Tyler had to speak up," Ruth said with disgust. "I haven't been able to get two words out of him all morning. But all of a sudden, Nate Purdy, the great medical god, is there, and Tyler has to talk."

"Yes?" Betsy said.

Ruth shrugged. "Tyler has the nerve to say I haven't been taking care of myself. I mean I've done everything my doctor's told me, absolutely everything. How could he say such a thing? I got so upset that I—I just got upset, that's all.''

Betsy studied her cousin. Ruth was pale as usual, but a hectic pink flushed her cheeks. She ran a brush through her dark hair, then turned to Betsy. ''Just give me a minute. To pull myself together.''

''Didn't Tyler want to come today?'' Betsy asked, trying to be tactful. ''He doesn't seem too happy.''

''He hasn't taken a Saturday off in weeks,'' Ruth said. They're having trouble with the venting system at the winery, and he thinks he has to be there every minute. I think he's actually forgotten how to have fun.''

''I guess he's got a lot on his mind.''

''I love him,'' Ruth said. ''But sometimes I sincerely wish he was less like his father and more like Cal. I told him that this morning. In exactly those words. *That* certainly didn't go over too well.''

No, Betsy thought apprehensively, it probably didn't.

At about half an hour before noon, something began to happen around their table.

Hutch was intent about making the chili, but he always managed to exchange jokes and stories with passersby. He was good at it, Betsy realized with admiration. He put people at their ease, drew them out, made them have a good time. Together he and Cal could be quite outrageous, and a small crowd formed to join the fun.

Lettie Mae Reese, the cook from the Double C, came by with her friend Mose. She teased Cal unmercifully, and he teased her back, and she eyed Hutch with grudging admiration.

''This boy,'' she said to Betsy, pointing at Hutch, ''knows what's what. He's one of a kind.''

I know that, Betsy thought with affection and pride.

Then she was startled by a loud sound. The high school principal had fired another shot into the air. "Let the tasting start," he cried in a melodramatic voice. "The judges are anonymous. They'll drift among the crowd and visit each crew. In the meantime, let the gustatory delectation begin!"

Lettie Mae picked up a paper cup and handed it to Hutch. "Ladle me out some," she said. "I had to pay five dollars for this spoon, and I intend to get good use out of it." She brandished her official Crystal Creek Chili Cook-Off Tasting Spoon.

"Our first customer," Hutch said. He half filled the cup.

Lettie Mae paused before tasting, to give maximum suspense to the moment. Hutch filled another cup for Mose. Lettie Mae took a spoonful from her cup, savored the aroma, stared at the chili critically.

Slowly she put the spoon to her lips, tasted its contents and closed her eyes as if in intense concentration. She swallowed and seemed to think even harder. She frowned.

"Well?" Cal asked pointedly. "What do you think?"

Lettie Mae opened one eye and stared at him. "What I know is that *you* had very little to do with creating this," she said. "You can't boil water."

She opened both eyes and looked at Hutch. "What I think is that *he's* gifted. Best I ever tasted. Better than mine, even."

Hutch grinned and Betsy hugged him. "My God," Cal said, pretending to stagger backward, "she's never said anything like that. The Last Days are on us. The world is at end."

Lettie Mae smiled serenely and winked at Hutch. Mose tasted his and his eyes widened in pleased surprise. "She's right. Mighty fine."

Others began to press forward for samples, and Cal, Serena and Ruth began to ladle chili into cups. Tyler had disappeared.

Mose was the first person to ask for seconds, but not the last. Soon more people were gathering around their table than anybody else's. Betsy felt a surge of excitement.

"I think," Serena whispered in Betsy's ear, "that he's a fabulous success. What do you think?"

"I think you're right. It's wonderful."

"Cal said Hutch could do it," Serena said. "We both knew he could. He's going to do great in this town. Just great."

Hutch took Betsy by the arm and drew her slightly away from the others. He thrust a paper cup of chili at her, a white plastic spoon stuck into it.

"Here," he said, pressing the cup into her hands. "Try it. See if I'm in the right business or not."

She took the cup and smiled up at him. "This is going to sound awful," she said, "and I hate to admit it, but I don't much like chili."

He looked into her eyes. "Hey," he said softly. "Until I came along you didn't much like sex, either."

She blushed. "Good point," she conceded. She took the spoon, raised it and put it into her mouth.

Her taste buds immediately seemed to sing out in delight. Not only did they sing, they danced, swooned, revived and danced again. She stared at Hutch in wonder.

"What do you think?" he asked.

"Ooh," Betsy said breathlessly. "My goodness!"

He raised an eyebrow skeptically. "Wow," he said. "The Big O word. That good?"

She gave him her most mischievous smile. "Well," she said, "almost."

THEY WON, of course. The hospital team came in as a surprise second. The deputies, third, grumbled that they'd been robbed and arrests were shortly in order.

The hospital team won first prize for showmanship, the high school band took second, the Cub Scouts third. Both Hutch and Beverly were presented large trophies that were truly garish.

Hutch mumbled, "Thanks," and looked embarrassed.

Beverly, reverting to her beauty queen routine, accepted for the hospital, thanking everyone, including her parents.

And then it was over. The crowd drifted away, the teams cleaned up and packed their gear.

Tyler reappeared without a word of explanation. Silently, he helped them. Betsy caught a whiff of whiskey on his breath. She and Hutch exchanged glances. There'd been rumors that one of the teams had been drinking pretty hard, and more than one crew had a bottle tucked under the table.

Ken Slattery came over to their table and invited them to a party that night at his and Nora's house. "Soon as we get shut of all these Cub Scouts," he said wryly. The children followed him like puppies, crowding around his knees.

Betsy felt a strange pang. The boys were about the same age as her child, and she remembered his Scout shirt under his jacket. She wondered if his childhood would be full of memories like this: afternoons in the town park,

Scout packs and contests and trophies and wild, happy excitement.

Hutch must have read her thoughts because he put his arm around her and nuzzled her cheek. "You all right?"

"Sure," she said and smiled as best she could. She knew she would often think of the boy who would be leaving Fredericksburg so soon. If he came seeking her someday, she would be waiting. It was all she could do.

"How about the party?" he asked. "Want to go?"

She tried to rub a chili stain off his shirt collar. "Sure. Cal and Serena are going, aren't they?"

"Yes."

She looked at Ruth, who seemed withdrawn as she concentrated on packing empty jars. "Ruth," Betsy said, "we're going to the party. Are you coming?"

Ruth didn't look up. "I'd like to," she said softly. "We haven't been out since that night at Zack's."

"Well, hell," Tyler said, "let's go then. We've shot the whole day. Why not the night, too?"

Betsy looked at him warily. He knelt on the pavilion's cement floor, scrubbing out the chili pot. His dark brows were creased together in a frown.

"We don't have to if you don't want to," Ruth said. Her tone was cool.

"If you want to go, we'll go," Tyler said without looking at her.

"All right," Ruth answered, an edge in her voice. "We will."

Betsy looked away. She could see the pain in both of them, and feared it sprang from their anxiety for their unborn child. She pitied them both and felt a sense of foreboding.

COMING TO THE PARTY had been a mistake, Ruth thought miserably. Tyler had immediately joined a poker game that Bubba Gibson had started in the kitchen. Somebody had produced a whiskey bottle, and Tyler'd been helping himself liberally.

It was unlike Tyler to drink, and Ruth was both repelled and frightened. She wished there were other family members here to help keep him in line, but there weren't.

His father and stepmother, J.T. and Cynthia, hadn't come. They were home where, Ruth couldn't help thinking, they had a happy, healthy baby to treasure.

Cal and Serena had left early. He'd had that I-want-to-make-love-to-you look, and he kept kissing and nuzzling Serena as if they were still honeymooners.

They want a baby, Ruth had thought, watching them. *And Cal will be lucky, just like always. Everything will go perfectly—for them.*

She hadn't felt envy. She'd felt nothing except a deadening emptiness. Cal and Serena had said their goodnights and left, their arms around each other.

At this very moment, Ruth supposed, they were probably in Cal's old room at the ranch house, making love wildly and ardently.

Betsy and Hutch left early, as well, giving the excuse that they had to drive back to Austin. But Ruth saw the way they looked at each other, and knew that they, too, wanted only to be alone and in each other's arms.

Hutch was totally inappropriate for Betsy, of course, but the two of them were so mad for each other it hardly mattered. They might not have a future, but their present seemed practically incandescent. They seemed to share not only passion, but true affection.

What secret did they all know that she and Tyler didn't? Why were the others so easy and playful and loving together, while she and Tyler seemed to grow more hopelessly apart?

She sat in the living room, listening to Ken and Nora talk and laugh with Martin and Billie Jo Avery. Mary Gibson and Virginia Parks were there, too, joining in.

But Ruth sat silent, feeling as isolated as if she were alone at the North Pole. She held a half-empty glass of fruit juice, which she finally set aside.

She heard Tyler's laugh from the kitchen. It was too loud, too reckless, like the laugh of some dangerous stranger. She wondered with aversion how much he'd drunk. Suddenly she could stand no more.

She stood, smiled weakly at the group in the living room and quietly told Nora that she needed a breath of fresh air. She went into the bedroom and got her jacket.

No one saw her when she left by the side door. She set off down the moon-drenched road toward her own house. The sky was luminously bright, strewn with stars.

Just as she looked up, one fell in a slow, silvery arc. It gave her a shuddery feeling. Her grandmother had used to say that every time a star fell, someone died. She shrugged away the thought. There were meteor showers in November, that was all. But she did not look at the sky again.

The temperature had fallen considerably, and by the time Ruth was near home, her teeth were chattering. She turned her collar up higher, walked faster. The way was familiar to her; she'd walked it dozens of times on her daily exercise route.

Yet at night it was different, and everything looked alien. Far away coyotes howled, and the sound echoed eerily on the night. She shivered.

At last she crested the last rise and saw the house, tall and dark-windowed, looking almost ghostly in the moonlight. Relief soothed her.

She quickened her pace and thought longingly of a warm bath, her flannel nightgown and the thick quilts on her bed.

A series of shrill yelps and howls pierced the night. Ruth stiffened in alarm. But alarm quickly turned to irritation. It was only the hound, Bogus, launching into one of his fits.

She was almost to the house. Out of the shadows, he came flying toward her, yowling with joy.

Ruth expected the dog to do its usual idiotic act and be jerked back by its chain. But as in some surreal dream, the dog kept coming at her, bearing down on her.

With a shock, she realized it had broken free. A long section of chain trailed, clattering, from its collar.

The dog bounded toward her and was upon her, almost before she could react. She sidestepped it and tried to swat it away, but the dog thought it was a game. He danced around Ruth in wild circles, barking and wagging his tail.

He wanted to jump on her, and the thought terrified her, because she knew he could knock her down. She sidestepped more desperately, but couldn't manage to keep him away.

She missed him, and then was horrified to realize that somehow his chain was wound around her ankles, and as he danced and leapt, the chain tightened, cutting into her.

She fought against being hobbled, trapped. She had almost managed to kick free of the chain when the dog sprang again. Its forepaws struck her chest so hard she lost her balance. Then, barking joyously, it jumped again, thudding into her from a different angle, knocking her forward.

She screamed as she fell. She hit the ground so hard that her breath was knocked away.

The dog was all over her, pouncing on her so that its claws jabbed her, even through her jacket. She curled into a knot, trying to protect her stomach.

The dog began licking her face. She felt its slathering tongue, smelled its hot breath.

Then she was conscious only of a stabbing sensation. Enormous pain rent her. It was sudden and agonizing, like being pierced by lightning. She writhed, but the pain became greater, overpowering. It broke her, and she plunged into unconsciousness.

The dog, disappointed at her lack of response, stared down at her quizzically, nosed her, then trotted away, its chain dragging on the earth.

Ruth lay alone, crumpled at the edge of the road, the cold wind stirring her hair. Overhead in the gleaming sky, one small star fell silently and died.

CHAPTER TWELVE

TYLER FOUND HER half an hour later. When he saw her lying at the road's edge, something in him died. It was as if he took a bullet through the soul.

He'd been slightly drunk, but shock stripped away all effects of alcohol. He screeched the truck to a halt, ran to her, gathered her into his arms and carried her back to the truck.

Fear possessed him. She was in a bad way, shuddering convulsively. Her water had broken, and her jeans were drenched. She moaned and kept saying, "The dog. The dog made me fall."

Even as he put her into the truck, the dog appeared, barking and trying to jump at him. He kicked it away, and it ran off yelping, its broken chain rattling behind it.

Blindly, hardly knowing what he was doing, he strapped her into the seat. He climbed in on the driver's side, gunned the motor, turned the truck around and drove hell-for-leather toward Crystal Creek.

"You're going to make it, Ruthie," he kept saying. "Hang on." But in truth he didn't know if he was helping her or making her worse. He only knew he couldn't bear to wait for an ambulance to come clear from town.

Ruth kept fading in and out of consciousness. Tyler had the shakes and the taste of gall at the back of his throat. His heart beat like a mad thing. He knew this was it—she was losing the baby. He was sick with dread he would lose her, as well.

He carried her, unconscious again, into the emergency room, and there he acted like a crazy man, because suddenly he didn't want them to take her. He was afraid to let go of her.

When they stretched her small form on the gurney and wheeled her away, he was sure she was dying and that he would never see her or hold her again.

He sat on a metal chair, put his fists against his eyes and cried like a child. People tried to help him, but he swore at them to leave him alone.

He wept for a full five minutes. Then he sat up, wiping his eyes, feeling spent, dead. A young nurse offered to take him to a waiting room in the obstetrical unit. Numbly, he let her. He was so drained that she might have been leading a hundred-year-old man. He felt unreal, a thin shell of a person with nothing left inside.

The young nurse brought him coffee. He drank it mechanically but couldn't taste it.

Someone had called his family. J.T. and Cynthia swept in, looking frightened and tense. Cynthia tried to hug him, but Tyler didn't want to be touched. He went rigid as stone in her embrace. She backed away, tears in her eyes.

His father said, "I'm sorry. Maybe everything'll be all right."

Tyler didn't look at him. Nothing was going to be all right. What did it matter if anyone was sorry?

Then Cal and Serena appeared. Cal was red-eyed and disheveled; Serena's hair was pulled back but coming loose and spilling wildly about her face.

Cal put his hand on his brother's shoulder and tried to say something. Tyler recoiled from him. "Get your hands

off me," he said, but would say no more. He refused to
sit. He stood and stared out between the window-blind
slots at the night.

He thought, *She's dying. It's my fault. She's dying. I
did it. Kill me, God. Leave her, take me.*

At last a grim-faced nurse came and said that Nate
Purdy wanted to speak to Tyler alone. "Come with me,
please," she said.

He walked down the long hall and knew how men feel
who walk to their executions. She showed him a small
coffee room and told him to wait. Dr. Purdy would be
there shortly.

She left him. Tyler didn't sit. He stood staring at a
vending machine. In its display windows were snack
foods in incongruously cheerful wrappers. They were
meaningless, absurd. The world was meaningless, cruelly absurd.

Nate Purdy entered. Tyler, stone-faced, stared at the
older man's expression.

Nate looked weary and grim. "Ruth's going to be fine,
Tyler. But the baby didn't make it. I'm sorry."

Tyler's knees sagged, and for a moment he thought he
would fall. He forced himself to stand straight. He put
his hand to his eyes, covering them.

She's all right, he thought. He felt muddleheaded.

"She had a hard time," Nate said. "But she'll get well.
There can be other babies."

Tyler gave a long, ragged sigh. He uncovered his eyes.
"I don't care about other babies," he said, his voice
tight. "I just want her to be all right."

"She will be," Nate said. "But *she* cares about other
babies, Tyler. She's taken this hard. She blames herself."

"Herself?" Tyler said bitterly. He turned from Nate. His eyes burned, and his throat ached. "How? I did it. I made her pregnant. I let her go off by herself tonight and didn't even notice. The dog jumped her. I wouldn't get rid of the damned dog. I wasn't going to let any woman push me around. God!"

He shook his head. Suddenly, he wanted for Nate to be gone, for everyone to leave him alone. He wanted to sink down at the table and just hold his head in his hands and thank God Ruth was alive.

"Don't blame yourself, Tyler," Nate said sternly. "She thinks now that if she'd followed my directions instead of somebody else's, it would have been different. She thinks if she hadn't tried to walk home tonight, it would have been different."

"Oh, hell," said Tyler hopelessly, and his throat ached harder.

"Nothing could have saved that baby, Tyler. Nothing that happened tonight made a difference. The child's been dead for at least a day. Maybe more."

Tyler had been rubbing his forehead. He stopped. He half turned to face Nate again. "What?"

"This child was already dead," Nate said. "She would have gone into labor soon, no matter what happened. Its little heart was malformed. So enlarged I could feel it through its chest with my fingers."

Tyler shook his head. He supposed he had given up on the baby long ago. He could accept losing the child. What he couldn't accept was what Ruth had been through.

"The only thing that could have saved that child," Nate Purdy said, "is God Himself. For some reason, in His wisdom, He decided not to."

Tyler said nothing. He was not sure Ruth would be able to live with it. If God was so wise, why had He made

Ruth suffer so much? And now she would suffer even more. His lip curled at the thought of God.

"Aren't you going to ask about the baby?" Nate asked.

"What's to ask?" Tyler said. The child was dead. What else mattered?

"It was a boy," Nate said without emotion.

A boy, Tyler thought. *We lost our son. Our firstborn son.* He shrugged. He could say nothing.

"Tyler, I'm sure it was his heart. The beat was highly irregular from the first. I'd like to have an autopsy. Ruth—doesn't want one."

Tyler spoke from between his teeth. "Do what she wants," he ordered, angry that Nate had brought it up.

"Sometimes it helps us learn—" Nate began.

Tyler cut him off almost savagely. "Do what she wants, dammit! No autopsy."

Nate was silent a moment. "I understand. Would you like to see him?"

The emptiness in Tyler seemed to turn over, a hollow shifting of nothingness. He didn't know if he had the courage to see the child. So he made himself say yes. "Yeah," he muttered. "Sure."

He was even more stunned after he saw the baby. It looked perfect. How could such a perfect child die?

He wanted to reach out, to touch the small, still hand and assure himself this tiny creature had existed, had been created, grown this large and been brought into the world. But he did not touch him. Seeing was hard enough.

Nate seemed to know he could take no more. "Go to Ruth," he said. "She's groggy. She's been sedated. But you should let her know you're here."

Nate led him down yet another hall. Tyler had the nightmarish feeling that he was in an endless maze of hospital corridors.

Nate opened a door. Tyler saw Ruth lying inert on a bed. An IV was attached to her arm.

"Go ahead," Nate told him. "Just ten minutes or so. I'll go talk to the rest of the family."

Tyler nodded and said nothing. He walked into the room and shut the door behind him. The only light came from a small lamp on a metal bureau.

Ruth lay with her free arm held over her now nearly flat stomach. She didn't look at him when he entered.

His knees felt weak again when he saw that she really was alive. He sat down heavily in the chair beside her bed. He reached for her hand, took it in his own.

For a moment he couldn't speak. "I'm sorry," he managed to say at last. "I'm really sorry."

God, what a pointless, useless thing to say, he thought. He wanted to tell her he loved her, but he didn't because he was afraid the words would make him cry again, and for her sake he had to be strong.

She turned her head and looked at him for a long moment. Her face seemed fragile and dazed, as if she couldn't yet comprehend what enormity had befallen her. Her dark eyes had a look of sorrow so profound that the numbness in Tyler engulfed him.

She was obviously drugged, but the drugs hadn't killed her sorrow. She looked into his eyes. Then she looked away.

She whispered, "I'm sorry, too."

Neither of them spoke again. They sat in the silence, holding hands, unable to say anything to each other.

"HOW IS SHE?" Hutch asked Betsy. She met him in the park after having been to the hospital to see Ruth. Cal had called them that morning.

Betsy looked shaken. He put his arm around her shoulders and began to stroll with her around the lagoon.

"Cal was right," Betsy said, obviously troubled. "She didn't have much to say. She doesn't even want her father to come for the funeral. She said it'd just be worse. She seems shut off in her own inner world."

"She's probably still in shock."

"I know. But then, at the end, when I leaned over to kiss her, she—she—hung on to me really tightly. And she said this thing that shook me."

He squeezed her shoulders sympathetically. "What?"

He had her safe and warm in the curve of his arm, but he felt her shudder, as if he couldn't keep her safe or warm enough. Her body tensed. "She said, 'You can't know what it's like. To carry a child inside your body and have it taken away.' She said, 'Be glad you don't know. I pray you never will.'"

Hutch swore softly. "I'm sorry."

She cast a moody glance toward the lagoon. "I wanted to say, 'I know exactly what it's like.' But I don't, not the way she does, because it was different for me. And she'd think I was a monster for giving mine away."

He stopped, took her by the shoulders. "Don't talk like that. Don't think like that."

She stared at him with earnest, pleading eyes. "Why's it so complicated, Hutch? I saw Tyler. He acts cold, but I can tell it's because he feels too much, and he's afraid to let it out. What is it about children that gets us so emotional?"

He shook his head, sighing, and fastened the top button of her jacket. "The way I figure," he said, "is nature wants it that way. People get emotional so the kids get taken care of. It's programmed into us. Some of us."

"What about you?" she asked. "Didn't you ever want children? Some men do. Tyler really does. Cal, too."

The question caught him off guard. "Me? I just looked at kids as something to tie you down. I wasn't one for bein' tied."

He put his arm around her and began to walk again. "Ever since I can remember, it was like there was something callin' me to come away. All the time."

"Even when you were little?" she asked.

He nodded, drew her closer. "Every time I'd hear a train whistle in the night—you know, that lonesome sound—I'd think, where's it goin'? What's out there? What am I missin'?"

"And?" Betsy prompted.

"So I had to go. I had to see."

"Why?" she asked, leaning her head against his shoulder.

He took a deep breath. "Because," he said, "life is experiences. There's so many different experiences you can have. Some people settle for a few. I couldn't."

She was silent a moment. "Your parents accepted it? That you'd drift around the way you have?"

"They didn't like it at first. But it was kind of a principle for me. Some people say heredity shapes you. Some say environment. Some say both. But I wanted *me* to shape me."

"They don't try to change you?"

He laughed. "No. Well, my mama drops hints now and then."

He gazed at the ducks gliding on the lagoon. "Now what's funny," he said, "is people always said I took after my Great-uncle Harlan. And I did. Same build, same colorin', same temperament. Though in truth we weren't blood relations at all. Everybody said I was just like him."

"Are you?" she asked, slipping her arm around his waist.

"Pretty much," he laughed. "He grew up in the Depression. Set off to see the world and make his fortune. Rode the rails with the hoboes. Went to the South Pacific in World War II. Did all sorts of stuff. Never quite made a fortune, but did well enough. Sure saw the world. He'd spin such tales, and I'd think, 'Man, I want a life like that.'"

"But," Betsy said, "he must have settled down somewhere along the line. He left you that money."

He shrugged. "We think he won it at poker. No. He didn't come close to settlin' until he was nearly seventy. Even then, he'd hear that lonesome whistle blow, and he'd have to take off and ramble for a spell."

"Wasn't he ever attached to anybody?"

"Not that he'd admit. Started havin' circulatory troubles in his eighties. Just checked himself into a veteran's home. Wouldn't ask the family for help. Guess he was lucky to have a place to go. Sometimes I see an old guy on the road, homeless maybe, and think, Harlan could have ended up like that. Glad he didn't."

"But your family would have helped him, wouldn't they?"

"Sure. But he was just too set in his ways by then. My granddaddy and my daddy loved him. They just didn't choose to be like him, is all. They were born to be family men. They were good ones. My granddaddy's gone, but

I'm lucky to still have my folks. I'll go see 'em at Christmas."

Betsy shivered again. "I'm supposed to go home at Christmas," she said. "I don't want to."

Hutch gazed down at her. She was probably thinking of Michael, as well as her family. Michael hadn't accepted her rejection, and it bothered her badly, he could tell.

"You look cold," he said. "You want to go have some lunch? Then go work on the bar?"

She toyed with a button on his jacket. "That's exactly what I want."

She studied the button, her eyes downcast, and her long lashes cast shadows on her cheeks. Her auburn hair lifted and fell like a flame in the breeze, and he gave in to the desire to touch it. She looked sad.

"What's the matter?" he asked.

She didn't look at him. "If someday that lonesome whistle calls you again, and you have to follow, I just want you to know I'll always remember you. It's like that song says. You'll always be gentle on my mind."

His heart wrenched unexpectedly, and he got a funny, hollow feeling deep within. He put his hand under her chin, and lifted her face to his. When their eyes met, his heart did that same damned, hurting thing.

He lowered his lips to hers. "You'll be gentle on my mind, too."

But as he kissed her, the realization struck him that he didn't want to say goodbye to her, not now, not ever.

It startled and bewildered him. He had fashioned himself to be like Harlan, a man meant to live and die alone, needing no one.

THEY GOT BACK to the apartment late. A note was taped to Betsy's door to see her neighbor in apartment 201.

Betsy knocked, and the neighbor, a pretty black woman, said a deliveryman had left flowers for her. She brought Betsy an absurdly large bouquet of white roses.

Hutch had to unlock her apartment door for her; the flowers were too cumbersome for her to handle anything else.

"Here," he said, taking them, "give me those. My God, who sent this? It looks like it belongs in the Pasadena Rose Parade."

"I don't know," she said. "Put them on the table. You're right. With wheels, we could drive this down the street. Where's the card? There's got to be one."

He studied her perfect profile, her shining hair. The world was full of men who would look at her with hungry interest. Smooth, well-bred and well-to-do men on the way up, out to establish themselves in a big way.

"Ah," said Betsy with a wary sigh, "here it is. Uh-oh. They're from my mother."

He nodded as if he'd half expected it. "A peace offering?"

"An attempt," she murmured. "Here. Look."

He took the card and read it. "Darling, I'm so sorry for what was said. You'll always be our own dear girl. We'll work this out. Please phone. Love, Mommy and Dad. P.S. Michael called to say he'll wait."

Betsy turned her back to the flowers, ran her hands through her hair. "She hasn't called herself Mommy since I was ten years old. Well, I'm not fooled. She let the mask drop. I finally understand what she really thinks."

Hutch put his hand on the back of her neck. "Sugar, she was upset yesterday. She regrets it."

"Not as much as I do," she said, her jawline stubborn. "And I won't marry Michael. I was crazy ever to think so."

He massaged her neck muscles, which were tense. "Betsy," he said, trying to choose his words carefully. "You never say much about Michael. But I think I understand." He paused. "Tell me the truth. He's gay, isn't he?"

She turned, looking up at him in surprise and unhappiness. For a moment he thought she wasn't going to answer, but at last she nodded. "Yes. I know he is. He's never told me, and I don't think he can really accept it. He must think if he gets married, everything will at least look ordinary. How—how did you know?"

He shook his head. "It was the only explanation. I knew he hadn't made love to you. Don't your parents even suspect?"

She sighed and looked away. "I doubt it. But they should have. That's why I could get along with him. He never tried to touch me."

"My God," he said, turning her face back to his. "You'd have settled for a life like that?"

She closed her eyes as if in weariness. "We were— friends. It would have made my parents happy. I think that for my mother it would have officially canceled out everything bad. 'Look at Betsy. Married to that wonderful man. Isn't she respectable? Haven't we done well? Isn't she normal?'"

His hands tightened on her shoulders. "It couldn't have been further from normal," he said. "It would have just been one more lie. Maybe the worst one."

She opened her eyes, smiling sadly at him. "I know that. Now. Now everything's different."

He folded her into his arms, rested his cheek against her hair. He said nothing.

"In a way," she said, rubbing her forehead against his shoulder, "I don't see how my parents couldn't know. He's *too* perfect, you know? Too handsome. Women look at him. But men do, too. And he looks back."

He held her more tightly. "Do you think he has lovers?"

She was silent a moment. "I think so. I tried never to wonder. That's how I grew up—trying never to think about unpleasant things, never to wonder. That's what we do in my family."

He regarded the roses with distaste. "How'd they get flowers delivered on a Sunday?"

The corner of her mouth curved downward. "My father's the kind of man that can get things like that done. It's amazing what money will do."

"I wouldn't know," said Hutch.

"Oh, Hutch," she said, resting her head against his shoulder. "I don't want to talk to them. I don't want to think about them. I wish we could find a secret little world where there was only you and me."

He kissed her temples. "I know," he said. "But we can't. It's all right. We've got here. We've got now."

"Hutch," she said, kissing his throat, "make love to me, please. Please."

"Oh, God, Betsy," he said raggedly. He kissed her so passionately that she gasped. Her hands moved up to touch his face, bring it even closer to hers, and her lips were hungry beneath his.

He swept her up and carried her into the bedroom. Then he kicked the door closed to shut out the smothering scent of white roses.

THEY MADE LOVE in a way that was both tender and frantic. Afterwards, they lay in each other's arms, not talking.

When the phone rang, it jarred like a warning siren on Betsy's nerves. She didn't want to answer the ring. She wanted only to hold on to Hutch.

His lips brushed hers. "You'd better answer it."

She nodded unhappily. "I'll take it in the other room," she said.

She rose, slipped into her white terry robe and padded barefoot to the living room. The roses dominated the dining room table, seemed to overwhelm it.

She picked up the phone. "Yes?" she said warily.

It was her mother. "Betsy? Where have you been? The hospital? Uncle Don called. About Ruth. The poor girl. Is she devastated?"

Ah, thought Betsy with weary cynicism, *so this is how the scene will be played—the family pulls back together in the face of crisis. Bygones will be bygones.*

"Yes," she said. "She's broken up. But the doctor says there can be other babies."

"Thank God," Margaret said. "There's nothing more important in the world than family. Children are the greatest gift there is."

Can't you hear yourself? Betsy wanted to cry out. Didn't her mother realize the cruelty in her pious-sounding words?

"My child was a gift to somebody else," Betsy said stiffly. "So I wouldn't know."

"Oh, Betsy," Margaret said, obviously pained. "I could shoot myself for the things I said to you. I didn't mean them. Truly, I didn't. Did you get the flowers? Dad went to special trouble to have them sent."

"Yes. Thank you. But if you didn't mean what you said, why did you say it?"

An awkward silence pulsed between them. When Margaret spoke, her voice trembled. "Sweetheart, I spoke a secret fear, that's all. It's not that we really didn't believe you. It's just that deep down, I suppose I always had this—this terrible fear."

"We should have talked," Betsy said. "I had fears, too."

"Betsy, your father couldn't talk about it. We thought it was best forgotten. Best for you, best for all of us."

"I can't forget," Betsy said. "I've never been able to forget it for a single day of my life."

"That's why it's important we do something *now*," Margaret begged. "Come home, and we'll talk about it. We'll work it out. You know how your father's never believed in psychiatrists? Well, he's agreed that we'd go with you to someone called a 'reality counselor.' Lacey Debbits took her daughter to him, and Lacey says the results were marvelous. Trisha was running around with that rock singer, but now she's completely back to her old self again."

Betsy frowned in disbelief. "A reality counselor?"

"Yes, and Dad's agreed to go to the first meeting with us. You don't know what a concession that is for him. That's how much he wants to help you."

"I don't want to go to a reality counselor," Betsy said emphatically. "And I don't want to come back."

"Now, Betsy," Margaret said in her most motherly voice, "we're not letting you stay there. We can't."

"What do you mean, 'let me'?" Betsy demanded. "I'm twenty-four years old. I'm staying."

"No," Margaret said firmly. "Dad's putting someone else on that job. There's no longer an opening for you at the Texas station. Come home so we can talk. You need it. I wish you hadn't kept it bottled up so long."

Betsy was aghast. "He's taking my job away? That's like blackmail. I won't come back. I'll find another job."

"Don't be ridiculous. Dad and I have talked this over. Your airline tickets will be couriered to you. We thought—"

"I don't *want* airline tickets," Betsy protested. "I'm staying here."

"And just what," Margaret asked pointedly, "do you intend to live on?"

Betsy's mind whirled crazily. She was hardly without funds. She had money from the sale of the condo she'd had while at Stanford. She had a small trust fund, as well.

"My condo money," she said stubbornly. "And the money from Grandma."

Margaret went silent. Betsy could almost hear her thinking. "It's because of this man, isn't it?" Margaret finally asked, her voice stiff.

"Yes," Betsy said, raising her chin. "It is."

"Well," Margaret said with false sweetness, "bring him with you. We can pay his fare if he can't afford it."

Oh, God, Betsy thought, pushing her hand through her hair. *I can't let them do this to me, to him, to us.*

"He's got his own business to take care of," she countered. "He won't come out to California at your beck and call. He's his own man."

"Is he?" Margaret asked. "Well, we'd see that for ourselves then, wouldn't we?"

Betsy pressed the heel of her hand against her forehead. She could see her mother's game. If Hutch came to California, her parents would belittle him in half a hundred ways, both large and small.

"He won't come," Betsy repeated. "Neither will I. I live here. I have a year's lease on this apartment."

"Leases can be broken. Dad's lawyers—"

"I don't *want* the lease broken."

"Just come see us for a week then," Margaret almost begged. "Bring this young man. He can spare a week for you, can't he? What's the matter, Betsy, won't he spare a week? Or are you ashamed of him? Don't you want us to meet him?"

Betsy sighed in exasperation. "I'm not ashamed. But you won't like him because you don't want to like him."

"We'd simply like to see what makes you think so much of him," Margaret said. "Just what it is about him that makes him so special that you'd throw over Michael."

"I liked Michael. I *love* Hutch. It's different."

"Different," Margaret said darkly. "Betsy, I'll be honest with you. After we talked, I cried my eyes out. I did. I cried until poor Dad got so concerned he called a doctor. I had to be—sedated. That's how upset I was."

Betsy felt guilt swarm through her, but resentment bubbled as well. "I'm sorry, but—"

"Let me finish," Margaret said, sounding as if she would cry again. "I discussed you with the doctor. I didn't tell him everything, of course."

You mean you didn't tell him about the baby, Betsy thought bitterly. *You say you're ready to talk, but are you, really? Will you ever be?*

"I said you had a history of broken relationships. When I told him about Michael and about this man, frankly, I—I broke down again. I must tell you, Betsy, I love Michael, and I'm terribly, terribly upset by all this."

Betsy found herself clutching the front of her robe almost convulsively. She wished she could tell her mother the truth about Michael, but she didn't know if she should betray his secrets. "I know, but—"

Margaret pushed on, ignoring her. "I told him I thought you'd taken up with this man as an excuse. That you're running away from marrying Michael."

"I'm not running away. It's just—"

"He agreed with me. He said that's exactly what it sounded like. And that man, Betsy, is a doctor. He's the one who said it sounded as if you needed help. Well, we were there for you when you needed help before, and I want you to know we're here again."

Betsy gripped her robe more tightly. "I don't need—"

"I'm getting upset again." Margaret's voice trembled, almost broke. "I won't argue. I'm not going to put myself through that again. But I'm pleading with you, Betsy. *Please use your head for once.* You're hurting us, but I'm afraid you're hurting yourself more. I'll call again, and I pray you'll be more cooperative."

"Mother, you shouldn't be so—"

"One thing I said before, I meant with all my heart," Margaret said, forging on in her shaking voice. "I won't apologize for it. Betsy, whatever you do, don't get pregnant again. You nearly ruined your life once. Don't do it again."

Betsy grimaced in distaste. "Mother, I'm not—"

"I have to hang up," Margaret said. "There are tears in my eyes. But I want you to know that your dad and I are here for you, sweetheart. We want you home where we can work all this out."

"If you'd just—"

"Goodbye. We love you," Margaret said with a little sob. She hung up.

Numbly, Betsy hung up the phone. She, too, had a lump in her throat, as much from anger as sorrow. She glared at the phone, then at the profusion of white roses.

Pulling her robe more tightly about her, she moved to the couch and sat down. Numbly, she put her elbow on her knee and her forehead in her hand. Her father meant to force her back to California. She refused, this time, to be forced to do anything.

"What's the matter?" Hutch said from the bedroom doorway.

"It was my mother again," Betsy said.

"What'd she do?" Hutch asked. "Lay a guilt trip on you?"

"I'm not sure 'trip' describes it. It was more of a grand tour. Or possibly an expedition or trek."

"I'm makin' trouble for you," he said. "I never meant for that to happen."

She raised her head, regarded him, and smiled sadly. He wore his low-slung, faded jeans and his shirt was unbuttoned. His hair tumbled boyishly over his forehead, but his face was serious, his beautiful, clear eyes troubled. He looked so lean and strong and handsome that it struck her as wrong that anything should ever bother him.

"If I'm sensible," she said, "I know that they have no right to do this. It's one thing for them to be concerned. It's another to try to run my life. But they've been running it for years, and back then, I felt so guilty—and I was so young—I let them. I'm grown now. If these are the consequences I have to face, I'll face them."

"I never meant to come between you and your family," he said.

"They're causing it. It's their choice."

She told him of their ridiculous proposal about the "reality counselor," about her father taking her job away. She vowed she wouldn't go back to California, that she'd find another job.

Hutch sat on the arm of the couch. He put his hand on her shoulder. "Look," he said gently. "You've got to think about this. You're right not to go back just because they snap their fingers. But you've got lots at stake here, Betsy. Your father wants you to understand the business. Part of it's going to be yours someday."

"It could fall into the sea for all I care," Betsy muttered, rubbing her cheek against his hand. "Ever since I can remember, we've all kowtowed to the money. My father, my mother. My brothers and I, it's like we've been born and bred to serve it. I'm sick of it."

His hand tightened on her shoulder. "You're not like an ordinary woman, sugar. You're like a princess. And me, I'm just a gypsy rover. I can't take you away from the kingdom. You belong to it, and it belongs to you."

"I don't want to belong to the kingdom," she said, tears rising in her eyes. "I want to be—be with you."

He let go of her hand. "I want you. From that first night, I've wanted you. But I can't keep you. I've got nothing to offer you."

"I've asked for nothing."

A muscle in his cheek twitched. "I know."

She bit her lip and stared at the hideous bouquet of roses. "It's the damned money," she said bitterly. "One reason things can't last between us is that someday I'm supposed to have all that money, isn't it? I might not have it for years and years, you know. My father could even outlive me. Who knows?"

"Maybe," he said, his voice level. "Maybe not. But the money's there, marked for you. You know what I've

got? A duffel bag of clothes, and a couple of books. I got
my van and about nineteen thousand dollars in the bank.
I got a run-down bar with a mortgage, and it's not ready
for business yet. That's it, Betsy. That's what I got.
That's all.''

"I don't care what you've got," she said with emotion, "I care what you are.''

"So what am I gonna do, Betsy? Marry you and ask
you to live in one room behind a bar? That's all the home
I need. But a wife? A family? That takes more.''

She turned her face from him, stood up. She moved to
the window. "I never said anything about marriage or a
family. Ever," she said, her back to him. Her heart beat
painfully hard.

"I know," he said. "You haven't.''

She pushed back the drape and stared out at the night
lights of Austin, twinkling like thickly scattered jewels.
"I've never asked you to change in any way.''

"I know that, too.''

"For years, I've let my parents rule my life," she said,
her throat tight. "For years, I've lived a lie because they
said I should. You're the only person I've ever been
honest with. I don't want them to drive you away from
me.''

She heard him rise from the couch, and felt his nearness behind her. She flinched when he put his hands on
her arms. All her muscles tensed.

"Nobody's driven me anywhere yet. We've just got to
face things as they happen. We've got to talk it out," he
said, his hands tightening on her. "Your mother made an
almost hundred-and-eighty-degree turn—she's willing to
talk, at least.''

"Yes," Betsy said, staring at the beautiful, cold lights
in the darkness. "About how she's right and I'm wrong.''

"Who knows?" he said almost fiercely, his voice close to her ear. "Maybe she'll change her mind again. Maybe she'll decide to let you alone. She'll think that you'll get this out of your system and then come home."

She turned to him, staring up into his eyes. "Is that how it'll end eventually? I get tired of you? Or you get tired of me? Then it's over and I go home? Or wherever in their kingdom they send me?"

He shook his head. "If they'd let you alone, and you loved me, and I didn't hurt your future, I'd never step aside and let you go."

She made a helpless gesture. "What's that supposed to mean? You're a man who doesn't make commitments, but you'd never let me go. What kind of mixed signals are those?"

His expression was troubled. He ran his hand over her shoulder, down her arm, took her hand again. "See," he said, "I've always figured you'd leave me, not the other way around."

She felt his hand, strong and hard, around hers, but she did not clasp it in return. She felt too torn, too bewildered.

She gazed up at him in incomprehension. "Me leave you? Why?"

He touched his other hand to her face. "Because I'm not your kind. But somebody'll come along who is. He'll be able to give you things. He'll—"

"Things?" Betsy burst out. "I don't want things. I've had *things* all my life."

He took her face between his hands. "Listen," he said earnestly. "I love you. But we're different. I'm like a bridge you had to cross. Between what used to be and what can be. I'm a—a transition for you, is all. Somebody's out there waitin' for you. Somebody right for you."

His body was too close, his face was too near for her to think clearly. Her senses filled with yearning awareness of him. Desire and hurt and fear warred within her.

"What if you're wrong?" she asked, her chin quivering. "What if, my whole life, there's never anybody I can love as much as I love you?"

"That won't happen," he said softly. "I follow my hunches, Betsy. And they're always good. He's out there. He'll find you. All I want is to be with you until he comes along. I can't hope for more. I never did."

"What if he *doesn't* come along?" she asked. "What if my parents *do* leave us alone? What if I *don't* stop loving you, ever? Do you mean what you said? You'd never let me go?"

He slipped his arms around her waist. "Yes. I mean it. But I can't believe it'll happen that way."

He kissed her, long and deeply. Then he whispered against her lips, "You said you were tired of lies, tired of pretending. Let's not pretend about you and me. All right?"

She gave a shuddering sigh, but kept silent, thinking *I'm not pretending. I love you with all my heart. I'll never want anyone else my whole life long.*

CHAPTER THIRTEEN

AFTER THE FUNERAL, Cal had to cut loose, somehow. He picked the least predictable horse at the Double C and saddled him up. He was a wild-eyed bay gelding named Hook, and if the damned thing decided to buck to hell and back, it was fine with Cal.

"Go after Cal," Serena had begged Hutch. "He scares me. He's set to do something crazy. I'm afraid he'll hurt his back again."

Because it was Serena asking, Hutch agreed. He told Betsy where he was going and went out to the barn.

"Want some company?" Hutch asked. Cal was swearing as he struggled to tighten the cinch on the skittish horse.

"Not particularly," Cal said shortly, jerking the strap. The horse tried to kick him.

"Too bad," Hutch said. "You got it. Which of these hayburners can I take?" He nodded toward the horse stalls.

"Oh, hell, take Grumpy," Cal muttered. "But hurry. I ain't waitin' on you."

Hutch shrugged, took down a bridle and went into Grumpy's stall. He knew the horse from rodeo days, had even ridden him in competition before. He slid the bit between the horse's jaws, buckled the bridle and led him outside.

Cal struggled to mount Hook, who kept circling and kicking out, not letting Cal get a foot into the stirrup. The horse's ears lay flat back against his head, and his teeth were bared.

Hutch vaulted onto Grumpy bareback. He watched as Cal finally subdued Hook and swung into the saddle. The bay took it bad-naturedly and danced more fiercely.

"Look," Hutch said mildly, "we all feel bad. There's no call to court suicide on that thing."

"He's courtin' suicide if he messes with me," Cal muttered. "And who sent you to look out after me?"

"Who do you think?" Hutch asked.

Cal reined the snorting Hook to a standstill. He tossed Hutch an unsmiling glance. "My better half, I suppose."

"You got that right," Hutch said.

Cal kicked the bay, who reared, then shot off at a trot that looked bone-shaking. Hutch sighed, kicked Grumpy, and caught up.

"Why'd your daddy buy that blamed thing?" Hutch asked, nodding at Hook.

"Didn't buy him," grumbled Cal. "Won him in a poker game from Bubba Gibson. Daddy's only hope is to get Bubba liquored up enough to let him win him back."

"Is he good for anything?" Hutch asked dubiously.

"Yeah," Cal said, leaning over the horn. "He can run like a son of a bitch."

He set his heels into the bay's ribs so sharply that the animal reared, then shot off at a gallop. Hutch speeded up Grumpy and hoped he wouldn't have to bring Cal home draped over Grumpy's saddle like a bag of feed. The day had been hard enough already.

He caught up to Cal and Hook nearly a mile later. The horse had veered to a stop at the sight of the mailbox at the end of the lane. He refused to pass it, and when Cal hit his hat against Hook's flank, the horse started bucking nastily.

Hutch gritted his teeth and watched. The horse seemed crazy, the man atop him seemed crazier still.

At last Hook subsided, weary. His bucks turned into kicks, the kicks into an ill-tempered sideways prancing, and finally the prancing died to mere steps.

Hutch rode up next to Cal. Cal's face was rigidly set, his breath ragged.

Hutch reined in Grumpy. "You feel better?" he asked without emotion.

Cal wiped his forehead, put his Stetson back on. "Yeah," he said tightly. He rubbed his eyes. "Jesus. I never been to a kid's funeral before. Jesus."

"You prayin' or swearin'?"

"I don't know," Cal said wearily. "And there's something I don't understand about funerals. Why does everybody in the world descend on the house bringing you hams and pies and deviled eggs? God, are we supposed to sit around and *eat* all afternoon?"

Hutch shrugged. "It's like a tribal rite. There's ceremony to these things."

"Yeah?" Cal asked grimly. "Well, I don't like it." He turned Hook to head across the meadow. Tired, the horse plodded, its head down. Hutch rode beside them.

"Tyler never told me," Cal said, looking off at the bare horizon. "He never said they were worried about the kid. Serena guessed, but I didn't believe her. I carried on like a damn fool in front of them about us havin' a baby. I didn't know. I feel like tearin' my tongue out."

"I don't think they told anybody," Hutch said.

Cal shook his head. "He hasn't really talked to me since it happened. For four days, he's hardly said a word."

"These things take time," Hutch said.

"He's not talkin' to anybody," Cal said moodily. "Not even Ruth. She's like a zombie. She's not talkin', either."

"She's talked some to Betsy. Not much. But some."

Cal kept his gaze fixed on the distance. "It's good she's got some kin here. I still think we should've had her daddy come."

"Might have been harder on her," Hutch said. Cal pulled to a halt. Hutch stopped beside him. The two men's eyes met briefly, but Cal, his face troubled, looked away.

"My brother's been drunk every night since this happened," he said tonelessly. "He's never been a drinker. He don't hold it good. I reckon that's what he's doin' now. Ruth's back at the house lookin' like a ghost, and he's off someplace—gettin' shit-faced."

Hutch nodded and said nothing. The funeral had been held this morning. Only family had attended, except for Hutch and Lettie Mae. Lettie Mae had taken it hard and cried silently throughout.

Ruth and Tyler's house was so ludicrously full of food brought by well-meaning friends and neighbors that it looked as if they were having a party. People kept dropping in after the service, but Tyler had disappeared.

Ruth hadn't asked after him. She didn't even seem to notice. She moved about mechanically, spoke just as mechanically.

She had stayed at the hospital two days, and had been out two. Betsy seemed the only person she allowed to register on her consciousness. She tuned out Tyler and the rest of the McKinneys as if they were reminders of something too painful to stand.

Cal pulled his hat brim down farther. "Ruth won't let anybody clean out the baby's room. It's like maybe she thinks this is a nightmare, and she'll wake up, and the kid'll be fine."

Hutch said nothing because there was nothing to say.

Cal urged Hook to a walk again. Hutch kicked Grumpy to stay abreast. "Damn," Cal said. "Damn."

"Look," Hutch said, "if Tyler's drinkin', maybe we ought to find him, sober him up—"

"No," Cal said flatly. "I tried to talk to him last night. I went over there, and he was alone in the den with half a fifth of bourbon. I said, 'Tyler, this ain't doin' one damn bit of good,' and he didn't say nothin', just looked at me. Like he hated my guts."

The two men rode on in silence. At last Cal said, "I put my hand on his shoulder. He jerks away, and all of a sudden, I know he wants to take a swing at me. I'm not gonna fight him. Enough's gone bad."

"You're probably right." Hutch thought a moment. "What did you do with the dog? Somebody said Tyler was goin' to shoot it, but it was gone. Did you take it away?"

Cal nodded. "I half wanted to shoot it myself. But it's only a dumb animal. I mean, hell."

"I guess," Hutch said and looked up at the empty, gray sky.

Cal gave a bitter, one-cornered smile. "You know what's funny? We think Serena's pregnant. She's done those home test doohickeys twice. They say she is. She's supposed to go to the doctor next week."

"Congratulations," Hutch said, trying to sound hearty. He failed.

Cal's lip curled. "I think we both knew the night it happened. Don't ask me how. We knew, that's all."

He shrugged. "If it's true, we shouldn't tell folks for a long time. It'd be too hard on Ruth and Tyler. I feel sorry for Serena. It's the kind of thing you want to get up on the roof and yell."

"I wouldn't know," Hutch said.

Cal turned and studied him, his eyes narrowing. "Just how you gettin' along with Cousin Betsy, anyhow? Aside from sweepin' her off her feet and movin' in with her?"

"I haven't moved in with her," Hutch said. It was his turn to look away.

"No," Cal said sarcastically. "You're just there every night."

"Well, that's gotta stop," Hutch muttered. "I'll be movin' into the room behind the bar. I'm keepin' that motel room, which is dumb, because I don't use it."

"Don't use it?" Cal asked in disbelief. "Then why keep it?"

"Because," Hutch said from between his teeth, "I don't want it to seem I haven't got my own place, that I'm livin' off her. That's *her* apartment. She pays the rent."

"You're crazy, man," Cal said, squinting at him. "Why live in that cracker box? Move in with her. Pay half the rent."

"I can't," Hutch said, an edge to his voice. "I don't have that kind of money. Besides, why drive clear in from Austin and back every day?"

"She knows you're gonna do this?"

"Yeah. We've talked about it."

"You seem mighty crazy about each other," Cal said slowly, with deliberation. "You sure you're not gettin' in over your head this time?"

Hutch's stomach gave a small, sickening pitch. "Naw. It'll end."

"You know," Cal said, staring up at the cloudy sky, "it don't have to end. You could break down and get married. It don't kill you. I'm livin' proof."

Hutch cast him a contemptuous glance. "I'm not marrying anybody who's gonna inherit a fortune."

"Some men," Cal said sarcastically, "wouldn't view that as a drawback in a woman."

"I'm not after her money, dammit."

"Who said you were?" Cal countered. "It's just I never viewed money as a strike against a girl, for God's sake."

"Well, she might not have it long, if she sticks with me," Hutch remarked, frowning. "Her mama and daddy don't cotton to me. What if they threaten to cut her off? I couldn't let that happen."

"Why not?" Cal said with a shrug. "Then you could marry her. You don't have to die old and alone with only your chili peppers to keep you company."

"I can't get her disinherited," Hutch retorted. "I'd hate myself. And she'd hate me for it later. What if we did get married, had kids? Every day, she'd be thinkin' of everything they couldn't have because of me."

"Well, she wouldn't have the kids if it wasn't for you, so it'd even out," Cal argued.

"No," Hutch said stubbornly. "It's her, too. Why should she give up everything? For a two-bit drifter with a chili parlor that might not even stay in business?"

"A woman could do worse," Cal observed.

"Not much," Hutch replied. "I see why her parents object. If I was them, I'd object to me myself."

Cal gave a derisive snort. "I've gotta hand it to you, Hutch, you outdone yourself this time."

Hutch cocked his eyebrow. "What do you mean?"

"You always play it so safe. You always fall for the woman you can't have. I remember Sandra Sparrow in Dallas. I remember like yesterday."

Hutch frowned harder. "Sandra Sparrow worked for an oil company, and they wanted to send her to China, for God's sake. She went."

"You could've gone with her."

"What would I do in China? I was makin' my livin' at rodeo. They got very little call for rodeo riders in China. No. She did what she wanted, I did what I wanted."

"What about that first one you had?" Cal asked. "The one you told me taught you the twenty-nine Tibetan secrets of pleasing a woman?"

"They weren't Tibetan," Hutch grumbled. "She found somebody else, is all. Besides, there was an age difference."

They rode on in silence, and Hutch remembered. The first big love of his life had been a beautiful woman he met his first year in the minor leagues. He'd been twenty, she'd been thirty-six. She was lovely, she was sexy, and she wasn't shy about telling him in bed exactly what she liked.

He'd been crazy for her. She'd said she loved him, too.

But an old boyfriend of hers showed up, widowed for a year and childless. He was forty-five years old, a corporate vice president with a fat stock portfolio, a house in Georgetown and a summer home on Martha's Vineyard. He proposed to her.

She told Hutch she might never get another chance for such security. She'd asked him to stay on as her lover. He'd passed on that. On the rebound, he'd almost gotten engaged, but after that he'd stayed determinedly free.

"Yeah," Cal mocked, "you've got it perfect this time. If she's got the money, you can't marry her. If she hasn't got the money, you can't marry her. Either way, you're off the hook. A neat trick, old hoss."

"I never set out to play any trick," Hutch growled.

"Well, you're sure playin' it on somebody," Cal answered. "Though I ain't sure who. Hell of a game, though. I gotta hand it to you."

"I'm not playin' tricks, and I'm not playin' games," Hutch insisted, anger rising.

"Oh, hell, forget it," Cal said irritably. "I'm in a piss-poor mood, is what. I guess I never knew anybody who lost a little kid before. Did you?"

Hutch sobered. He thought of Betsy, who'd had an unwanted baby planted inside her by force, had carried and borne it in shame, had obediently signed it away and been haunted ever after.

"Yeah. Sort of," he said without emotion.

Cal had gone somber again. "Did it take a long time to get over it?"

Again Hutch thought of Betsy. The same sickening pitch twisted his stomach, and a twinge shot through his heart.

"Yeah," he said softly. "I reckon it did."

HUTCH LOVED Betsy. Betsy loved Hutch. That didn't change an iota. But other things began to change, slowly and subtly.

For the first time, he spent the night at the bar instead of her apartment. It was so he could get an earlier start on repairs in the morning. She missed him terribly. She found it hard to sleep without him.

Betsy had bought herself a used car, complete with fuzzy dice hanging from the rearview mirror. She supposed it was the first used car to disgrace her family in forty years. The car was a clunky gray sedan, but she took great if slightly perverse pride in it.

Her mother had continued to call. At first the conversation was much the same. But it, too, began to alter and the calls came less frequently. Margaret sounded more resigned, less insistent.

"Go your own way," Margaret said at last, her voice full of weariness. "Your father says you'll get this out of your system, then come crawling back. So does my doctor. I can't keep torturing myself. We'll be here when you come to your senses. I just pray it's soon."

In a way Betsy was relieved, in a way worried. She knew her parents had relented in hopes that the love affair would die a natural death. She wondered, fearfully, if they were right.

Being in love was wonderful, but it opened up a whole new set of insecurities. They roiled within her as she pulled her car up in front of the bar. It was midafternoon, and Hutch, as usual, was at work remodeling.

The front door was unlocked, and she stepped inside. Hammering rang out, and the scents of plaster dust and freshly sawed wood hung in the air. Hutch was putting up new drywall, and the interior was perceptibly brighter.

He was hammering a piece of molding into place and hadn't heard her enter. "Hi," she said, almost shyly.

He turned to her and grinned. "Hi, sugar," he said, tossing the hammer aside onto a roll of insulation. He held out his arms. "Can I hug you? Or are you too dressed up?"

His jeans and blue work shirt were dusty, the shirt darkened by sweat. His hair fell across his brow, and he had a smudge on his left cheekbone. His blue-green eyes shone with pleasure, and Betsy's heart leapt.

"I'm never too dressed up," she said, going to him. "Hug me to bits."

He put his arms around her. "Hug my Bets to bits," he said, bending to her. He kissed her until she was dizzy with the taste and scent and feel of him.

"Can you stay?" he asked, drawing back and smiling down. "God, I missed you last night."

"I missed you, too," she said, her throat tightening. "Oh, Hutch, I'm almost afraid to tell you this. I've got a job offer—finally."

His smile faded. "Jeez, Betsy, does that mean I'll see even less of you? Is that what you're afraid to say? You got something that'll keep you in Austin nights?"

She swallowed. "No," she said, gazing up at him worriedly. "Just the opposite. The job's here. In Crystal Creek. At the radio station."

"Are you kiddin'?"

"No," she said, toying with the rumpled points of his opened collar. "At KRCW. Selling ads. If I take it, I'll be working here five days a week. The office is only two streets away."

"What do you mean, if you take it?" he asked, a frown line appearing between his eyes. "Don't you want to? If you don't like sellin', don't take it."

She gripped his shoulders. "I want to. I don't mind selling. My dad made us all learn it. I can do it."

His frown line deepened. "Then what's the problem?"

"The problem is—" she faltered, took a breath, and started over. "The problem is I don't want to seem like I'm crowding into your territory. That I'm chasing you."

He laughed and pulled her more tightly against him. "You don't have to chase me. You already caught me."

"You won't mind? Honest? Because I don't want you to feel that I'm trying to hover over you or anything like that."

"Betsy," he said in a low voice, "I want you around. I'd hate havin' you in Austin all day every day."

She sighed with relief and put her arms around his neck. They held each other, and he kissed her hair, nibbled her ear, nuzzled her cheek. He opened the coat collar, lowered his mouth and kissed her throat.

Betsy's pulse pounded beneath his warm lips. He unbuttoned her coat the rest of the way and put his hands around her waist, pulling her closer.

"Hey," he said breathlessly, drawing back again, desire in his eyes. "You know what? If you sublet your apartment in Austin, you could move here, to Crystal Creek."

Betsy, too, was breathing hard. She nodded solicitously. "I—I thought of that, too. But then it'd really look like I was chasing you."

He arched a dark eyebrow. "You're kind of crazy, you know that?"

"I mean," she said, "my apartment's fancier than I need. I could get a much more reasonable one here. But I didn't want to seem—"

"Plumb crazy," he said and kissed her. "Lord, I wish I had a bigger place. We could live together, really live together."

"Your place is hardly big enough for you," she said and kissed him back.

"I know," he murmured, nuzzling her ear again. "We couldn't even fit your clothes in the closet. We'd be like sardines."

"Absolutely," she said. His hands were under her sweater now, caressing her bare flesh.

"So that'd be impossible," he said, unsnapping her bra.

"Impossible," she breathed, as his hand moved beneath the lace, caressing her, cupping her breast.

"Which is really too bad," he said, trailing kisses along her jawline, "because like I said, I *really* missed you last night. I missed you like crazy."

"I missed you, too," she said, unbuttoning the top button of his shirt, then the next. She slipped her hand inside to rest against the warm hardness of his chest.

He gasped slightly, pressing closer to her. "Betsy, are we going to make love?"

"I certainly hope so," she said dreamily, her face against his throat. She realized she had never been so happy in her life.

THEY MADE LOVE wildly and tenderly and crazily in the tiny back bedroom. The bed was too small, and Hutch knocked his elbow nearly through the wall. The calendar fell down, got mixed in with the sheets. There was little heat in the room, and afterward Betsy and Hutch lay in each other's arms, shivering and laughing.

"It's too small and too cold in here for a lady like you," he said, wrapping the blanket more firmly around them. "Brr."

She snuggled closer, basking in the heat of his naked body. "How's your elbow?" she asked with concern.

"Hardly broken at all," he said, kissing her beneath the ear. "What happened to the calendar?"

"It finally fell to the floor," she said, rubbing her cheek against his shoulder. "But I think a couple of months got torn off."

"Time well spent," he said. "Ouch. Maybe I did break my elbow."

"Let me see."

"No," he said, holding her tight. "I'm fine. I like you where you are. I love you where you are."

"I love you, too," she said contentedly.

They lay silent for a moment. "We could have some mighty interestin' lunch hours with you workin' in town," he said.

"*Mighty* interestin'," she teased, mocking his accent.

But when he spoke again, his voice was serious. He took her hand and held it against his chest so she could feel the strong, steady beat of his heart.

"Bets," he said softly, "I know a place—a real house. We could move in together. What do you think?"

"A house?" she asked, pleasantly surprised. "A real house?"

"It's little. It's not fancy. It needs work. If you don't want to, I'll understand. Everybody in town'd know about us."

"I think they know about us now," Betsy whispered, tracing her finger along his collarbone. "I don't think we're fooling anybody."

"Vern Trent looked in on me one day, saw how I was doin', told me about this house. I wasn't gonna fool with it, but if you're livin' here, it'd be worth it. And I could pay my half."

She inhaled sharply. She hated it when the subject of money came up. She wanted to say the stupid money didn't matter. But she knew he had his pride and so she said nothing.

"It's a little ramshackle brick place," he said, stroking her hair. "Owner's out of town, but won't sell. It's his home place. He needs a tenant who's handy, could fix it up. Could you stand that?"

She pulled back from him slightly so she could gaze into his eyes. "You and me? In a real house?"

"Come here," he said, gathering her back into his arms. "It's cold with you clear over there. Vernon says the guy'll rent it out, a hundred fifty a month to somebody who'll put it back in shape and keep it that way."

"A hundred and fifty?" she asked in wonder. "That's great! But if you fix it up, it's like you're working two jobs. You're doing more than your share."

"Hush, and just tell me," he said. "Would you? Live in that little brick house?"

"Yes," said Betsy, pressing her lips against his throat. "Oh, yes."

HUTCH WAS ELATED, yet uneasy. He showed Betsy the brick house, an eccentric little Victorian cottage with an overabundance of fretwork, all of it needing paint. The porch, with its curlicued woodwork, sagged sadly, and cracks zigzagged through the masonry. The lawn was thick with dead weeds.

She'd looked at it with such shining eyes that he might have been showing her a castle. His arm around her, he felt an odd pride in the place himself, and took irrational pleasure in her liking it.

They peered into the dusty windows, commented on the funny little rooms with their strange nooks and crannies and faded wallpaper. He looked in the window of the largest bedroom, thought of sleeping with her there every night and found he was smiling.

They'd gone back to the bar. She'd changed her fancy clothes for jeans and a sweatshirt to help him work. She'd never worn jeans much before, and he thought she looked cute as hell in them.

They bought sandwiches and soft drinks at the supermarket deli, brought them back to the bar and picnicked
on the bare floor. They talked about how to fix the bar,
how to fix the house. They laughed, they flirted, they
were serious by turns.

But he said he should stay in Crystal Creek for the
night, because he should talk to Vernon as soon as possible about the house, and get to work on the bar at the
earliest hour; he'd be working double-time now.

Betsy nodded reluctantly and said she should go back
to Austin. She needed to talk to her landlord about sub-
letting, and get ready to start work. The station manager
had said if she wanted the job, he'd like her to begin as
soon as possible, even before the week was ended.

Against their wills, they parted, but only after so much
kissing and touching that they ended up making love for
a second time in the ridiculously small bedroom. The
calendar fell off the wall again, and lost another two
pages.

Then he'd watched her bundle up in her coat, walked
her to her funny little car and stared after her as the tail-
lights disappeared into the night.

He missed her so much it scared him. Head down, his
hands jammed in his jacket pockets, he walked to the
nearest pay phone and called Vernon Trent.

"I want to rent that house on West Street, after all,"
Hutch told him. "You can start drawin' up papers."

Saying the words gave him a discomfiting feeling in the
pit of his stomach. He hung up the phone and headed
back to the bar.

His boot heels on the concrete sent faint echoes
through the deserted streets. He stared up at the stars and
waning moon.

I'm renting a house, he thought, with that same feeling in the pit of his stomach. *I'm renting a goddamn house. I don't believe it.*

Never before in his life had he done such a thing. He hadn't even waited for Betsy to sublet her apartment.

They needed a place in town, and they needed it now. He couldn't handle taking her to that cracker box of a room behind a half-gutted bar.

He'd told himself before that he needed no more than that cell of a room, but now he did. *They* did. They needed a home.

A home, he thought ominously. He'd never called any place home since he'd left his parents' house to go to Harvard. Since his minor league days, he'd lived as Spartanly as possible.

He'd been with women, but never had he found himself in such a position—deliberately setting up housekeeping with one, no matter how much he'd liked her. But Betsy wasn't other women. Betsy was—

His.

The thought struck him so forcibly he felt it like a physical blow. His midsection tightened, and he sucked in his breath through his teeth.

She's mine, he thought, stunned by amazement. *I'm hers.*

He, who'd never wanted belongings and had guarded his freedom so jealously, now possessed someone. And was possessed by her.

NEWS TRAVELED fast in Crystal Creek. Vernon Trent told his wife, Carolyn, that Hutch was renting the house on West Street, and he'd heard the radio station had offered Betsy a job. He opined that Hutch and Betsy

Holden were probably setting up housekeeping, sure as God made little green apples.

Carolyn told her sister-in-law, Cynthia McKinney, who told her husband, J.T. Later, when Cal phoned to ask how Ruth and Tyler were doing, J.T. mentioned the news to him.

Cal passed the news on to Serena, who found it most intriguing. Hutch was moving in with someone? *Hutch?*

When Serena later called Tyler, to see how things were, she said something about it, only in passing.

Tyler showed no reaction to the news, but when he hung up, he told Ruth, who did. She looked worried and said that she hoped her aunt and uncle didn't hear of it. Their uneasy tolerance of the affair might quickly disappear. Ruth had come to like Hutch, and it was clear he loved Betsy.

Ruth was still concerned the next morning when her father called from California to see how she felt. She forced herself to sound as cheerful as possible.

When Don Holden asked about Betsy, Ruth was grateful for a change of subject. She told him of Betsy's new job and said Betsy and Hutch might soon be keeping house.

"Don't tell Uncle Ron or Aunt Margaret," she told her father. "This is confidential. Just between you and me. She needs to work this out on her own. Ron and Margaret'll just get upset and try to interfere. It's Betsy's life."

Don agreed that he wouldn't tell his brother. He assured Ruth that he had no intention of alarming Betsy's family.

Yet when Don Holden hung up the phone, his conscience reproved him. He was deeply worried about his own daughter, and knew that his brother and sister-in-law were, in their way, just as distressed about Betsy.

Don Holden had long thought of Betsy as resembling her father—quiet, repressed and with a too-tight grip on her emotions. Her recent rebellion was incomprehensible to him.

Ruth seemed to have taken a liking to Betsy's young man, but that's what fortune hunters were skilled at—getting women to trust them. It was one thing for Betsy to have her little fling. It was another for her actually to flout all convention and live with him. Moreover, it didn't sound like Betsy at all.

The more that Don brooded, the more he thought that if *his* daughter were getting into such a mess, he'd want to be told. In the end, he yielded, believing he should do as he would wish done to him.

He dialed his brother's number and told him, with reluctant frankness, that the situation in Crystal Creek had grown more serious. Betsy, it seemed, was about to take up living with that man.

Ronald Holden was silent for an emotion-charged moment. He was an aloof, stern man, and when he finally spoke it was with cold passion. "Enough is enough. The time has come to put a stop to this. I'd sooner see her dead than carrying on this way."

CHAPTER FOURTEEN

BETSY WAS EUPHORIC. She'd started work—almost. On Friday, the station manager had sent her out with the sales manager to meet clients and potential clients.

She was to begin full-time on Monday. In the meantime, her landlord, in an incredible stroke of luck, had found someone who wanted to sublet her apartment and who would take possession in December.

All day Saturday Betsy and Hutch worked furiously, not on the bar, but on their little house on West Street.

Together they scrubbed down the odd but charming kitchen. The wallpaper was faded and tattered, spiders had spun webs in every corner, and the linoleum was buckled and full of bulges.

But Betsy loved it. Quaint handmade cabinets lined two sides of the room, and a funny little table came down out of the wall to reveal shelves behind it. The window looked out on a dogwood tree that Hutch said would flower in spring and turn bright colors in fall.

She paused for a moment from cleaning the window glass. She turned, sat on the edge of the sill and looked up at Hutch.

He was in jeans and white T-shirt, perched on top of a ladder, expertly detaching the light fixture. She watched the play of muscles in his sinewy arms, the lazy way he swung one booted foot, as if he were playing a game, not working.

"You said the plumbing looks good?" she asked.

"Yep," he said with satisfaction. He put the screwdriver behind his ear, pulled a pair of wire cutters from his belt and started snipping. The old light fixture came loose. "Here," he said, handing it down. "Throw this away, will you, baby? I gotta replace these wires."

Betsy took the cracked fixture and stuffed it into the trash can. She put her hands on her hips and looked up at him. "What are you going to replace that with?" she asked. "Should I go out and buy a new one?"

"Naw," he said, doing something complicated with the wires. "We'll go to a flea market, buy us an old, funky one. To go with the house."

She turned back to the window. "We need curtains. I wonder if anything's on sale this close to Christmas."

"Don't buy 'em at the store," he said, sticking the pliers back into his belt and using the screwdriver again. "We'll go to a yard sale or something."

"A yard sale," Betsy said meditatively. She picked up her cloth and cleaner and began to work on the window again. "You know, I've never been to a yard sale. Or a thrift shop. I went to a flea market once. I bought this lamp made out of an old duck decoy. I thought it was a hoot, but my mother threw it out. She said I was being tasteless."

"Your mother'd want to throw *me* out, most likely," he said. "As bein' tasteless."

She paused again, staring out at the dogwood tree. Her parents didn't know she was moving in with Hutch, and she knew they would object.

"I—feel funny keeping this from my parents," she said. "Like I'm slipping into a whole new set of lies."

He came down from the stepladder and took up another cloth. He moved behind her, leaned close and cleaned the top of the window, where she couldn't reach.

"If you feel wrong about this, sugar," he said quietly, "you shouldn't do it. Do you need to think it over more?"

She resisted the desire to lean back against him, savoring his warmth, his strength.

"Nothing I've ever done with you seems wrong," she said. "I feel as if they force me to keep the truth from them."

His chest brushed her shoulder, and she could feel his breath on her hair. "Sugar, you can keep them happy, or you can try to make yourself happy. It doesn't sound like you can do both."

"I know," she said moodily. "I wish it wasn't that way. But it was, even before I met you. I suppose I would have married Michael. Because *they* wanted it. Not me."

"Some night," he said, his voice rueful, "when the wind is blowin' through the cracks in these old walls, and the furnace has broken down for the fifteenth time, you may wish you hadn't chosen me."

She turned to face him. "Never. I'd never wish that."

He set the cloth down on the windowsill. "Oh, God," he said. "Don't look up at me that way. It puts wings on my heart. It flies off and leaves me."

She smiled, but what she had to say was serious. "I want us always to be honest."

"I know. Me, too."

"The money," she said, "my money, that I actually have. It's not much compared to what my folks have."

He stroked her cheek with his knuckles. "It seems like a lot to me. When I'm not bringin' anything in yet."

"I understand," she said. "But we've worked it out, pretty well, haven't we?"

He nodded and put his arms around her. She sighed and pressed her cheek against his chest.

"This isn't cleanin' any windows," he said against her ear, "but I think you need a snuggle break."

She wrapped her arms around his waist. The feel of him was familiar, dependable, yet at the same time exciting. A rush of affection swept through her.

Friday night they had worked on the bar and picnicked on pizza. And they'd talked frankly about the money.

Hutch had nearly nineteen thousand in the bank, and he was sure he could get the bar in shape and open on that amount. He could also cover many of their living expenses.

They would split the rent. He would pay their utilities, gas, electricity and water. Betsy would do the grocery shopping, and they would split the bill down the middle.

For her part, she was in charge of furnishings, and whatever she bought was her property. Hutch declared her the Empress of Home Entertainment, and all major decisions concerning things like VCRs and corn poppers were hers.

Betsy felt Hutch was paying more than his share, but she understood that was the way he wanted it. She had more money—$21,000 in the bank from the sale of her condo, and $1500 a month from her trust fund. Soon, she would be drawing a paycheck from the radio station, as well, although she knew it would be small.

"Hutch," she said, rubbing her forehead against his chest, "if an emergency happened—if you suddenly needed money, would it bother you to borrow from me?"

He held her more tightly. "Probably. We'll cross that bridge if we come to it. Let's hope we don't."

"Right," she said, hoping with all her heart. He was more independent than any man she'd ever known.

"Hey," he whispered, "how about I take you out honky-tonkin' in Austin tonight? We haven't danced for a while. I miss it."

"I miss it, too," she said.

"Then we'll go to your place and make love in a real bed and sleep late in the morning for a change."

"Sounds wonderful," she said.

"So give me a kiss to last me till then," he said, putting his finger under her chin and tilting her face up to his.

"Gladly," she said. God, she thought, he had beautiful eyes.

He lowered his lips to hers. "Betsy," he breathed, "I do believe you're learnin' to love simple pleasures."

HUTCH WOKE EARLY, although he'd promised Betsy they'd sleep late. Through a gap between the bedroom drapes, he could see the sky was still black.

The morning was almost eerily silent. There were no traffic sounds, nothing. Then, barely audible, he heard it—the lonesome whistle of a distant freight train.

Where's it going? he wondered automatically. *What'll they see that I won't see? What'll they learn that I don't know?*

He turned toward Betsy. She lay, a small, dark shape, curled like a child and clutching her pillow. He raised himself on his elbow and stared down at her. The nightlight cast the dimmest of glows, and he could see her lashes dark against her cheeks, and her hair tousled on the pillow.

With a long sigh, he took her into his arms, drawing
her close so that she lay with her body cradled against his.
He stared past her into the shadows. He still couldn't get
over the fact—he was renting a house. They would soon
be in it, together.

In the distance, the train whistle blew again, as if calling him.

Betsy's perfume tickled his nostrils. She wore some
scent he loved; it smelled like the lilies of the valley that
used to grow in his parents' yard back home.

Home, he thought uneasily. He and Betsy were making a home.

Betsy stirred slightly, her silky back moving against his
chest. She made a small noise that sounded vaguely sad.
He held her tighter, as if willing her dreams to be happy,
not haunted.

Yet he felt haunted himself. Somehow he'd slipped into
acquiring things and responsibilities he hadn't planned
on.

He was used to traveling around the country keeping
everything he owned in one duffel bag and one van. Now
he had a bar to fill with restaurant equipment, and Betsy
was talking with happy innocence about curtains and
throw rugs and bedspreads.

Curtains and throw rugs and bedspreads. Restaurant
equipment and mortgages and insurance. How had he
come to this?

Sounding nearer now, the train whistle called again,
ghostly, yet inviting.

Betsy stirred slightly. "Ummm," she murmured
dreamily. She put her hand on his bare thigh to give him
a drowsy caress. His heart pounded, and he drew in his
breath sharply.

He couldn't quite believe her, really. She never crowded him, never made demands, never asked for any real commitment from him, expected no long-lasting promises.

The train sounded, farther away again, the whistle fading, leaving him behind. He wondered where it was going, what was to be seen there, what a man might learn there.

He remembered walking on the beach in Galveston, finding himself between jobs, between destinations, but not worrying, just enjoying the sunset, not a care in the world.

It's been a long time since I've seen Galveston, he thought. *It's been a long time since I've been to the Gulf.*

He found his hands rising to cover the soft curves of her breasts. The train whistle sounded one last time in the distance, then was swallowed up by silence.

He was filled with emotions he didn't understand. He pressed his lips against the back of her neck and kissed her. "Betsy," he whispered, "could you stand to make love again? I need you, sugar."

He kissed her again, pulled her more tightly to him. "Ummm," she said again and was silent a moment. But then she turned to him and wound one arm around his neck. She pressed her soft, full lips against his hungry ones.

She gave herself to him, completely, generously and sweetly. She asked no questions, only trusted him, loved him and let him love.

IT WAS TUESDAY evening and already dark. When Ruth came in the back door, Tyler was sitting at the kitchen table, eating leftovers.

"Where have you been?" he asked. He didn't smile in greeting. Neither did she. She took off her car coat and hung it on the back hall peg.

"I went to see Hutch and Betsy's house," she said without emotion. "And to invite them for Thanksgiving. Cynthia said I could. I wouldn't mind having some of my own family around."

She moved to the counter to pour herself a mug of coffee.

"I didn't know where you were," he said. "You could have left a note."

She turned to face him, leaning against the counter. "I didn't think I'd be this late. And I never know how late *you'll* be."

He always worked until after dark these days. At least he'd stopped drinking. He quit the day after the funeral, as if he'd simply switched his emotions off and was going on with life as usual.

She couldn't turn off her feelings, only try to crush them down. She'd become Nate's patient again, and she was trying to be obedient and take it easy. But she'd grown sick of sitting in the empty house. It seemed to imprison and smother her, and she'd fled it.

She sipped her coffee without really tasting it. She couldn't help comparing the perfection of her kitchen to the chaos of Betsy's. Yet Betsy's was warm and full of laughter, and her own seemed hollow and cold.

Betsy and Hutch had shared their supper with her. Peanut butter sandwiches and root beer, that was all. They ate sitting cross-legged on the kitchen floor, and Hutch told such outrageous stories that Ruth had actually laughed.

She had thought perhaps she would never laugh again and was grateful to him. She'd felt oddly content with them in their funny little house and hadn't wanted to leave.

"So how are they?" Tyler asked. His dark eyes flicked up and down her body, as if he was taking the measure of a stranger.

"They're like kids playing house," she said, hoping she didn't sound envious. "Everything's fun for them. The place is a dump, but it's a charming dump, and she loves it."

Tyler said nothing, only arched a cynical eyebrow, as if he couldn't imagine Betsy in a dump, no matter how charming.

"He's fixing it up," Ruth said. "It'll be something when he gets through. It's got potential. He's really very good at that sort of thing, you know."

"No," Tyler said stonily. "I don't know."

She shrugged off his tone, as if she didn't care. "They showed me what he's done with the bar. It's amazing."

Tyler said nothing. He finished the leftovers, pushed the plate away, picked up his coffee mug.

"It *is* amazing," Ruth said. "*He's* amazing. I think he could do anything. It puzzles me that he's content with so little. Why he dreams so small."

Tyler's lip curled. "Maybe he's smart."

"What do you mean?"

"Nothing," he said. "Forget it."

She knew what he meant. Tyler's dreams had been big, but they'd turned into burdens. The construction was dragging on forever. Everything was behind schedule. Everything.

She looked away, feeling guilty and resentful. The dormant seedlings should be put out before the truly cold weather set in. It was demanding work, with every vine needing to be placed by hand.

If things were normal, she would be helping him, planting by his side. But Nate forbade any such work for six weeks, at least. Suddenly weary, she wondered if things would ever be normal again.

Why did Tyler have to keep driving himself so relentlessly? Couldn't he be more realistic? And couldn't he tell that she needed him?

"You're pushing too hard," she said, trying to sound calm and rational. "You always push too hard."

"Yeah?" he said cynically. "Well, if I don't push, nothing's going to get done. That's the bottom line."

Ruth sighed and looked away. She didn't understand why they couldn't talk anymore. It was as if an evil spell had been cast upon them. She stared moodily into her coffee cup.

"Ruthie," Tyler said. "I'm sorry. I've been leaving you alone too much. Maybe you're right."

"No," Ruth said, hating her own selfishness. "No, you're right. I shouldn't criticize."

He rose from the table, came to her. "I was worried when I came home and you were gone. I worry about you."

"Don't," she said. "I'm fine. This just takes time."

"I guess I should be glad you went out."

She shrugged. The trip to Betsy's was the first time she'd left the Double C since the funeral. She'd had to pass the cemetery. She'd had to pass the hospital. She couldn't speak of it.

Tyler put his hand on the back of her neck. "Are they coming? Hutch and Betsy? For Thanksgiving?"

"No," she said, still staring into the cup. "They say they need to work. And they have plans."

"Plans?" he asked, rubbing her taut muscles.

Ruth tried to smile. "They're crazy. They're going to put up wallpaper and eat chili."

"Doesn't sound like much of a Thanksgiving," Tyler said.

Ruth was silent. She envied them. Their holiday would be small, eccentric, intimate, full of laughter.

Hers would be crowded. She would be surrounded by the clannish McKinneys, gathered to celebrate a holiday that seemed a mockery to her.

They'll all pity me, she thought unhappily. *They try to be kind, but they're too kind. They don't know how much their pity hurts.*

Besides, J.T. and Cynthia's baby would be there, a happy, healthy baby, almost a year old now. Ruth didn't know if she could stand it. Then there would be her pregnant sister-in-law, Lynn, and Cal and Serena, trying with all their might to conceive a child....

"I don't want to go," she said bitterly. "I dread the idea. I don't want to celebrate Thanksgiving. I don't feel thankful."

"Ruth," he said, taking her by the elbows.

"I don't," she said, looking up at him defiantly. "And I don't see how you can, either."

"I'm thankful you're alive," he said.

"Are you?" she returned. "I suppose I should be, too. But all I can think of is that our baby's dead."

There, she'd said it. It was the first time she'd actually said it aloud. Tears rose in her eyes.

"That's it, Tyler," she said, her chin trembling. "How can I be thankful when our baby's gone?"

He gripped her arms more tightly. "Did you ever think maybe it was a mercy?" he asked, his face rigid with control. "That he might have lived, but only a little while. Then we would have lost him, and that would have been worse—"

"No," she said, shaking her head. "I don't want to hear such a thing—"

"You need to hear it," he said, not letting her go. "If he'd lived, he probably would have had to have surgery. Extensive surgery. And he might not have survived. At least he didn't have to go through that. He didn't have to suffer."

Ruth was too overcome to speak. Again she shook her head impotently. She didn't want Tyler to say any more.

But he did. "He might have suffered, Ruth. Suffered a lot. And we'd have lost him and been in up to our necks in debt for hospital bills, and—"

Something snapped and broke inside Ruth. How could Tyler mention money, for God's sake? How could he even think of money in connection with the child? Did he think of nothing but bills and money and financing the damn winery?

She tore herself out of his grasp. "Don't talk to me," she choked out.

"Ruth, we have to—"

But she shut his words out. For the first time, she let her sorrow burst free. Sobs strangled her, and she couldn't get her breath. Tears scalded her eyes; she could barely see. She fled from Tyler and ran into the bedroom. She slammed the door behind her, locking it because she didn't want him to follow.

She threw herself on the bed and wept uncontrollably. She felt violated, robbed, betrayed, bereft. She was thankful for nothing.

She didn't want the hypocrisy of a Thanksgiving with the too solicitous McKinneys. She didn't even want to see them. The last time she had been with them all was the day of the funeral, and they reminded her too forcibly of everything she had lost.

She hated the Double C for being the scene of all her grief. She hated the whole state of Texas.

I miss my father. I miss home. And home is not here. It's California.

She wanted only one thing—to escape back to her real home. To flee this place and all its people. Most especially to be free of Tyler, whom she no longer knew if she loved or hated.

IN CRYSTAL CREEK, Hutch and Betsy got caught up in an impromptu waltz in the kitchen to the music of the radio.

"Watch out," she warned, laughing, "you almost stepped on that scraper."

"I saw it. Have I ever tripped you up yet?"

"No," she said, "never."

He whirled her around, holding her tighter. "And you don't mind hangin' wallpaper and eatin' chili for Thanksgiving? That's not a misstep?"

"It's a wonderful step," she said, slightly breathless, "It sounds perfect."

"Good." He smiled. He waltzed her into the living room and then into the bedroom, then into the closet, where he stopped, pulled her closer and kissed her until she was more breathless still.

"I love you," he said against her lips.

"I love you, too," he breathed.

She could no longer even imagine life without him.

This would be the most splendid Thanksgiving she'd ever had. Nothing could ruin it.

CHAPTER FIFTEEN

WEDNESDAY, the day before Thanksgiving, Hutch worked alone in the bar, painting. Betsy was in the neighboring town of Claroville, selling ads.

Yesterday she'd bought a bed with an elaborate iron headboard in need of repainting. He was to pick it up during his lunch hour. They'd assemble and repaint it tonight.

My God, I'm getting domestic, he thought wryly. *Nobody'd believe it.* He didn't believe it himself.

He wasn't surprised when a knock sounded at the door. Vern Trent often stopped in to shoot the breeze.

"Come in," Hutch called. Cal and Serena were due in at the ranch for Thanksgiving. They might stop by, too.

But it was a stranger who entered.

He was a small, compact man of about thirty-five. His clothes were expensive, his head was bare, and his brown hair expertly barbered. He was handsome in a hard-faced way.

"Are you Malcolm Hutchison?" he asked. His voice was clipped, untouched by a Texas accent.

Hutch set down the paint roller. He looked the guy up and down, and his vibes told him this was not a sociable visit. He saw the man's hazel eyes, and he knew why.

"I'm Hutch," he said evenly. "Who are you? Kin of Betsy's?"

Surprise crossed the man's severe features, but a controlled coldness swiftly replaced it. "I'm her oldest brother, Mitchell. Mitchell Holden."

He stepped toward Hutch and extended his hand. Hutch shook it, but knew this was no gesture of friendship. It was more like the acknowledgment of two fighters about to start the first round.

They released hands. Hutch thrust his thumbs into his belt, cocking his hip. Mitchell was shorter and slighter than he, but he had the air of a man who played rough.

"I suppose you're here about Betsy," Hutch said.

"Of course," Mitchell said. "You're the one?"

Hutch looked him up and down again. "I'm the one."

Mitchell took Hutch's measure just as coolly. "Well," he said with a little smirk, "you're unexpected. I'll give her that."

Hutch shrugged one shoulder. "So are you. What exactly do you want?"

"To talk, that's all," Mitchell Holden said. He looked with obvious distaste around the half-remodeled bar. "Is there a place around here we can talk?"

Hutch cocked his hip at a more rebellious angle. "This place is good as any. You want to talk about Betsy? Okay, talk."

"Here? Fine, if you feel safer on your own turf."

Hutch folded his arms across his chest. "I feel safe on any turf. Now, what you got to say? Does she know you're here?"

"Not yet," Mitchell said. He stroked the scarred bar top, then rubbed his fingers together fastidiously to clean them. "So this is how you'll make your living? Selling chili, I'm told."

"You're told right."

"Hmm," Mitchell said, gazing about the disordered room. "So this is what you've got to offer my sister."

"This is it. This and me."

"Yes," Mitchell said, unbuttoning his coat. He began to pace slowly across the room, examining it critically. "And you. You seem to have cast quite a spell over my sister. She's going to be a very rich woman someday. You know that, of course."

"I don't care about her money," Hutch said. "I care about her."

Mitchell smiled. "A noble sentiment. It has a nice ring. It's worked well on her, obviously."

He stopped and meditatively tapped his foot against a mousetrap. "You know," he said, still smiling, "if you care about her, you *should* care about her money. I wouldn't want Betsy to fall into the trap of thinking it doesn't matter. It does. It always has. It always will."

"I'm not with her because of the money," Hutch said. He shifted his shoulders restlessly because anger was rising in him, hard and cold.

"Perhaps," Mitchell said. "But that's not the point. She's with you *in spite* of the money. Careless of her. Thoughtless. If you're concerned for her, you don't want her to be careless or thoughtless."

Inwardly Hutch swore, and his stomach tightened, "All right," he said in a harsh voice. "Get to the point."

Mitchell walked to the bar and leaned his back against it, his hands resting on either side. "I was speaking of traps, Mr. Hutchison. My parents feel that Betsy has them in a trap. A very painful trap."

Hutch frowned. "She's not doin' this to hurt them."

Mitchell raised his eyebrows speculatively. "No? Not consciously, perhaps. My sister's a complex person. More complex than you suspect. As is demonstrated by this little—rebellion. We're told you and she are going to live together. Is this true?''

Hutch's stomach knotted more sinisterly. "Yes," he said, staring at Mitchell.

Mitchell's mouth took on an ironic slant. "My parents are conservative people. They're offended."

Hutch shifted his shoulders again. He put his hands on his hips. "We're adults. I love her. She loves me."

"Love," Mitchell said, arching his brow derisively. "But I understand you don't want to marry her. And she doesn't want to marry you."

Hutch nodded. "Right. We're happy the way we are."

"My parents aren't happy. My mother, in particular, is upset. Which, in turn, upsets my father. They've always been anxious for Betsy to marry. To marry someone appropriate."

"Decisions like that are hers, not theirs."

Mitchell glanced up at the ceiling thoughtfully. "We're concerned that Betsy's decision isn't completely rational. Up until now, we've kept my sister's reputation spotless."

Hutch's mouth tightened in disgust. So Mitchell, too, pretended that Betsy's child never existed.

"Morality's always been important to my parents," Mitchell said, training his cold gaze on Hutch. "Extremely important. Betsy's shaming herself and them, both. What we don't understand is why."

"I think," Hutch said, "that appearances are more important to your parents than morality. She's plenty moral. She's good, she's honest, she keeps promises, she doesn't use people."

Mitchell was unfazed. "Has it struck you that she's using you? To keep from accepting responsibility?"

Hutch's eyes narrowed. "She's acceptin' responsibility just fine. Your parents can't stand it because they don't control her any longer."

"My father learned on Monday morning about the two of you planning to shack up—"

The term *shack up* angered Hutch. He took a step toward Mitchell. "I think you could choose your words better."

"I call a spade a spade. Are you afraid of words? And answer me. What can you give my sister? You certainly can't support her in the style to which she's accustomed."

"I love her. You don't ever seem to have accustomed her to that. Which is too bad. 'Cause she's lovable."

Mitchell cast him an almost conspiratorial look. "You talk a good game. No wonder she picked you. You're perfect. You give the illusion of integrity while you drag her down."

"There's no way on God's earth I'd try to drag her down."

"Then you're doing it without trying," Mitchell said. "I've seen that 'house' you're going to live in. It's a travesty. My God, if you want to degrade her, why don't you just tar and feather her, ride her through town on a rail?"

Hutch's lip curled militantly. "How in the hell do you know where our house is?"

"My father has ways of finding out things," Mitchell shot back. "He's a resourceful and efficient man. He had a check run on you. He learned about the house. I drove past it. Really, you expect Betsy to *live* there?"

"I expect Betsy to decide."

Mitchell laughed. "She must be like a child on a camp-out. At first, roughing it's fun. A diversion, a recreation. But she'll tire of it very soon."

"I'm startin' to tire of *you,*" Hutch said.

"Hear me out," Mitchell countered. "My father understands the situation. He sees you and Betsy have us in a bind."

"We don't have anybody in a bind," Hutch said tightly.

"Then Betsy does," Mitchell countered. "Because what, precisely, Hutchison, are we going to do about you? We don't want Betsy to make a fool of herself, and we don't want her to break from the family. But almost any move we make will guarantee just that."

"I think you should go," Hutch said. "If you don't want this rift any wider, leave."

"I said hear me out. My father's not a fool. He could threaten to disinherit her. She might give you up, but she'd hate us. We don't want that."

"Why do they want to control her so bad?" Hutch demanded. "Why in hell can't you let her—"

"Now," Mitchell said smoothly, "we could try to buy you off, but if she ever found out, she'd never forgive us for that, either."

"You can't buy what isn't for sale," Hutch said.

"Everything comes down to money, one way or another," Mitchell returned. "And what can't be bought, can usually be broken. We know your finances. They're shaky. My father could crush you like an insect, you know. He could ruin you in a dozen different ways."

"He could try," Hutch said.

"He'd succeed," Mitchell answered with perfect confidence. "But Betsy would resent that, too. So we're reduced to two alternatives, Hutchison. The first is that you think it over and let her go, for her own good. End this charade before it becomes any more ridiculous—and painful—for my parents."

"And what," Hutch snarled, "if I'm good for her? A hell of a lot better than you think?"

"Then that," Mitchell said coolly, "brings us to the other alternative. If you're so good for her, if you care so much for her—marry her."

Hutch was so stunned, his ears rang. *"What?"* he said.

"Marry her," Mitchell repeated. "Why not? You say you love her. You want to live with her. You don't want to create trouble between her and her family. You don't want to take a chance that she's disinherited. It's simple. Marry her."

Hutch stared at Mitchell as if the man was mad. "You've just spent fifteen minutes telling me I'm not good enough for her, and now you want me to *marry* her?"

"If the two of you have to have each other, why not? It's better than ruining her reputation and setting the family against one another."

"You're crazy," Hutch retorted. "Why would she marry me? I've got hardly anything. You said so yourself."

"That could be changed," Mitchell said. "Oh, you'd have to sign a prenuptial agreement. You'd have to learn the family business. But my father can find a place for you. There's a station in Manhattan, Kansas, he's thinking of buying. You and Betsy could start there—"

"I don't want to go to Manhattan, Kansas," Hutch retorted. "And I don't want to work in television—for your father or anybody else. And we don't want to get married."

"How do you know?" Mitchell asked smoothly. "Have you asked her?"

"No, but we've talked—"

"Doesn't she love you enough to marry you?"

"That's not the question."

"It's part of the question," Mitchell insisted. "Or is she using you to play her usual game? No commitments. What's the matter? Aren't *either* of you mature enough to make a commitment? And the rest of us have to live with the consequences?"

"The rest of you could mind your own business."

"My sister is my business," Mitchell countered. "In some cultures, I could kill you for what you're doing with her. Instead, I'm offering you a civilized alternative."

"We don't need an alternative. This is blackmail—"

"Blackmailers extort money, Hutchison. I'm only trying to encourage responsible behavior. Now, my father will give Betsy her job back in Austin—"

"What if she doesn't *want* her job in Austin?" Hutch demanded.

"Then she's not very practical, and you wouldn't want her to be impractical, would you? And there's the question of that house. My father can provide you with something more suitable until Manhattan's ready. He can also take this place off your hands."

Hutch stepped close to Mitchell and took him by the lapels of his topcoat. "I don't want anything from your father. Nobody takes this place off my hands. And you get lost and leave both me and your sister alone."

Mitchell's snake-flat gaze didn't waver. "Let me be frank, Hutchison. Betsy's not what you think. Her past is seriously flawed. Now so is her present. We don't want her future to be."

Hutch jerked him closer. "What are you saying?"

"She's not as cool and innocent as she seems. She slipped once before. She had an illegitimate child. She gave it away. She needs to be settled. Have children of her own—real children. You see, you don't really know her. She has her secrets. She needs to be protected from herself."

A red mist seemed to fill the room. "I know her better than you ever will," Hutch snarled. "And she *did* have a real child, you sorry son of a bitch."

He wanted to hit Mitchell's smug face. He wanted to throw him across the room so hard that he'd carry bruises for a month. He resisted, but barely.

Instead, he grabbed the back of Mitchell's coat collar, hauled him away from the bar and frog-marched him to the front door. He pushed him outside. Mitchell's face was no longer confident, but fearful.

"I'd get out of town, if I were you," Hutch said. "Before you go and make something happen to you."

He slammed the door, then walked to the bar and put his elbows on it. He put his head in his hands, his heart beating hard.

Oh, God, he thought, *now I've done it. I nearly punched her brother. I threatened him. I've just made a bigger mess of things.*

"HE THREATENED you?" Betsy asked, horrified. Mitchell had tracked her down through the radio station. Her beeper commanded her to call a coffee shop in Claroville, and when she did, Mitchell came on the line. He said he'd be waiting there for her. She'd been stunned, but she'd met him.

"Yes," Mitchell said with resentment. "This man has the potential for violence. What have you got yourself involved with this time?"

"He's not violent," Betsy insisted. "You must have said something—"

"I told him the truth. I said you'd screwed up before and Mom and Dad didn't want you doing it again."

"Mitchell!" she cried, clenching her fists on the table top.

"I also said he ought to act like a gentleman and marry you," Mitchell told her. "I said Mom and Dad were willing to help you out. That they wanted to see you settled and with children of your own. He seemed to find that offensive."

"Married? Children?" Betsy said, astonished and outraged. "How could you?"

He ignored the question. "Don't worry. I won't tell Mom he actually made a threat. She's upset enough. She's spent the past week in bed. Nerves."

"Nerves." Betsy shook her head. "Oh, really, Mitchell, why are you all carrying on so? Don't you know what century this is? People live together all the time."

"Not in this family," Mitchell said. He held up his hand and pointed at his thick gold wedding band. "See that? It's a symbol. That I care enough about my wife to promise to love and honor her my whole life long. That's the kind of promise a real man makes. A real man is responsible, Betsy."

Offended, Betsy turned her face away from him.

"And so is a real woman," Mitchell said, his voice angry. "She can commit to a husband. And children. Betsy, Mom and Dad just want to see you settled. That's all they ask. I'm going to be brutally honest."

"I suppose if somebody in the family's going to be honest, it'd have to be 'brutally,' " she said.

"Betsy, for years nobody talked to you about what you'd done. We were trying to spare you. We didn't want you to have to think about it."

"Not think about it?" she demanded. "How could I not think about it?"

"Because it's the sort of thing you put behind you," Mitchell said with conviction. "How were we to know you were sitting around obsessing about it?"

She flashed him a glare. "I wasn't obsessing. I was trying to face the reality of what had happened."

"You've got Mom worried sick," he said. "She thinks you've been secretly torturing yourself for years about this kid and that you're still punishing yourself. That's why you won't get married and have kids of your own."

"Now Mom's playing psychiatrist," Betsy said impatiently. "This is too much. Really, Mitchell."

"*Really,* Betsy," he said sarcastically. "I think she's right. You were set to marry Michael. We were all happy about it. Then you turn around and take up with this crazy cowboy with hardly a dime to his name. And he's no more ready to make a commitment than you are. How's that look to *you?* From where I sit, it looks damned immature. And more than that, it's self-destructive."

Her chin jerked up rebelliously. "It's not self-destructive. He's the best thing that ever happened to me."

"Do you really believe that?" Mitchell challenged.

"Yes. I do."

"And you really think you love him?"

"Yes. I do."

"Then prove it," Mitchell said, narrowing his eyes. "Marry him."

Betsy felt bullied, and she refused to stand for it. "I don't *want* to get married."

"See?" Mitchell said triumphantly. "My point exactly. This isn't really a relationship you've got. It's an escape from relationships. And what's more, it's kind of sick. You've got the upper hand with this cowboy. He's no threat to you whatsoever, because you know he's not your equal."

"Not my equal?" Betsy cried. "He's the equal of any man I know. He's better. He's—he's—"

Mitchell leaned across the table, his expression defiant. "Do you love him enough to have his child?"

The question took her aback, stymied her. She stared at him, stunned. She thought, *Hutch's child. Our child.*

"Well?" Mitchell said, as if daring her. "What's the answer? Do you love him enough for that? Yes? No?"

"I—I haven't thought about it."

"No? Well, you should. You're obviously sleeping with him. What happens this time if you get pregnant?"

She tossed her head angrily. "You have no right to ask such questions."

"You should be asking them yourself," Mitchell said. "Mom and Dad might come to accept your living with a guy, even a guy like that. Even though it looks like you haven't got a scrap of pride. But another child out of wedlock? They won't accept that, Betsy. I guarantee it."

"And so what happens then?" she flung at him. "They disown me?"

"I can't say what they might do," Mitchell said ominously. "But I'll tell you what they're willing to do. They're willing to tolerate this man if you've got the maturity to marry him. Dad's going to give you back the Austin job. He'll spring for a better place for the two of you to live. Mom'd die if she saw that house. And Dad's willing to make room for Hutchison in the organization. He can send you to Kansas. Maybe within a year."

"My God," Betsy cried. "You told him *that?* No wonder he threw you out. How dare you?"

"No, Betsy. How dare you turn down an offer that generous? Mom and Dad are bending over backwards."

"They're bending over backwards to run my life."

"You're shutting them out," Mitchell accused. "But they're trying to take you in. They want to come see you. They want to meet him, God help them. Dad wants to talk to him. About the organization. About the money. About everything."

"No," Betsy said, pushing away from the table. She stood and glowered down at her brother. "I won't have it. They will not descend on us and ruin our lives."

"They're coming because they love you. And you're supposed to start the Austin job in two weeks. Dad's got to give the other guy that much notice. And a hefty piece of severance pay."

She buttoned her coat, shrugged her shoulder bag into place and clutched the strap. "I'm not taking the Austin job," she said with spirit. "I've got a job."

Mitchell, too, stood. "Selling ads at that two-bit station? Betsy, Dad's sorry he pulled the Austin job away from you. He realizes you think he was trying to be pushy. He's sorry, and he's giving it back. It's a peace offering. He's even throwing in a raise—as an apology."

"He's still being pushy. I won't stand for it." She turned her back on Mitchell and marched toward the front door of the café.

He followed her. "Mom and Dad'll be down here to talk to you about it. You and Hutchison both."

She pushed the door open and stalked out into the cool afternoon air. "Mitchell," she said, "you're insufferable."

"I'm your big brother. I want you to be happy."

"Then leave me alone. Leave *us* alone."

"My God, Betsy, is that your car? That clunker? Where'd you find such a piece of junk? What's becoming of you? I think Mom and Dad are right—this whole thing is some juvenile way to spite them."

"Mitchell, I will live my own life, dammit."

She unlocked her door, got into the driver's seat. She tried to slam the door, but Mitchell held it open. "Answer me something," he said, his jaw set at an ugly angle. "Hutchison knew about that kid. You told him, didn't you?"

Once again, his question caught her short. But she raised her eyes to lock with his. "He knows. Yes."

"Is that part of his charm? He somehow accepts it?"

"Yes," she said coldly. "Unlike some people."

"We accept it. We've accepted it for years. And it cost us a lot. We're willing to accept Hutchison, too. If he's man enough. And you're grown up enough."

"Mitchell, let go of that door," she ordered. "This is infuriating. I won't discuss it anymore."

"One more question, Betsy. *Would* you marry him? If he asked? Or is that why you'll live with him? He won't ask—so you'll settle for the best you can get?"

Of all Mitchell's questions, this one stung most. It was closest to a truth she wanted to keep hidden even from herself. She *would* marry Hutch if he asked. But she had promised him not to think in those terms, and she'd tried to keep her promise.

"The subject's closed," she told Mitchell. "The last word's been said."

"No," he said grimly. "It's just started. You haven't seen anything yet."

But he closed the door.

She drove off and left him standing in the middle of the sidewalk, staring after her.

Angrily she realized that she had started to cry. She headed the car toward the highway. It was after five o'clock, and she wanted nothing more than to go home. Home to Hutch.

But when she reached the house it was dark and empty. He was gone. She drove to the bar. It, too, was unlit, its doors locked.

She looked, half-panicked, up and down the empty street for some sign of him.

There was none.

He's gone, she thought in despair. *They've driven him away.*

CHAPTER SIXTEEN

HUTCH DIDN'T GET HOME until half past seven. He walked in the kitchen door, then stood there. Betsy was standing by their odd little table that let down out of the wall. She'd just set down a mug of coffee. Now she stared questioningly at Hutch, the coffee forgotten.

He made no move toward her to embrace her, even to touch her. "Cal came by," he said with a shrug. "We had a beer. I lost track of the time."

Although Betsy was deeply relieved to see him, she was hurt, too. They'd needed to talk, but he'd let her come home to an empty house. Why? Because he'd been out drinking. It seemed too much like a bad country and western song to her.

She clenched and unclenched her fists nervously. "My brother," she said, "he said he saw you."

His mouth took on a self-mocking twist. "I nearly punched his lights out. I came within an inch of it. I shouldn't 've thrown him out. I took a bad situation and made it worse. I'm sorry."

"Don't be," she said almost fiercely. "If I were a man, I would have hit him. I'll never forgive him."

Again, he shook his head, his expression troubled. "Don't feel that way. He thinks he's doing it because they love you."

She stared at him. "Hutch, you don't believe what he said for a minute, do you? That they want us to get married? You don't, do you?"

He shook his head, his expression troubled. "No. It's the last thing they want. I could tell by the look in his eye. He'd sooner meet me in hell. He's playin' head games. Reverse psychology."

She wished he would take her in his arms. He seemed somehow different to her, distant, as if Mitchell's visit had made him draw back from her.

"I know why they sent Mitchell," she said. "He talks so fast your head spins."

She saw Hutch tense. "He said you needed children," he said. "And you will someday. I knew it was true as soon as he said it."

"Someday," she said, a lump in her throat. "Not now." But she could not imagine herself wanting anyone else's children. Only Hutch's. The thought frightened her because it meant she loved him too much and in a way she'd never intended.

"I think I'll be kinda jealous," he said quietly.

Don't say things like that, she wanted to cry out. She fought the desire to go to him, hold him and be held by him.

"My parents are coming," she said, swallowing. "He said so. That they want to meet you, talk to you."

"Oh, Lord."

"Hutch, it's a mean game they're playing. They'll pretend to kill us with kindness, when all they really want is to come between us."

His upper lip curled at a corner. "I never met a woman with such a family. They just won't let go of you, will they?"

Betsy looked into his eyes but couldn't read them. "I've never seen them like this before. The way Mitchell talks, they all think I'm this neurotic who can't deal with the past, that I'm punishing my parents and using you, and—"

"No," he said wearily. "Don't talk that way. They're the ones actin' crazy, not you."

"Maybe if they *did* meet you," she said. "Maybe then, they'd understand about us. Not right away, but eventually."

He put his hands in his back pockets, his face grim. "Don't fool yourself. They won't accept somebody like me. They'll never understand. But if you're stubborn enough and still willin', maybe we can ride this out."

"Stubborn enough? Still willing?" she asked, wounded. "Maybe? What do you mean?"

"Just that," he said, nodding. "They're gonna be on your case—hard. You got to decide if it's worth it."

"Worth it?" she echoed in disbelief. "I don't understand."

"If it's worth all this hassle. I never wanted to come between you and your family—"

"My family's carrying on like a pack of rabid jackals," Betsy protested. "It's hard to worry about their feelings, when they don't care about mine."

"Listen," he said, his beautiful eyes serious. "You got to keep one thing in mind. They're concerned about your future. And with me, there's not much of a future."

Betsy stared at him in disillusionment. "What's the matter?" she asked, searching his face. "Why are you saying this? You want to make it clear you're free? I've always known that."

"That's not what I meant," he said, "I just meant your family's a permanent thing, and I'm—"

"Yes," she said, more sharply than she'd intended. "You're anything but permanent. You won't ever belong to anybody. Except yourself."

"I told you once," he said, "I'm like a bridge you got to cross. But when I start doin' you more harm than good, then you have to consider—"

"I have to consider what?" she demanded. "Selling my soul to them? Doing whatever they decide? Taking their silly job in Austin?"

"I didn't say that. But the job in Austin's better, and you know it. I just want you to be aware—"

Betsy turned her back and bit her lip. Why was he acting like this? Had Mitchell convinced him that she was more trouble than she was worth? Made him feel trapped? "How can you say it's better?" she asked. "It's a bribe, a sop, a farce. You must have had more than one beer. Or is that why you went out? To show me that this isn't worth it for *you.*"

He came up behind her and took her by the shoulders, turned her around to face him. "I never said that," he said. His eyes searched her face. "I went out to talk to Cal. About you. We're gettin' ourselves in a complicated situation here."

She stared back, still unable to read his expression. "And what did Cal say?"

And why, she wanted to ask, *did you go out with him, when I needed you here so much?* But she couldn't say such a thing. It would sound too possessive.

"Cal's always got easy answers to hard questions," Hutch said, his lip curling again. "He can't understand."

"If he can't understand, why'd you have to spend so much time with him?" she asked, then wanted to bite off her tongue.

He gave her a perplexed frown. "What do you mean? That's not like you."

She shook her head in confusion. "Nothing. I'm sorry. Mitchell said some damning stuff to me. About my past, my folks, you. That I'm with you because I'm too immature to make a real commitment, things like that."

"We're committed to each other for here and now," he said. "Isn't that enough?"

She stared up at him, a new sort of pain flowering in her heart. Perhaps it *wasn't* enough. Perhaps she had been a fool to think it could be.

"Of course it's enough," she whispered, looking away. "We've always agreed on that."

"Good," he said. "Now what we've got to do is figure how to lead our own lives without your family interferin'. Especially when they're dead set on doin' just that."

"They're going to be angry," she said, staring at the torn-up kitchen floor, the tattered walls. "And they're going to be determined. They won't let us alone. Unless I cut off relations with them."

He put his hand under her chin and forced her to face him again. "I don't want you to do that."

Why? she wondered unhappily. *Because it shows I love you too much? Because it makes our relationship too serious, and you'll feel like I'm making a claim on you?*

A small wave of rebellion surged through her. "If your family had told you not to wander, to stay home and mind the gas station, would you have done it?"

"Betsy," he said, shaking his head, "that's different."

"Is it?" she challenged. "What if they'd had money and said they'd cut you off if you left? Would it have stopped you?"

"I didn't have to make those choices. You do. Don't do anything about your family that you'll regret," he said earnestly. "Promise me that. Will you? Will you promise?"

"I won't do anything about them I'll regret," she said, hating the words even as she spoke them.

"Good," he said. He bent and kissed her. She found the kiss bittersweet.

"But what about the hassles?" she asked, her throat tight. "That worries you. How do we handle it?"

He frowned, looking dissatisfied. "Better than I did today, I hope. If it's best, I'll stay out of their way. It might be easier all around."

Frustration burned in her chest. "But their story is they want to know you. How, if you stay out of their way?"

He smiled sardonically. "They don't want to know me, sugar. They'd just as soon I didn't exist."

What was he doing? she wondered in distress. He seemed to be separating himself from the problem, telling her to handle it alone.

"All this is happening because somehow they found out we're going to live together," she said unhappily. "I suppose Ruth let it slip."

"Don't blame Ruth," he said. "She's grievin' so hard she probably didn't know what she was sayin'."

"I'm not blaming her," Betsy objected.

Then, almost without thinking, she let the words pop out of her mouth, as if to test him. "I just meant that if we don't live together, maybe they'd leave us alone."

His frown deepened. "Not live together?"

"Right," she said, hoping he'd object. "Suppose we didn't live together? Then maybe they'd go back to pretending to be tolerant."

"Is that what you want?"

"It makes sense, doesn't it?" she asked. She had the odd, dizzying sensation that her heart was turning to stone. She hoped it would. Maybe it wouldn't hurt so much.

He stared at her. She thought she saw hurt and disbelief in his eyes, but she wasn't sure. "But you already sublet your apartment. We've got this place."

She shrugged. "I could rent it by myself. You could move back to the bar. You used to say that was plenty room enough for you."

"I agreed to fix it up here."

"Fix it up," she said airily. "I'll pay you. That'd be fair."

"Pay me?" he said, barely parting his lips.

"Why not?" she said. "Or, if you think you could afford it, you could keep it. I could move someplace else. Someplace better. That'd make my family happy, too— wouldn't it?"

His hands moved to her shoulders, gripped her a little too tightly. "You *want* us not to live together?"

"It's a thought. It solves a lot of problems."

His eyes moved over her face, studying her. When he spoke, his voice was bitter. "Do you think so? Maybe it would."

"And maybe I should even take the job in Austin," she said, squaring her jaw. "That'd make them *really* happy—wouldn't it?"

"Betsy," he said, his nostrils flaring, "what in hell are you saying?"

"I'm just offering some ideas," she retorted. "Some what-ifs. What if I stayed in Austin? I wouldn't want to stick you with the rent for this place if you can't handle it. I could still pay my half. It'd be fair. And I can afford it."

He clenched his teeth, his lip curling. The muscles in his arms tightened as if he were going to shake her. But he didn't. "Why the hell are you talkin' about money?" he demanded.

"Because maybe we *should* talk about money," she challenged. "I mean, it's always defined things, hasn't it? That I have it, and you don't? That's why you don't want me to break with my family. I might lose money."

Anger flared briefly in his eyes. "That's only part. They're your family, and they care about you—"

"Maybe," she said, nodding. "Although they've got a strange way of showing it. But still, there's the money. I'm supposed to let it run my life. Well, if that's all that counts, how do you fit into the picture?"

"I love you," he said, almost savagely, his fingers digging into her shoulders.

And I love you, she thought miserably. *I love you too damn much for my own good, and I can't have you. Not really.*

"I love you, too," she said, her voice shaking. "But I don't see where it's getting me."

"Why's it have to get you anywhere?" he asked. "Why can't we just enjoy it for what it is?"

"Because other people won't let us."

"Betsy," he said, his face rigid with control, "slow down. Think, for God's sake. You say you resent them, but you're doin' exactly what they want."

"You're the one who said maybe we could weather this," she shot back. "Well, maybe we can, and maybe we can't. You claimed I'd move on someday. That I'd want more than you can give. Maybe I do want more. But I can't ask for it. So maybe the time's come—just sooner than we thought, that's all."

All he had to do, she thought, was tell her that she was wrong. All he had to do was say he loved her as much as she loved him. All he had to show was that he wanted her in spite of her impossible family.

Instead, he let go of her, his hands dropping to his sides. He stepped back from her, and raked his hand through his hair. "All right. It had to come. I tried to fight it. Maybe it can't be fought. It's gotten too complicated."

"I should go back to Austin for the night—alone," she said, fighting the choking sensation in her throat.

He turned from her, walked to the window and stared off into the darkness. "Your brother'll probably be waitin' for you," he said.

She tossed her head as if it didn't matter. "He probably will."

He stood, his back to her, looking at the ragged wallpaper. "He might try to talk you into goin' back with him."

"He might."

"Will you go?"

"I don't know."

"When will I see you again? Betsy, are you walkin' out on me?"

She took a long, ragged breath. "I don't know that, either. What do you want me to do?"

She waited for him to ask her not to go. He said nothing. He did not even turn around. He just kept staring off into the night. She realized, sickly, that he must be waiting for her to leave.

When he spoke, his voice was flat, without emotion. "I don't want you breaking with your family over me. I can't let you do that. You'd be givin' up everything. For nothing. You're right. I can't give more."

Tears burning her eyes, she took up her coat and purse. Blindly she made her way to the door, pushed her way outside and walked as quickly as she could to her car.

I was making a fool of myself for him, she thought emptily. *I'd have done anything for him, split away from my parents, lived with him and for him and never asked anything in return.*

Yet she knew she would turn around in a second if he called out for her to come back. But he didn't.

"Let him keep his precious freedom," she said aloud as she slammed her car door shut. She drove away from the little house that had almost been theirs.

ON THANKSGIVING DAY, Tyler and Ruth didn't show up at the ranch house for the family gathering. They didn't answer their phone. Cal drove over to their place to see what was the matter.

He hoped nothing serious was wrong. He was already in a grim enough mood. Last night he'd tried to talk sense into Hutch, but doubted that he'd succeeded.

The house was silent, and after he'd rung the bell for almost three minutes, he wondered if it was broken. He knocked on the door. Nobody answered. He pounded as hard as he could.

At last the door swung open. Tyler stood there, in jeans and a work shirt. He was unshaved, his face grim.

"What're you doing?" he demanded. "Trying to wake the dead?"

Tyler looked like hell. His eyes were bloodshot, with dark circles under them. Deep lines etched his forehead, and Cal was disturbed; he honestly couldn't remember those lines being there before. It was as if his brother had aged five years in a week.

"They're waitin' for you over to the house," Cal muttered. "We couldn't get a phone call through. What's wrong?"

Tyler stared at him for a long moment. Cal couldn't tell if his expression was of hostility or disgust or unhappiness or all three tangled together.

"Ruth's gone," he said, his voice harsh. "She left me."

Cal felt as if the porch had been jerked out from under him. He looked at his brother in disbelief. "*Left* you? When?"

Tyler's mouth twisted. "Night before last. In the middle of the night. She's gone back to California."

"Jesus, Tyler." Stunned, Cal shifted his shoulders against the November wind. "Can I come in?"

"No," Tyler said. He made a move as if he would shut the door, but Cal's hand shot out to hold it open.

"I'm comin' in," he said. "We should talk."

"I don't want to talk. To you or anybody else."

Cal ignored him and forced his way in. A disorderly collection of boxes and large plastic bags cluttered the living room. "What's this?" he demanded.

"The kid's stuff," Tyler said bitterly. "I'm getting it the hell out of here."

Cal shook his head. "Tyler, you shouldn't be doin' something like that today."

"I want it out of here," Tyler said, clenching his fist. "Same as I want you out."

Cal didn't intend to leave him by himself. "Why'd she go?" He nodded toward the boxes, the stuffed sacks. "Did she have to get away from all this?"

"I told you," Tyler said, his jaw tightening. "She left *me*. She said so in the note. She said not to call, not to follow."

Cal hooked his thumbs into his belt. "So what you gonna do?"

"Not call, not follow," Tyler said. "Look, would you go? I'm not in the mood for company. Especially yours."

Cal gritted his teeth and ignored the personal barb. "What do you want me to tell the others?"

"Tell them anything you damn please. I don't care. And tell them to stay away from me. Like I said, I don't want company."

"Why're you doin' this to yourself?" Cal asked, his eyes narrowing. "Why don't you get your sorry ass in gear and go after her? I would."

"I don't care what you'd do, you smug son of a bitch," Tyler said scornfully. "Mind your own stinking business, and get out of my house."

Cal stood straighter, met his brother's glare and nodded, as if to himself. "You got a real burr under your saddle lately when it comes to me," he said quietly. "You mind tellin' me why?"

Tyler regarded him contemptuously. "Because, like I said, you're a smug son of a bitch. Always have been. You've messed in my business enough. So how about you get out, for a change?"

Cal's nostrils flared, and as much as he pitied Tyler, he felt a wave of anger rising against him. "How have I messed in your business, hoss? It's news to me."

Tyler crossed his arms. Idly he kicked a bag. It fell open, and Cal saw a pair of large, fuzzy stuffed rabbits, dressed in overalls—toys for the baby. The sight of them made something tighten in his throat.

"For starters," Tyler said, "you got a piece of my winery. If it'd been up to me, it wouldn't have happened. If you're going to be a partner, be silent, will you?"

Cal swore. "First, it wasn't just up to you to sell shares. It was up to Daddy and Cynthia and Ruth, as well."

"Don't talk about Ruth," Tyler warned, a dangerous glint in his dark eyes.

"Well, don't blame me about her. And I didn't put money into your winery to insult you. I did it to help. I told you—you can buy the damn shares back."

Tyler gave him an unpleasant smile. "What I don't understand is how a guy like you, who never did a decent day's work in his life, ends up richer than Midas, expecting us all to kowtow."

Cal's anger flared higher. If it hadn't been for the sight of those pathetic rabbits, he might have hit Tyler, something he hadn't done in years. "Tyler," he said, "that ain't fair, and you know it. Serena and me, we've worked—"

"You can't even talk good English," Tyler exploded. "Or you won't. God knows I worked my butt off through school, and you slid along, not givin' a damn. Daddy tried to send you to college, but you couldn't be bothered. Had to follow your damn rodeo. Then you marry somebody with brains and talent, and wham! Everything falls in your lap. You never did one damn thing to deserve it, but you get to play the conquering hero. It makes me sick."

Only those damn rabbits are saving you, Cal thought bitterly. *Those damn, sad, stupid rabbits.*

He took a deep breath for patience. "Tyler," he said, shaking his head, "I've had more than my share of luck, that's true. But do you think you were an easy act to follow? You, the perfect son? I *couldn't* do as well in school as you. Daddy was always fussin' at me. I could never do anything right."

"I stayed here and worked this damn ranch while you chased all over hell and back," Tyler accused. "You know how many times Mama cried over you, afraid you'd get your fool neck broke?"

Cal took another deep breath. "I do know. That's why I wanted to make it up. Nobody ever took me serious, you know that? Not until Serena did. But I never did anything to try to make you look or feel small. I swear that, with God as my witness."

Tyler said something obscene.

Cal stared at the rabbits, which had pink satin linings in their floppy ears. "Tyler," he said tightly, "your problem is you can't bend. You can't ask for help, you can't accept it when somebody offers."

Tyler swore again, only with less passion and more weariness. He rubbed his forehead. "Nothing bad ever happens to you. Everything's perfect for you." He smiled his bitter smile again. "Even your marriage. God, you were the worst womanizer in seven counties. But *your* marriage isn't breaking up. It's ironic, is what."

Cal stepped closer, put his hand on his brother's shoulder. "You really feel sorry for yourself, don't you? God, you should see yourself. I used to look up to you."

"Leave me alone," Tyler said, trying to wrest himself away.

Cal held him fast, stepped closer. "If I got a good marriage—and I do—it's because I work at it. You think everything's easy for us? It's not. She's got a sister, nieces, that worry her half-crazy. There's a streak of sickness runnin' through that family, bad sickness."

"Cal, just go, will you?" Tyler said, warning in his voice. "You're going to push too hard. And then I won't be responsible for what I do—"

"Shut up and listen, dammit," Cal ordered. "You got no corner on sufferin' in this world. Serena and me have plenty of problems, big and small. She's quiet in the morning, I'm not—sometime's she'd like to kill me. She squeezes toothpaste careful, from the end. I like to squeeze it in the middle, I like the way it feels. She does everything careful. I don't. We can make each other crazy sometimes. She takes weeks to make a decision. I make 'em so fast I scare her."

"Get your hands off me," Tyler said, trying to shove him away. "I'm going to knock your block off. I mean it."

Cal grabbed him by the shirtfront and slammed him against the wall so hard that a nearby bookcase shuddered, and books spilled to the floor. "I'm gonna knock *your* block off," he said in Tyler's face. "Because I'm tryin' to help you, you stubborn bastard."

Tyler tried to resist, but Cal slammed him against the wall again, harder than the first time. He winced when he heard his brother's head strike the plaster, but hauled him away and knocked him to the wall a third time and held him there.

"Serena ran off from me once," he said. "I didn't sull up like a possum and gripe about how unfair the world was. I went after her, by God. And I talked to her. I've seen you with Ruth. You act like you got a poker up your ass. You're the goddamn great stone face. Have you ever, since this sorry business with the baby, have you ever once told her that you loved her? Even once?"

Tyler tried to push him away, but Cal swung him around and knocked him into the corner and pinned him there. "I asked you a question, Tyler. Did you say you loved her? Or were you too busy hiding your feelin's from everybody—includin' yourself?"

"None of your goddamn business," Tyler said, gasping for air. "If you don't let go of me, I'll kill you, I swear."

"I haven't punched you since I was fifteen years old," Cal snarled. "But if I have to fight you, I will. You know what's wrong with you? You think bein' a man is never showin' any feelin' except like this. I could say I love you, and not be embarrassed. But I don't think you could ever say it to me. Could you? I love you, Tyler. Do you love me? I love Serena and Lynn and Daddy and Lettie Mae and a whole lot of people. Can you say that? Can you come out and actually say it?"

Tyler was silent. He stared at Cal with angry, wary eyes. "You're crazy," he said at last. "You know that? You're crazy."

Cal pressed him harder to the wall. "You know what I did when the doctor told me Serena was gonna be well? I cried. And I ain't ashamed. I know you cried when that baby was dead. They told me at the hospital. But you'd never admit that, would you? Did you ever tell Ruth you cried?"

Tyler's lip curled, but he said nothing.

Cal's patience broke. He shook his brother angrily. *"Did you ever tell her?"*

Tyler stopped resisting. He gave a grimace of pain that Cal knew wasn't physical.

"Did you ever tell *anybody?*" Cal demanded. "Can't you ever unbend, you damn fool? Are you so stiff-necked proud you're gonna let her get away? You love her. She loves you. Go after her."

"She doesn't want me," Tyler said, shutting his eyes.

"She does. Trust me. She's runnin' so you'll finally break down and chase her. She's askin' if you care about her, Tyler. Don't you get it? What are you gonna tell her?''

Tyler opened his eyes. He stared at Cal in anguish. "She doesn't want me," he repeated.

"Tyler, you damn fool, she does. I've seen it in her face. I *know* it. You used to say I was born understandin' women. I reckon I got your share, man. 'Cause if you don't go after her, you ain't got a brain in your head. Go to her.''

Tyler said nothing. He looked into Cal's face as if seeing his brother for the first time.

"Go to her," Cal repeated. "Now. Don't wait. Show her you care. You got to let her know.''

Tyler was silent again for a long moment. He swallowed. Then, gruffly, he said, "Will you ask Cynthia and Lettie Mae to get this stuff out of here?''

He nodded at the boxes and sacks of baby things. His voice shook. "I should have done it before she came home from the hospital. I never thought of it. I never—''

"You weren't thinkin' straight," Cal said, putting his hand on Tyler's shoulder again. "None of us were. I'll see to it. I promise. Does this mean you'll go to her?''

Tyler sighed and leaned his head against the wall. He looked exhausted, wrung out. "Yeah.''

Such relief surged through Cal that for an instant, his knees felt almost weak. "I didn't mean to get rough," he muttered. "I'm sorry."

"It's okay," Tyler said. He was still breathing hard. He stared up at the ceiling, not looking at Cal.

Cal studied him, sorry for his brother's emotional pain, sorry that things came so hard for him.

He drew Tyler into his arms and gave him a short, masculine embrace. "I meant it, you fool," he said gruffly. "I love you."

Tyler said nothing. But for a few seconds the men held each other. Then they drew apart.

Cal picked up his hat from the floor, where it had fallen. "I'll tell everybody she's feelin' blue, that you might take off for California for a few days. Call me. Let me know how things go, okay?"

"Yeah. Sure," Tyler said.

Cal moved to the front door, opened it. "Good luck," he said, not looking at his brother. "She'll want to come home with you, I know. I know that."

"We'll see," Tyler said, his voice controlled again. "And Cal?"

Cal turned and gave him a parting glance.

Tyler's mouth twitched and he swallowed again. "Thanks."

Cal only smiled, a little sadly. Then he left.

LATE THAT NIGHT, at almost midnight, Tyler boarded a plane. He sat in tourist class, trying to adjust his long body to the cramped seat. It was the first flight he could get out of Austin because the airlines were crowded with holiday passengers.

The Fasten Seat Belt sign was on as the plane lifted from the tarmac, and a pretty blond flight attendant sat in the jump seat across the aisle, facing him. She smiled at him and said she'd soon be up to take his drink order. He shook his head to tell her not to bother.

"Then how about a pillow?" she asked. "Want me to get you one from the overhead when I can move around?" He said no, thanked her and turned to stare out the window.

"Going all the way to San Francisco?" asked the woman, seeming determined to be friendly.

Tyler nodded. He saw the lights of Austin falling away beneath them. Once in San Francisco, he'd rent a car to drive to the wine country. He tried to calculate the time and distance it'd take him.

"Business? Pleasure? The holiday?" she asked.

He turned to look at her, his face taut. "I'm going to bring my wife home. She's visiting her father."

"Oh," she said, clearly disappointed.

He nodded absently, as if to himself. He turned back to the window, thinking of what he must say to Ruth.

I love you. He kept telling her that over and over in his mind. *I love you.*

This time he swore he'd get it right. He looked at his wedding ring and twisted it once for luck.

I love you, Ruth. Let's go home. Together, let's go home.

CHAPTER SEVENTEEN

MITCHELL HAD LEFT a note for Betsy at her apartment. He wouldn't wait for her to make up her mind, he'd written. He'd wanted to be home for Thanksgiving. A man's place was with his wife and children.

Take some time to think over the Austin offer, the note had said. She had the whole holiday to decide. Mitchell had added that he was sorry if he'd caused her distress and asked her forgiveness. He'd signed the note "With love."

Betsy passed the night feeling hollow and spent. She wanted the phone to ring and for the caller to be Hutch. She wanted to hear a knock at the door, to open the door and see him standing there.

But the only person who phoned was her mother, who said she and Betsy's father would fly to Austin in two weeks, that they were anxious to see Betsy and meet her young man. Her mother acted as if everything were perfectly normal, and no stresses tore at the family, no conflicts strained it.

Oddly, Betsy found herself responding in kind. It was easier. *We're all so good at pretending,* she thought. *Maybe that's how we're meant to spend our whole lives. Nobody will ever be honest or will ever want to be.*

But she could not pretend happiness over the break with Hutch. She had precipitated it, but it was as if he had wanted her to leave. He must have sensed they were getting too deeply involved, that her family would make things too complicated, and he wanted out.

Well, she thought with dark irony, at least he had always been honest about wanting his freedom. Honesty was what she'd said she wanted.

That night she couldn't bear to sleep in the bed they'd shared. She remembered him too vividly, his touch, his taste, his strength and gentleness.

She slept curled up on the couch and had uneasy dreams. She woke up miserable with missing him. What would happen, she wondered, if she drove back to Crystal Creek, told him she was sorry?

No, she thought, shaking her head. It wouldn't be the same. She'd finally realized she wanted to love him and be with him all her life. He wanted his freedom. He had let her leave. He hadn't tried to stop her or come after her.

If she went back, she would be living another lie, pretending she didn't want him as much as she did. She would be clinging to him pathetically and without pride, taking whatever she could get, never daring to ask for more.

He would feel smothered, and she would resent that he would always love his liberty more than her.

The apartment seemed to close in on her. When she looked out from her living room window, Austin's skyline seemed coldly alien. She could see which building housed her father's television station.

Suddenly she knew that she had to get out of the apartment. She put on her coat and went out. She walked all afternoon, along the river, downtown, up and down Sixth Street with its artsy shops and jazz bars.

She ducked her head and walked more swiftly when she passed the occasional bar from which country and west-

ern music issued. The sound brought back too forcibly
the memory of being in Hutch's arms and dancing all
night long.

They'd moved so perfectly together. They'd made love
so perfectly.

Hutch, she thought with a pang too strong to be
created by infatuation. Numbly she noticed that lights
were starting to come on; evening was falling.

She shoved her hands more deeply into her pockets and
started back toward the apartment. Had she been a fool
to think she could be happy with Hutch in a small town?
Living in a run-down rental house and selling ads for a
tiny radio station? Had she deceived herself?

Her apartment seemed abysmally silent. She switched
on the television, but every channel was full of Thanksgiving programs or football games. She turned off the
set.

She realized, rather numbly, that if she wasn't with
Hutch, she didn't want to stay in Texas. The whole state
seemed haunted. She'd been granted one glimpse of her
child, then had to relinquish him, maybe forever. She'd
had her affair with Hutch, and now it was ending.

She could still go to New Hampshire, she supposed. Or
back to California. Maybe she'd even talk to the idiotic-
sounding "reality counselor." Perhaps she needed to,
because without Hutch, reality no longer felt real.

She made herself eat something, tried not to think of
the impromptu picnics she and Hutch had shared, the
laughter, and the touching, both sweet and sexy.

If he hasn't called, if he doesn't show up by midnight,
she thought, *then I'll know it's over.*

She knew that setting a time limit was stupid, but she
didn't care. If she didn't hear from him by midnight,
she'd make plans to leave Austin. She'd simply vacate the

apartment early; the new tenant would be there in a few weeks. She'd have to do something about her car, her ridiculous car. Her bank account would have to be closed, the post office notified, her phone turned off—

The phone rang. Startled, she stared at it and could only think, *Hutch*. She glanced at her watch. It was exactly eight o'clock, four hours until midnight. She realized she was praying to hear his voice.

When she lifted the receiver and said hello, her voice trembled. But it was her mother who answered her, all sweetness and cheer.

"Betsy! I'm so glad to find you home. We tried earlier. You were out."

"Yes." *I was out alone. Hutch and I are over. You helped make it end. Should I hate you, forgive you, thank you—what?*

"Did you and your friend have a pleasant day?" Margaret asked brightly.

"Yes," Betsy lied. She didn't want to tell them the truth yet. It was too new and hurt too much. Besides, lies were easier. They were, she thought bleakly, what her family did best.

"We had the traditional old-fashioned feast," Margaret said. "Turkey, ham, sweet potatoes, cranberry sauce, pumpkin pie.... Cook did herself proud. We're all just stuffed.

"This is one of my favorite holidays," Margaret burbled. "We've got Mitchell's family here. We just wanted to talk to you and wish you and your friend well. Is he there? I'd love to say hello, start to get acquainted."

Betsy's heart twisted painfully. "He's not here right now," she said.

"Too bad," said Margaret. "But we'll see him soon enough. Well, everyone wants to say hello, then I want to talk to you again. We have a surprise. And then your Dad's going into his study, because he wants to have a private little chat with you. So, talk to you in a minute, dear.''

Betsy's sister-in-law, Bridget, came on the line, talking about Mitchell and their children. ''I guess that's what I'm most thankful for,'' she said. ''That Mitchell's such a good husband and father.''

Betsy considered Mitchell a distant husband and a somewhat grumpy father, but knew that Bridget was sending the approved family message: *Find a steady man. Stop playing with fire. You don't know the value of things.*

Mitchell took the line next and reemphasized the thought less subtly. ''Bridget and I took the kids to a special service this morning. The sermon was on 'individual responsibility.' It was good. You should have heard it.''

You should have heard it. Yes, Betsy thought bitterly, that's probably exactly what Mitchell thought.

Margaret took the phone again. ''This is the first Thanksgiving you've ever been away,'' she said a bit mournfully. ''It makes me feel—well—sad.''

It's the second time, Betsy thought in sick amazement. *The first time, I was in Utah, sixteen years old and pregnant. Nobody called me that day except Mitchell. He said you couldn't phone, it would have made you too sad.*

But Margaret seemed really to have blocked the truth from her mind. ''What matters, of course,'' she said, ''is that you're happy. I know I was upset with you at first when you broke up with Michael. I overreacted, and so did Dad. But we want to make it up to you.''

Now what? Betsy thought, her muscles tensing nervously.

"Mitchell says you're driving a perfect old horror of a car, and there's no need for that. You don't need to do without. We're making arrangements for a new car for you. A Corvette convertible. All you'll have to do is go in to the dealer next week and pick out the color."

Betsy felt sickened. A Corvette? Hutch could never afford such a car; it was a gift designed to rub in the fact.

"I don't want a new car."

"Betsy," Margaret said, clearly hurt, "we want you to have it. To show you we love you and you'll always be our daughter, no matter what. Please. Don't you dare say no."

Betsy put her hand to her forehead. She felt as if she was being bludgeoned to death by too much kindness, all of it calculated and cold-blooded.

"No," Margaret almost cooed, "you wouldn't refuse something we want you to have so much. I'd worry to death about you in some old used car. I really would. Now hang on. I'm going to switch you over to Dad."

Betsy grimaced slightly. She hadn't talked to her father since she'd come to Texas. He did not much like phone conversations about anything except business.

"Hello," he said, his voice gruff.

"Hello," said Betsy.

"This is your mother's idea," he said, "not mine. She wants me to talk to you."

Betsy gripped the receiver more tightly. She had no idea of what he might say.

"First," said Ronald Holden, "she wants me to express my support for you and so forth. Frankly, I don't approve of what you're doing with this man, but if he's going to be a part of your life, I suppose I'll have to accept him. Very well. But he has to accept our terms, too."

No, he doesn't, she thought with something almost like satisfaction. *He's free of you, of me, of all of us.*

"So that's that," her father said. "This next business is not pleasant for me. Your mother insists that you have some sort of complex about what happened to you when you sixteen. She thinks you resent us for not talking about it. Is this correct?"

Betsy realized that she was standing as straight as a soldier at attention before her general. "I wouldn't call it a complex," she said as evenly as she could. "Everybody pretends it never happened. That's not healthy. It did happen. It changed my life."

"That's where you're wrong," he said. "It most certainly is healthy. Think of it as damage control. Your life did not change. You can live like any normal girl, and nobody needs to be the wiser. If you choose to dwell on it, I find that unhealthy, frankly."

"I'm not dwelling on it," she objected. "I'm facing it. And we're not just talking about me. There's a child involved."

"No, Betsy," he said firmly, "there is not. The child is not involved with us, we are not involved with the child. You don't have to worry about it. It's taken care of."

Anger rankled hotly in her breast. "Not *it*, Dad. *He*—he's a *he*. A human being."

"He's a human being who was a mistake. I'm sure he's been placed with a caring family to whom his background doesn't matter."

"You're sure?" Betsy challenged. "I doubt that. You don't really know, do you?"

"I'm reasonably sure," he amended. "Which will have to content you. None of us needs to know more. Nor does he need to know about us."

"Why?" she asked, raising her chin defiantly. "Why would it be so terrible? What if he wants to know someday?"

"The adoption was closed, Betsy. For your good. He won't come troubling you. If that's what's bothering you, you needn't worry. You can put him out of your mind."

"Bothering?" she asked. "Dad, that's not what concerns me. If he turns up at my door someday, then—"

"He won't," Ronald Holden said with conviction. "Nor will he show up at mine. He can't trace us, which is how we want it. I'm certainly not going to have him appear on my doorstep someday trying to extort money—"

"Money?" Betsy cried in horror. "Don't tell me everything happened this way because of money, for God's sake."

"Watch your language. Money's a consideration, of course. I don't want him popping up demanding a share of what isn't his. I don't want to see him at all, ever, under any circumstances. None of us do, and that should include you."

"I can't believe you're saying this." Betsy shook her her head in disgust.

"The other consideration has been your welfare."

"Then why have I always been treated as if I have this shameful secret?"

"Because it *is* shameful. And you should be ashamed."

The words jarred her. She felt light-headed, almost giddy with emotion. Rage warred with a wild, strange feeling of something like liberation.

"I'm tired of being ashamed," she said, her heart pounding. "I'm tired of being treated like I can't take care of myself. You wanted me to marry Michael. You didn't care if I loved him or not."

"He was suitable," her father answered coolly. "But you chose to reject him."

"Michael's not acceptable," Betsy shot back. She'd held the truth back far too long. Only Hutch had ever guessed it. *Hutch,* she thought, her throat tightening.

She took a deep breath. She no longer worried about betraying Michael. He would have used her, and she would have let him. "I'm not the only one with secrets," she said. "Michael's gay. And I don't exactly find that 'acceptable' in a husband."

There, she thought. *The truth's out at last. What do you have to say to that, Dad?*

"Don't be ridiculous," he scoffed. "I know his father."

"What's that got to do with it?" Betsy demanded, bewildered by his lack of logic. "I tell you, he's gay. We went together a year. He never tried to do more than kiss me. But I've seen the way men look at him, and the way he looks back. But he's like I was, afraid to displease his family. He likes me, but he doesn't want me sexually. He wants to pretend everything's fine between us. But it isn't. He knows it, and I know it."

"Don't be ridiculous," her father repeated. "Stop shifting the blame. So he isn't oversexed. Good for him. Sex isn't everything."

He won't believe me, she thought, stricken and angry. *He won't even listen.*

Her heart thudded madly in her chest. "Let me get this right. What I did was shameful. You don't want the child I bore ever to come near you—or your money. And you would have told me to marry Michael even if I came to you and said I thought he was gay."

"He's not gay," her father snapped. "Stop obsessing about sex. That's what got you into trouble in the first place."

"You know," she said, her voice shaking, "Mom used to always tell us that you were quiet, but proud. That you worked so hard because you loved us so much. And that your standards were so hard to meet because you cared so much for us. She made it seem as if you were the most important person in the world to please. She always acted like you were a god. I believed it. And when I thought I'd failed you, I tried twice as hard to be what you wanted. Now I wonder why."

Silence was her only reply, but it seemed to pulse with displeasure.

"You're cold and hard," she accused. "Mother's the only one who's ever gotten through to you, and God only knows how she did it. Probably by pretending to be this frail, fainting flower, which she most certainly is not."

"Don't you speak against your mother," her father ordered. "You've put that woman through enough misery. You will speak of her with respect."

"I don't want you to come here," Betsy said. "And I don't want a car. Do you think you can buy me? Do you think it's your money I need? It's not. I'm not sure you're capable of giving me what I need."

"That tone is unnecessary," Ronald Holden said icily. "That tone is offensive."

"I'm sorry to say this," she said, her voice shaking harder. "But I have to have time away from you. I want to be on my own. Maybe for a short time. Maybe long. So don't come see me. Don't phone me. Don't send anybody after me."

"Betsy, don't dictate to me."

"Then don't dictate to me," she answered. "I mean it. I want to be on my own. Completely."

"You have no idea what reality is," he said with contempt. "On your own? Completely? You'll come crawling back. Then your mother will cry and forgive you, like she always does. That woman's a saint."

"I will never crawl back," Betsy retorted. "I swear that. I may walk back someday, but it'll be of my own free will. I'll never crawl for you. Not anymore. In my mind, you've had me crawling for years."

"Balderdash," he snorted.

"Did you hear what I said?" she returned passionately. "I said you had me crawling in my mind for years. Don't you care that you've done that?"

"Did you hear what I said?" he demanded angrily. "I said balder—"

She hung up. Her knees shook, and her vision was blurred with tears that she refused to shed. She tore the phone cord out of its plug because she knew her mother would soon be calling back, doubtless in tears, and she could stand no more of it.

She would not stay in Austin, because they'd come after her or send someone for her again, and she refused to tolerate it.

She would pack, take her car and start driving—east, away from Texas, farther away still from California. Florida was east. She had college friends from Florida. One in Tampa, one in Key West. Maybe she would go to one of those places, maybe not. She didn't care where she went.

Blindly, she started filling her suitcases. She was supposed to be back to work at the radio station on Monday. She would have to phone and tell them she had to quit. She would take care of whatever other details she left behind by phone or mail.

She would write to Ruth later; Ruth had too many troubles of her own to be involved with Betsy's.

She started lugging suitcases down to the car. There was food left in the cupboards and refrigerator. She would pay the landlord to deal with it. She loaded the suitcases into the trunk and went upstairs for more.

As she took up the second pair, she glanced at her watch. It was three minutes after midnight. Hutch hadn't come. Of course he hadn't—what had she expected?

She took the second set of suitcases to the car, loaded them and went back to the apartment. She was hauling a valise and two suit bags across the parking lot when she heard a familiar rattle and clatter.

Hutch's van swung into the parking lot, and its headlights caught her in their glare.

It's too late, she thought illogically, *it's after midnight.* She opened her car door, threw in the valise and struggled to hang the suit bags. She didn't want to look at the van because it might be a hallucination, a cruel trick her mind was playing.

The van screeched to a stop. She heard its door creak open, heard boot heels ringing against the pavement. She didn't turn around. Under her breath she cursed the stubborn suit bag for not hanging on the hook.

Then Hutch's arms were around her from behind, pulling her close to him, and his voice was low in her ear. "What are you doin'?"

She tried to pull away. He held her fast, his face pressed against hers.

"I'm leaving," she said. "Go away."

"Where? California?" The night was cold and his breath was hot against her skin.

"Just away. Florida, maybe. Let go."

He swung her around so that she had to look at him. He held her tightly by the shoulders. "Florida? Why?"

"To get away from my parents. I have to break away from them. At least for a while."

He shook his head. The wind stirred his long hair. "I didn't want you to have to do that for me."

"I didn't do it for you," she flung at him. "I did it for me. Your name didn't even come up. Now let go. I'm getting out of here."

"No," he said, bringing his face close to hers. "Don't. Stay with me. Please."

His voice was so earnest, almost pleading, that it wrenched her apart. She looked into his eyes, feeling helpless. "Hutch, let's not pretend. I'm through pretending. We can't get back together. You know it better than I do."

"I love you," he said. "Do you love me?"

The parking lot was well lit, and she could see the intensity in his eyes, the fierce set of his mouth. His barely restrained emotion shook her, made her fight to keep up her defenses.

"We come from separate worlds," she said. "We have to go separate ways."

"I love you," he repeated. "Do you love me?"

"I'd tie you down," she said. "I come with too much luggage." She glanced down at one of the suit bags. It had fallen at her feet. "Look at it all," she said sadly, as if her bags were packed with troubles, not clothing.

"Betsy," he said patiently. "Answer. Do you love me?"

She closed her eyes. She was, after all, going to be honest from now on. "Yes," she sighed. "I love you."

"Then come here," he said, drawing her into his arms. "Because I can't let you go. Not forever. One day was bad enough. My God, we lost a whole day. A whole day with you. I lost it."

Tears burned her eyes again, and she pressed her face against his jacket, fighting them. "We can't do this."

He kissed her hair. "Tell me," he said in a tense whisper, "did you ever think of marrying me? Did you ever want that? Is that what you meant when you said you wanted more than I could give?"

"Yes," she admitted. "But I know you're not that kind. I knew from the start."

He kissed her ear. "Is that why you said those things? You were hurt because you thought I didn't want you enough?"

"No," she lied and wondered if the truth could be any worse. "Yes. Oh, I've got no pride, saying that. I shouldn't say that."

"I said things to you I didn't mean," he murmured against her cheek. "Because you scared the fool out of me, Betsy. You made me think about gettin' married. You made me think of children. You made me think things I never thought before, feel things I never felt. Would you have me?"

She drew back from him as if he'd stung her. She stared at him, her lips parted in surprise.

"Would you have me?" he asked. "Would you marry me?"

Her heart pounded so hard it almost shut off her breath. "Why are you saying this?" she asked. "You don't mean this."

"Betsy, I love you. I want to marry you. I used to wake up sometimes in the night and just look at you, touch your hair."

His fingertips stroked her hair, then settled along the line of her jaw. "Lord knows we were careful makin' love, but mistakes happen. I thought, what if she gets pregnant? And I'd think, I couldn't let her go through that again. I started seeing us in my mind's eye. You and me and a little kid. A kid with your eyes."

"No," she breathed, her heart beating harder. "With your eyes. I'd want him to have your eyes."

"Once," he said, his voice strained, "we were makin' love, and I thought, what if I slipped up, just once? And you got pregnant? Then we sorta *should* get married. It'd be like a sign, it'd be like fate. But I couldn't do that to you."

"You want your freedom."

"You're my freedom," he said. "Kiss me. For God's sake, kiss me."

Trembling, she raised her mouth to his. He brought his lips down upon hers with an ardor that made her half-faint.

Then he gathered her more tightly into his arms, his cheek against hers.

"Every minute I was with you," he said, "was like it wasn't enough. I didn't just want to make love to you. I wanted to live with you. And I kept thinkin' someday I'd have to let you go. I made myself believe I could."

He pressed his cheek more firmly against hers, as if assuring himself that she was really there.

"Yesterday," he said, "when your brother said you needed children, I thought, yes, she does. And how can I stand it if they aren't mine? But I can't marry her. Then Cal dragged me out and gave me his desperado speech, which almost made me crazy—"

"His desperado speech?" she asked, hardly understanding what he was saying. All she could think of was how much she loved him.

He took a deep breath. "There's a song about it. It says freedom turns into a prison if you're too afraid to care enough about somebody. He kept sayin' I ought to marry you if I felt the way I felt. And I kept sayin' I couldn't. There was the money and all. And he'd say, what's the matter? Didn't I have the *cajones* to deal with a little money, more or less?

"Betsy, he was makin' way too much sense. I loved you so much, I felt trapped, cornered. Yet somehow, in some crazy way, that made me want you more. Everything he said was right, but after that ruckus with your brother, I was dead set not to agree. I was a damn fool."

"I'm so sick of the money," she said, gritting her teeth. "They can cut me out of everything if they want. The choice is theirs."

"Sugar," he said, his hand roaming possessively over her back, "I don't care if you have the money or don't. If it ever comes to you, we'll put it in a trust fund for the kids or something. Not let 'em have it till they're old enough to deal with it—be sensible about it. We'll figure it out. We'll handle it."

"There may not be any money," she said. "I really did make a break from them. I had to, Hutch. My father told me something about the adoption tonight that I never knew."

Haltingly, she told him of what Ronald Holden had said about not wanting any illegitimate offspring making claims on his money. And she told him, too, of her father's refusal to believe the truth about Michael.

"Sugar," Hutch said, "you did right. If they come down here, we'll face them together. I was wrong to say you shouldn't chance a split with them. You knew better than I did."

She slid her hands around his neck and laced them in his hair. "Once you told me that you didn't want either heredity or environment making you. You wanted to make yourself, according to your own lights. That's what I have to do, too."

"Betsy, for half an hour after you left the house last night, I thought, 'My God, that was a close one. She nearly nailed you, Hutch. You got away just in time.' And then I started to miss you so hard it hurt."

"I missed you, too," she said, touching his face.

He took one hand, kissed it on the palm and held it. "I started playin' dumb games in my head. Like if you didn't come back last night, that meant it was supposed to be over. But you didn't, so this morning, I said, 'Okay, if she's not back by noon, it's supposed to be over.' Did you ever hear of anybody so stupid?"

"Yes," she said, smiling for the first time. "Me. I did the same thing. Only I made it midnight tonight."

"Then we're both late, aren't we?" he asked.

"Better late than never," she said softly.

"I can't promise you riches," he said. "Only that I'll love you as much as a man can love a woman. If you'll have me."

Tears rose in her eyes, and this time she couldn't blink them back. "I'll have you. There could never be anybody but you."

He swallowed. "Okay," he said. "Then I got something for you. To make it official. Will you take a ring?"

"A ring?" she asked in surprise.

He dug into his pocket. "Don't laugh at it," he said. "It's the best I could do for now. Nothin' open but the hockshop on Thanksgivin'. Maybe someday we'll trade it in for a fancier model."

He held up a ring between his thumb and forefinger. It was a thin gold band with tiny chips of diamonds set into it. "You can't see the diamonds too well unless the light's just right," he said ruefully. "Will you wear it for me?"

"I'll wear it for you forever," she said, gazing at it through her tears. He took her hand and slipped it onto her ring finger.

"My God, Betsy," he said, wiping her tears away with the back of his hand. "We're engaged. Want to get married before anybody can kick up a fuss?"

It was crazy, she knew, but it felt right. It felt more right than anything in her life. The vibes, as Hutch would say, were right, exactly right. She nodded.

"I can't afford a honeymoon," he said. "I can't take you to Niagara Falls."

"We're too busy for Niagara Falls," she said. "We've got wallpaper to hang."

"Right you are," he said and kissed her until she forgot about wallpaper, Niagara Falls and everything in the world except him.

In the distance a train whistled its lonesome invitation, but neither of them heard it.